SINS OF THE FATHER

SINS OF THE FATHER

AUBREY MALONE

First published November 2022

ISBN 978-1-913144-41-8

:

PENNILESS PRESS PUBLICATIONS
Website:www.pennilesspress.co.uk/books

1

I grew up outside a small town in Galway. My father was a farmer. He always said he hated farming but I didn't believe him. Some people are good at re-inventing the past. I remember him being happy at it when he was young.

He talked about his own father a lot. I never knew him but I heard so much about him growing up I felt I did. His mother was English, his father Scotch-Irish. One of his brothers joined the British Army. As the saying went, 'He took the shilling.'

There was no richer landowner in the area. Nobody ever knew how he got to be like that. He had no special skills. The expression people used was 'self-made man.' It covered a multitude.

He came from Antrim originally. Nobody knew why he moved to Galway. There was a rumour that his father beat him, that he ran away from home. He was said to have married the first woman he met in Galway. She was a landlady. He didn't have any money in those days. She was said to have put him up for free. They married shortly afterwards. It would have been a scandal if he was seen coming out her door for too long without them tying the knot.

Her family had land. He farmed it with her brother. Their father was dead. After the brother died it all came to him. There was an uncle in Down who laid claim to it at one stage. He even went to court about it with some old document that suggested he was

5

entitled to it. My grandfather fought the case and won. It turned out the document was forged.

In later years he got into property. He ploughed the money he made from selling his crops into buying houses. The people who worked on the land did them up for him. Afterwards they were sold at a profit. Such a cycle continued all his life. He always claimed luck was on his side but my father thought that was false humility. 'He knew when to buy and when to sell,' he said, 'That was his secret.'

My father's life went the other way. He had money when he was young and then he lost it. I only have a vague memory of being wealthy. In my early years we had a lot of stock on the farm. We had to sell most of it when we became poor. That happened so suddenly it was a shock to us all.

One day my father went into town to cash a cheque and it didn't go through. I was only seven at the time. He came home in a state of despair. I remember his face as he came in the door. He looked as if he'd lost all belonging to him.

He fell into a chair. There was a piece of paper in his hand. He said to my mother, 'The cheque bounced.' I didn't know what 'bounced' meant. I only knew it with reference to a ball. He said it meant something different with a cheque.

My mother was washing the dishes at the time. I was playing with my toys. Greta, my sister, was doing her homework. Neither of us took it in.

We had to sell a lot of our land to make ends meet. I didn't miss the wealth because I hadn't had much experience of it. It was different for my father.

His world was turned upside down. I said to him once, 'Was it the money you missed or the power it brought you?'

Maybe it was neither. What he missed most, I always thought, was the aura his grandfather created around himself. It made people look up to him and at times fear him. My father had both of these reactions too. He regarded his father the same way the people who worked for him did. They saw him as someone who could turn on you if you didn't do exactly what they wanted.

After my father lost his money he had to let his farmhands go. There was no such thing as compensation in those days. They went to England with practically nothing in their pockets. A lot of them lived sad lives over there. Some of them became victims of drink and some of depression. Most of them eked out humble livings.

Emigrants weren't made very welcome in England in those days. It wasn't like America. Everyone knew about the 'No Irish, no blacks' signs on properties that were available to rent. Even in places that let the Irish in put up their prices once they heard the accent.

Many of them were beaten up. The thinking was, 'If you were Irish you were in the IRA.' When a bomb went off somewhere it was worse. They had to lie low. If a man had a pregnant wife it was even be harder to get a place to live. Many families had to sleep rough. A lot of babies died.

Some of the men made good. They banded together in Kilburn and Cricklewood, anywhere they felt at home. They were accused of taking English jobs. Fights broke out in pubs. It didn't matter what England had done to us for 700 years. This was now and they were in their country. John Bull still ruled.

The lucky ones earned money on shipyards and building sites. They often married English girls. After a few years they came home. They'd have English accents, bringing children with them that spoke that way too. Or else they'd have a combination of an Irish and an English accent, the kind you heard sometimes on soccer programmes where there were interviews with players who'd made their names with the big English clubs.

With prosperity came confidence. 'Jack's as good as his master,' my father said. It was almost as if they had to apologise for doing well. He didn't have much time for them if they came to the farm to see him. When he knew them before they'd have been dressed in overalls. Now they were often in three-piece suits. He expected them to be cap in hand to him but that was a ridiculous expectation. The tables had turned.

I tried to make them feel welcome but I was aware of him glowering in the background. 'They'll be addressing me by my Christian name yet,' he said. That would have been the last straw for him. I could see such a day coming.

He only saw the successful ones. When they presented themselves to him with their new wives and their new lives it made him think everyone who went away must have turned out like that. He forgot about all the ones who fell by the wayside.

He almost denied them the right to earn money in England despite the fact that the English had colonised us for so long. He referred to them as English Irishmen. His father was different. He'd been more like an Irish Englishman. I couldn't understand the difference. Maybe it boiled down to the fact that his father got rich under what he called the *ancien regime*. He became the beneficiary of that when he inherited his fortune.

'I made their lives possible,' he said to me, 'If it wasn't for me they wouldn't have had the money to emigrate.' But what good was it if they couldn't bring it home? Ireland was our country. Was he afraid they'd become as rich as his father was while he was like they were when they had nothing?

We lived about a mile from the town. That was near enough to be accessible to it and far enough away from it for us to be able to have our own lives. The people who lived near us liked dropping in when they felt like it. It was the way people behaved in most country areas but it didn't suit my father. He wanted to see them on his terms rather than theirs.

People from the town saw me as a culchie and people from the country thought of me as a townie. I wasn't sure what I was myself. Inhabiting the middle ground suited me. It meant I could have the best of both worlds. I went into the shops when I wanted to and enjoyed the world of nature when I didn't.

I knew fields better than buildings. I learned how to drive a tractor before I started driving cars.

never happen again after the cheque bounced. If we went anywhere now we had to come back the same day.

My father said a lot of his friends deserted him when he lost his money. It made him cynical about people. He rarely socialised afterwards. People called to the house to discuss business with him but that was only now and again.

His sister Betty was the only person who came to see us on any sort of regular basis. She lived about a mile from us on her own. My father didn't get on with her. He made cruel jokes about her.

'She made a lot of men happy by not marrying them,' he said. That was cruel. She was one of the kindest people you could meet.

She never talked about her past. She'd been engaged to be married once but my grandfather made her break it off with the man. He was a plumber. The idea of his daughter marrying a labourer would have been unthinkable to him. He married someone else afterwards but it wasn't a happy marriage.

Betty regretted breaking it off with him. 'I ruined things for myself,' she said to me once. I felt sorry for her. She'd have made a great wife. The opportunity never came her way again. She wrote to the plumber after my grandfather died to say the way was clear for them now if he wanted her. He did but it was too late. There was no divorce in those days. She wouldn't have written to him if she knew he was married. People had been afraid to tell her. It was embarrassing for her not knowing. As if she hadn't suffered enough already.

The only other member of the family was Setanta. He was our dog. My father told me he was a setter but he looked like a mongrel. He was probably cross-bred. We rescued him one day from a man who threw him from a car. We were out driving one day when it happened. He was thrown into a ditch. We never knew if the person who did it wanted to kill him or not. He was skin and bone at the time.

I brought him with me everywhere. He became like a brother to me. I told him things when I got upset. The way he crooned made me think he understood me.

Greta told me it was stupid to think a dog could understand you talking to him. I argued with her about that. In fact I argued with her about everything - who'd get the bathroom first, where we'd sit at the table, who'd get first choice of food. I argued with her even when there was nothing to argue about.

She was four years older than me. My mother said that was behind it. Boys didn't like their sisters to be older than them. It seemed like more than four years. I looked forward to getting older. It wouldn't matter so much then.

She always made me out to be in the wrong. Most people went with her. She sounded mature. I didn't. After a while I didn't bother trying to make them see my side of things. It was too much like hard work.

She had to be better than me at everything. Even religion. God was her special friend. At Mass she looked like she was about to take off on a chariot to heaven when she prayed. Coming down from

Communion her hands would be clasped so tight you could see her knuckles whitening.

She loved the nuns. When she was in their company she looked like one of them. They kept praising her. She licked up to them. I saw it as false. Was I jealous? Religious people had easy lives.

She gave out about some nuns behind their backs. Would they like her as much if they knew that? I told her she was two-faced. She didn't see it. I didn't think she realised it. That's how immersed she was in it all. She slept with an easy conscience,

Everything came quicker to her at school than it did to me. She piped up the answers while I scratched my head in confusion. At home she talked about current affairs. She listened to *The News* as if her life depended on it. If there was some tragedy in a far-away place she almost shed tears.

Anything I told her about myself was of no interest to her.

'Why do you never talk to me?' I asked her one day.

'I would if you spoke about important things' she said.

Most days after school she'd have her head buried in some book. If I asked her what it was she'd say, 'Research.' She did research for school projects. I never understood them. They were beautifully presented. She won prizes for them. The teachers gave her trophies. She put them on the window for everyone to see. I could see her being a teacher herself when she grew up. School was the centre of her life. If she made an ink-blot in one of her copies she panicked.

Anytime I looked at her she told me I was distracting her. It was supposed to be a study-room for both of us but it really belonged to her. I usually went up to my bedroom to get away from her. Sometimes I wandered from room to room trying to get interested in something. If I passed my mother she'd look at me as if to say, 'You've let me down again.'

She had conversations with my father late at night when they thought I was asleep. They talked about what would become of me if I didn't get some direction in my life. My father would tell her not to fret. I was still only a child. It did no good.

She tried to interest me in things. The more she tried, the less interested I became. I hated when people told me what to do. That was why I got on so well with my father. He had his own weaknesses. He didn't preach to me about my ones.

I escaped from both of them to my bedroom every night. I listened to a transistor under the blankets. Frank Sinatra comforted me. He was like the brother I never had, singing songs of loss I felt were for me alone.

On the nights I couldn't sleep I read. Books were like pills I took to make me forget what might happen at school the next day. They were substitutes for company. Especially female company. Some of my classmates were already going out with girls. I was too confused in my head to think about having a relationship with anyone. It never struck me that a woman might help me sort myself out. The priests in the college told us to beware of the temptations of the flesh.

Greta became fascinated with religion when she got into her teens. It sneaked up on her without warning. She started reading about the lives of the saints. When she gave out to me now it was because I did something against God rather than her simply flying off the handle. She started looking for reasons for everything. I preferred her the old way. At least you knew where you stood. And you didn't get a lecture afterwards.

She acted as if God was a private friend to her. When we sat in the church I felt she was having these intimate spiritual experiences I could never know anything about. She'd screw up her eyes as if she was in a trance. She never went into any detail about what she'd been through. It was too precious to share with me.

My mother wanted me to be like her at school. I told her I couldn't. 'Are you jealous?' she said.

One night she came up to my room when I was lying in bed. She said she had a surprise for me.

'I'm going to enter,' she said.

'Enter what?' I asked her.

'A convent, dummy.'

I couldn't imagine anyone less likely to become a nun.

'Don't look so miserable,' she said.

I thought she was fooling herself about her vocation. It was as if she needed the attention. I didn't expect her to last more than a few months.

A party was thrown for her. I tried to look sad that she was going. My mother was in tears. Greta milked the situation

I wondered if she wanted to become a nun to escape from the world of men. 1 couldn't remember her ever having been on a date. The only people who called to the house for her were her female friends. She'd been on group outings with boys but that was all. Was there something she was afraid of in the company of men?

'Why are you doing this?' I asked her.

'I don't have a choice,' she said, 'God wants me to work for him.'

I refused to go to the train station with her the day she went away. She said she'd never forgive me. I didn't care. It was all too much of a farce.

At school the problems got worse.

'Where were you the day they gave brains out?' the Dean said to me, 'If it was raining soup you'd be out with a fork.' He told me he didn't hold out many prospects for my future. I was advised to go down to the local hardware shop and get myself measured up for a shovel.

I pretended I was sick to get out of going to school. My father usually let me stay at home if I looked bad. Education was a waste of time in his eyes. He said the only thing you needed to know in life was how to write your name on the back of a cheque.

The Dean taught us Latin as well as being a Dean. He chased me around the room if I missed the conjugation of a verb. He'd come after me grabbing at my hair. Sometimes he pulled lumps off it. Everyone laughed when he did that. It was like a circus act.

On the days we had Latin I hid in the bicycle shed at the back of the gym until the class was over. Sometimes he found me. If he did he dragged me into his office by the neck. I got six slaps on each hand for trying to escape class.

He had a cane that was shredded at one end to make it more painful. He used to pull it out of his cassock like a sword-fighter drawing a sword out of his scabbard. Then he'd swish it up and down a few times to test it. It made a sound like the wind.

I kept staring at him no matter how much pain I was in. That made him furious. I got a kind of strength from it. He knew I didn't care. I was getting the better of him no matter how hard he struck me.

The pain didn't come until a second after the blow. It took that time for the message to get to my brain that I was hit. Afterwards it started to tingle. It was like pins and needles. I sat on my hands to get them back to normal. It was like when you burned yourself or when your foot went to sleep. You had to wait for time to pass.

Sometimes I used to pull my hand away as he was about to hit me. That drove him crazy. He thought it made him look like a fool. Every time I did it I got an extra slap. One time I got nine on each hand. That was my record. I boasted about it. The most anyone else ever got was seven.

I only told my father about the beatings once. It was after he hit me across the face one day after banging into him in the corridor. It was an accident. He came up to the school the next day.

'If anything like this ever happens again I'll lay you out,' he said.

The room went quiet. Then he walked out.

For the rest of the term the Dean didn't acknowledge me. He corrected my work but never handed it back to me himself. If I passed him in the corridor he looked the other way. I didn't know which I preferred, being hit by him or being treated as if I didn't exist.

My mother got more upset about my school work after Greta went off to the convent. If there was a red mark on any of my exercises she came down on me. It wasn't like her. My father said she was missing Greta. He was probably right. I'd see her checking the calendar for the dates of her visits home. There were only three a year.

At Christmas it was as if we killed the fatted calf when she got came home. The world had to stop as she told stories about life in the convent. It was an enclosed order based in Belfast. She brought photographs of herself that she'd taken with the other nuns. Some of them spent most of their time praying. Others did gardening in the grounds. Greta wanted to go to a school to teach biology. It was her best subject.

Her visits got rarer as the years went on. My mother started to miss her more. It got to the stage where she had to go on tranquillisers. I wanted to help her but I didn't know how.

The sixties ground to a close. Suddenly everyone was talking about free love. The dark days of the past seemed to be over as far as Ireland was concerned. Priests stopped giving sermons about hellfire and damnation. There were singing priests in pubs, Elvis imitators. It was a long way from the Redemptorists at retreats. The second Vatican Council blew out all the cobwebs. My father thought they blew out too any of them. 'They threw out the baby with the bath water,' he claimed.

Greta became taken over with it all. She kept saying, 'Celebrate! Celebrate!' There was a charismatic Renewal Group in her convent. She became its main facilitator.

My father wasn't impressed. 'Any day now,' he said, 'she'll come in the door singing *Guantanamera*.' It was a song that was popular at the time. There was a nun on a television series who went around the place on a motorcycle singing it. She reminded him of her. Whenever she came on he'd say, 'There's Greta.'

He hated the church of 'kindness to the cat.' When he heard of a nun who left the cloisters to marry a priest he nearly had a seizure. He said they were all tumbling the wildcat up and down the aisles now.

His world was simple. When he went to Confession he expected to have the wrath of Jove unleashed on him instead of the tolerance of Jesus. He often said he'd like to have been a priest so he could scare the daylights out of parishioners from the pulpit. 'When I do something wrong I like to be told about it,' he said, 'I don't want it explained away.'

It was the same in matters of the law. Criminals who were as black as the ace of spades were getting off with a warning because they said they hit their head off a stone when they were young.

'They blow away half the population,' he said, 'and then they get a good lawyer for themselves. They say, "I'm sorry, Your Honour, I was temporarily insane at the time." A custodial sentence is abandoned. Instead they get assigned to a Social Worker. He brings them into a pre-fab and they have a cup of tea and a chat. It comes out that they were fed on bottled milk instead of the breast when they were babies. That's what caused all the problems. They serve two years in a detention centre and then they're on the streets again.'

When I asked him what his solution to this state of affairs was he said, 'It's simple. We need an Ayatollah.'

2

Most of my father's ideas came from his own father. He idolised everything about him. That created a distance between them. He felt guilty about the fact that he could never live up to his expectations. He took fits of trying to farm the land but he couldn't keep it up. It just wasn't in him.

I heard once that he disappeared for a year one time. Nobody knew where he went. He didn't talk to us about it. His father was fit to be tied. He never had much patience. He put out a search for him but it went nowhere. Then one day my father appeared back home as casual as you like. He'd probably have been forgiven if he had an excuse but he didn't give him one. Things were never the same between them after that.

My grandfather died of a heart attack when he was in his fifties. He was saying the rosary at the time. My father never recovered from the shock. I couldn't understand why he took it so badly because of the distance between them. He said he loved him but I felt he had more fear than love.

He didn't think he was properly appreciated in Galway.

'He employed half the county,' he said, 'but he was never thanked for it. Today he's seen as someone who was only interested in money.'

To him that was blinkered thinking. He believed his motive was to improve his worker's circumstances rather than his own. When he died, the obituary of him that was printed in the local newspaper portrayed him more as a capitalist than a philanthropist.

'I'm going to set the record straight,' he said, 'I'll write a book on him.' There were loads newspaper clippings about his achievements around the house that he planned to use as research.

My mother was given a blow-by-blow account of the book anytime he could get her to listen to him. Sometimes I saw her ready to explode as he told her about it.

'The house is falling down around your ears,' she'd complain, 'and here you are talking about a book.' She told him he'd be better off tilling the soil than busying himself with the study of a man few people cared about.

'That's the whole point,' he said, 'Nobody cares about him.'

He devoted himself so much to it that the farm went to seed. His passion for it increased as he got older. In time it took over his life. It put him into good form if Greta or myself listened to him talking about it. All you had to do was go into a room and he'd buttonhole you. He was like a doll that was wound up. We didn't need to contribute anything. Being there was enough.

He claimed the obituary of his father was the work of a twisted mind. He carried it around with him in his wallet. 'It drove me to drink,' he told me. That might have been an excuse. He'd had a problem with drink for years. It became chronic when he got into his forties.

'He doesn't miss it if he doesn't have it,' my mother said, 'As soon as it passes his lips and it's like a match to a flame.'

He went on binges that lasted weeks. Labourers were employed to look after the farm when he wasn't able to work on it but they didn't do a good job. My mother said they slacked off as soon as he took his eyes off them.

He had problems paying them. Drink took away his money as well as his health.

Any time he went missing my mother gave me the job of tracking him down. I usually found him in the snug of a run-down tavern. He'd be there for hours. Publicans let him stay inside during the holy hour and after closing time. If his form was good he entertained the other drinkers with his stories. Other times he slunk into a corner and drank alone.

If he didn't get home by midnight my mother would be beside herself. The drink became like another woman in their relationship. It was an unspoken third party she could never hope to challenge. She knew if she asked him to give it up he'd only drink more. He had that kind of stubbornness. She told him she'd leave him if he didn't stop. He didn't believe her but she carried through on her threat once. It was after he was coming off one of his worst binges.

'That's it,' she said, grabbing her things. She said she was bringing myself and Greta down to her brother's house in Wexford. It was near the beach in Curracloe. He pleaded with her not to go but it was no good. She had her mind made up. She marched us down to a house where a taxi driver lived. He'd been booked to bring us.

I'll never forget the journey. There was a smell of leaking petrol. Second gear was broken so we had to go from first to third. It meant we were crawling a lot of the time. My mother chain-smoked all the way. It was lashing rain outside. The drops were like pellets against the window.

The car had a slow puncture. It felt as if we were hitting bumps on the road every few seconds. I didn't think we'd make it to where we were going.

The driver didn't talk and neither did my mother. She just kept looking into the distance. Her foot was hopping up and down the way it did when she was nervous. Greta was with me in the back seat. She was chewing chocolate mints.

'Where are we going?' she kept saying. 'Why couldn't I bring my tennis racquet?'

We passed through town after town. I wanted to stop so I could buy some sweets but I wasn't allowed.

'If we break the journey,' my mother said, 'We'll lose too much time.'

Eventually we saw the sea. She told the driver to stop. We went into a roadside café for chips. She went into a toilet to do up her face. Greta and myself played Xs and Os on serviettes. The paper was too soft to play properly.

I kept thinking of my father sitting alone in some bar. Would he be drinking? Maybe he'd stop now. Shock did that to some people.

My clothes were sticking to me because of the rain. I asked my mother if I'd be able to get something dry in her brother's house. 'Maybe,' she said.

We reached it finally. I'd never been there before. It smelt like the sea. I didn't like it and I didn't like him either. He acted friendly to me but I didn't believe it was real. I felt he was only being nice to me because of who I was.

He didn't like my father. I heard somewhere that he wanted my mother to leave him. They were total opposites. He'd been in the IRA as a young man. I heard him asking her if my father ever hit her when he had drink taken. He seemed to nearly want him to have.

We put our clothes on radiators. I watched the steam rise from them. We had towels wrapped around us. As soon as it got dark we were sent to bed. We were put into bunk beds that were too small for us. Greta took the top one. The mattress slumped so much her bottom was almost down on top of me.

I couldn't sleep. There was music from a nearby dance-hall. The waves kept crashing after it stopped.

The next morning was sunny. It was often like that after rain. Everything looked scrubbed clean outside.

I told my mother I wanted to go home. She said we couldn't. I sat with Greta in a conservatory playing cards.

It started raining again.

'Does it ever stop?' she asked her brother.

'For a while,' he said, 'Then it starts again.'

She spent most of the day talking to him. They spoke in low voices so Greta and myself couldn't hear what they were saying. We sat looking out at the rain falling into the sea. It was too wet to go out.

Anytime I went up to my mother to ask her something she put her finger in the air as if to say 'Hush.'

I asked her when we were going back.

'I don't know,' she said, 'I'll tell you after I ring your father.'

He rang her instead. I knew by the way she spoke to him that things were better. At the end of the call she said she was going to give him another chance. Her brother was disgusted.

We went home that night on the train. The taxi driver had gone back to Dublin. He'd got a call for another job. My mother was excited on the journey but I saw fear in her eyes too.

When we got to the station my father was waiting for us. He put his arms around us all.

'Thank you for coming back to me,' he said. He lifted myself and Greta up. He was strong enough to lift the two of us together.

'How are my little chickens?' he said. He had a present for each of us. I got a soldier. He gave Greta a small box of sweets.

When we got to the farm there was a meal on the table. I didn't know if he prepared it himself or not. It was unlikely. He hardly knew where the cooker was.

Over the next few months he didn't drink at all. He said he was happy being off it but I wondered. So did my mother. She was proud of him for fighting it.

One day he told her where he'd stashed a bottle of whiskey. He asked her to pour it down the sink.

She told Greta it was only a matter of time before he went back on it again. When he did he drank more than I'd ever seen him do before. He didn't even seem to be enjoying it. It was as if he was on a mission to kill himself.

Sometimes he drank so much she had to put him to bed when he came home from the bar. At times like that I hardly recognised him as my father. His eyes would be back in his head and his voice muffled. He'd look at me as if he didn't know who I was.

The next morning he usually forgot everything. Greta would be looking daggers at him. My mother would act as if nothing happened. That was her way of dealing with it.

She told me not to tell people about these nights. Maybe they knew anyway. We lived in that kind of area. Everyone knew everyone's business. You could tell by the way they went on.

The people I went to school with looked strangely at me when his name came up in conversation. They made excuses to get away. That upset me. I wasn't ashamed of him. My mother said he had an illness. He was never violent with drink. It made him sentimental. She said the real person came out when they drank. The only one he did damage to was himself.

One time when he was asleep after a binge I saw her taking £20 out of one of his pockets. I didn't blame her. If she left it where it was it was going to end up in the publican's till.

She needed it for food. If she asked him for money for a school book one of us needed he'd throw his hands up in dismay 'We can't afford it,' he'd say. He had a different sense of things when it came to drink. That was a necessity to him. Food was a luxury. Everything was back to front.

In the bars he bought drinks for strangers. He even bought them for people he didn't like. His personality changed with alcohol. Another person took over when he was telling a story. He became an actor giving a performance. The next morning he'd be back to himself.

Drink often made him sick. That didn't make sense to me. I thought people drank because they enjoyed it. My mother made me promise I'd never let it pass my lips. I said I never would. I told her I tasted it once and it made me sick. She smiled when I said that. I liked it when she smiled. Her whole face lit up. It showed how happy she could be even with all the problems we had. But then things would get bad again and the smile would go away. He'd become a prisoner of his need and turn into the other person.

I remember the worst day of that ever. It was a day when a storm was blowing. It was so strong it was knocking trees down. The raindrops were like golf balls.

I watched drivers abandoning cars. People were putting plastic bags over their heads to keep themselves dry. One of our outhouses had its roof lopped off.

My father had a hangover from the night before but he said he was still going to go to the bar. He said he was going to drive to it. My mother tried to stop him.

'It's not safe,' she said, 'You'll crash.'

He said he didn't care. She begged him not to go. She was shouting at him at the top of her voice but he didn't pay any attention to her. .

She hid his trousers in the loft to stop him going out. He was standing there in his pyjamas, shaking her to make her tell him where she put them. She refused.

He went upstairs to Greta's room and put on a pair of jeans she had. I followed him up. They were a few sizes too small for him. He could hardly get them on. They clung to his legs.

He had trouble walking down the stairs. My mother shouted at him as he came into the kitchen. I wasn't able to look at him. There was a mad look in his eyes. When he was going out he banged the door so hard we thought he broke it.

We looked out at him getting into the car. Every time he opened the door it blew shut. His hair was wild in the wind. He threw himself into the car and drove off. It lurched towards the main road. My mother burst into tears.

'This is the way it's always going to be,' she said. I asked her if she was going to follow him. She said there'd be no point.

She did once but it did no good. He only drank more. I told her I'd go after him. She just said, 'If you want.'

I followed him into the town. It took me nearly half an hour. I knew the bar he liked best. It was a run-down place in a back street. I remembered him being in it before. He only went there when he wanted to be alone.

As soon as I got in the door I saw him. He was ordering a drink at the counter. It was his favourite place to be. He liked looking at the optics. Some people were behind him in a group. They were laughing at him but he didn't seem to be aware of it. He just drank his drink without looking round, gazing into the middle distance as it worked its magic on him.

After a few minutes he caught my eye. He looked at me through a mirror that was beside the optics. I was afraid he'd be annoyed with me but instead he beckoned me over. He ran his fingers through my hair. Suddenly he seemed to become aware of the people around him.

'This is the heir to my millions,' he said.

He lifted me onto a stool.

'What would you like to drink?' he said.

I asked him if I could have a Club Orange. He laughed.

'I wish it was all I ever drank,' he said.

I told him the taste of it was nicer than alcohol. That made him laugh again. He said he used to drink it when he was my age

'Are you here to bring me home?' he said.

'Mammy is worried about you.'

'Tell her I'll be back soon.'

A man with a fiddle started to play a song. He put his hands over his ears.

'I hate Irish music,' he said.

'Would you not come home?'

'I don't feel right until I get drink into me. You know that.'

He lowered a glass of whiskey. It was as if he was drinking water. He sucked in his breath. Then he asked for another one.

'Don't ever get like me,' he said to me.

He seemed to be in pain. I asked him why he drank it if he didn't like it.

'You wouldn't understand.'

The music stopped. He started to talk about my mother. He talked about how he first met her, chasing her around all the counties of Ireland until she said yes to his proposal of marriage.

The more he talked, the faster he drank. When he started to slur his words I told him I thought we should be going home. He said, 'You go. I'll be back after you.'

'You shouldn't drive,' I said.

'Don't worry. Someone will bring me.'

As I was leaving I saw him carrying a glass of whiskey into a corner of the bar.

I ran home. There was debris all over the streets from the storm. I saw broken umbrellas in bins. There was a strange quietness around everything.

When I got back to the house my mother was still crying. She asked me how he was.

'Fine,' I said.

'Was he drinking much?'

'No.'

I didn't want to make her any more upset than she was. She kept talking about how good a man he was if it wasn't for the drink. I told her she didn't need to say that.

Greta hadn't been in the house when he went up to her room. She was now. 'Where are my jeans?' she said. My mother pretended they were lost.

We sat looking out the window at the devastation the storm caused. There was a car across the road that was half way down a ditch. It had been abandoned. One of the fields was like a river. A tree in the meadow seemed to be only a fraction of its original size. The water was almost half way up the bark.

My mother told us to do our lessons. We tried to but we couldn't concentrate. After a while we heard a car pulling into the farmyard. It was a black one belonging to a guard.

'It's him,' she said, 'Thank God it's unmarked.

He was asleep in the passenger seat. The guard woke him. He walked him to the door.

'Was he any trouble?' my mother said.

'He never is,' the guard said, 'He just had one too many.'

She thanked him. He doffed his cap to her. We watched him driving off. She brought my father over to a chair.

'He's wearing my jeans,' Greta said.

She started crying. My mother told her to wet the tea. I stood watching him. He was breathing hard.

The kettle boiled. I brought him over a cup of tea.

'No,' my mother said, 'Not now.'

She tried to take the jeans off him but she couldn't. They were too tight. She had to cut them off with a scissors.

'They were my favourites,' Greta said through her tears.

'Sorry, darling,' my mother said, 'I'll buy you another pair.'

She took his trousers down from the loft and put them on him. He woke up. His eyes were glazed. He didn't seem to recognise us for a moment. Then he did.

'Sorry,' he said to my mother, 'I love you.' Then he fell asleep again.

After that day he started to be out more. He was drinking spirits all the time now. I heard my mother crying in the night. If he woke up I'd hear her talking to him. Then it would stop and there would be the steady drone of his snoring. I don't think she slept on these nights. If I went to the toilet I'd see a chink of light under the door.

She was often up with the doctor, filling in forms with him and asking him questions about places she was thinking of sending my father to where he could get help. Sometimes she gave him a pill after his meals. I heard Greta saying that if he took a drink after one of them he'd get a heart attack

One day a car I'd never seen before arrived at the door. A man got out. My mother invited him in. Then she went upstairs. Greta and myself stood looking at him. He had sad eyes and a thin build.

'What are you here for?' I asked him.

'Your daddy,' he said.

My mother came downstairs.

'Is he ready?' the man said. She nodded. A few minutes later he came down. He had a case in his hand. The man took it. He put it in the boot of his car.

My father put his arms around my mother.

'I'll see you soon,' he said. He gave Greta a hug.

'You're the man of the house now,' he said to me.

I asked him where he was going but he didn't say. He went out to the car. My mother waved at him. She was crying. The car scrunched over the gravel path and onto the road.

'Where is he gone?' I asked my mother.

'Somewhere to get well,' she said. Greta seemed to know. I wasn't told. 'It's for the best,' she said.

She was more nervous in the days afterwards, losing her temper over nothing and pulling me up for chores I forgot to do around the house. When I asked her what was wrong with my father she said it was his drinking. Everything would be fine when that was sorted out.

I kept asking her when he'd be coming home but she told me she didn't know, that it was up to the doctors. They were charging a huge amount of money to take care of him. She was worried that we wouldn't be able to pay the bills.

She asked me would I mind if she got a job to ease the blow.

'How could I?' I said.

She said it would mean I'd have to fend for myself a lot of the time. I didn't mind that either. In a way it was like a compliment to me. It meant I'd be the man of the house like he said.

35

She got a job in an office in the town. It paid well but she was away often. She had to get up while it was still dark and walk a half mile to the nearest bus stop. She was often gone all day. It was a strange time for me, coming in from school to an empty house for the first time in my life, seeing notes on the table to heat up a dinner that had been left for me on the Rayburn. Greta would often be home before me. Other times she'd be out with her friends.

I walked around in the silence as I waited for the sound of the bus pulling up outside and then her key in the door. She always asked how I got on at school after she came in. No matter how much news I had I didn't feel she was hearing it. She was a stranger to me now, dressed up in official clothes and with lots of make-up on her.

We bought a carpet with the money she was earning. It was the first thing we'd been able to afford for years. It was moss green with rainbow designs on it. We put it in the living-room. I was almost afraid to walk on it in case I put a mark on it.

Men with posh voices came into the house to talk to her. One of them said he was hoping to open a branch of their company in another town in the county.

'It'll help to pay the bills,' she said to me.

I couldn't think about things like that. My father was on my mind all the time.

'I hope he'll be home soon,' I said.

She said, 'Me too.'

We visited him whenever we could. He was usually too drugged to speak much. When we were leaving he always clenched my hand. He'd usually be biting his lip as if to say he'd let us all down. I wanted to tell him I loved him no matter what he did but I could never get the words out. I'd end up just sitting there waiting for the doctor to tell us it was time to go. My mother would look at him silently, hating and loving him with her huge, tired eyes.

Just as we were about to give up hope he started to get better. The old fire came back into his cheeks. One of the doctors said he'd turned a corner, that the worst was over. He told my mother he'd never drink again. By the look on her face I knew she believed him. She said, 'All you can do is try. Nobody asks any more of us than that.' She looked at him with love in her eyes. I felt my heart beating with excitement as I watched her. The lines disappeared from her face.

'You'll be fine,' she kept saying to him, 'You'll be fine, you'll be fine.' It was like an echo.

That's the last memory I have of her, sitting there at the bedside quietly hoping. Shortly after he was released from the hospital we were involved in a car accident and she broke her neck as a result of it and died.

3

I still see the bridge in my dreams. When we got to the top of it a car hurtled towards us on the wrong side of the road. I let out a scream at my father to swerve but it was too late. We hit it head on. It sent us spinning across the road into a wall. Greta and myself were thrown on top of each other in the back seat. My father's door flung open. He was thrown clear but my mother went through the windscreen. She was dead before the ambulance arrived.

I wasn't able to grieve properly for her. A doctor told me I was in shock. Greta did enough crying for both of us. 'There must be a reason why it happened,' she said, 'Nothing happens without a reason.'

My father couldn't go to the funeral. He was in Intensive Care at the time. Maybe it was for the best. He'd have fought with her brother. Greta spent a lot of time talking to him at it. He blamed my father for the accident.

The next few days were days of waiting. He had a lot of injuries but they weren't life-threatening. For a while the doctors were worried about internal bleeding. He was on a high dose of morphine for the pain. It left him drained of energy. He drifted in and out of consciousness as they did tests on him. After a few days he was moved into an ordinary ward. He had to be fed through a tube.

'I wish I died with her,' was the first thing he said to us when he was able to speak.

We tried to comfort him but he was inconsolable. He just lay in his bed looking at a photograph of her that he kept in his wallet. He said his memories were like knives piercing through him.

We stayed by his bed as he recovered. His neck was in a brace for a while. After the stitches were taken out he said, 'I don't have any feeling in my legs.'

The doctors couldn't say what his long term injuries would be. We prayed that they wouldn't be bad but our prayers weren't answered. After a month in the hospital he was told he'd be spending the rest of his life in a wheelchair. He was paralysed from the waist down.

When he heard the news first he was too drugged to care. Then they took him off the pills and he raged. Doctors watched his room around the clock until they felt he wasn't a danger to himself.

When they said they were letting him home I trembled. I felt he'd be like an animal let loose. They talked to Greta about catheters, bedpans, incontinence. I didn't want to know about things like that. She took it all in.

We converted a room so he could sleep downstairs. For the first few weeks he hardly said a word to us. We left trays of food at his door. Sometimes he picked at it but more often than not he left it untouched.

We looked forward to the day he'd be able to sit in his wheelchair. He said he didn't care one way or the other. District nurses came to the house to check on him every few days. They turned him to stop him getting bedsores.

One day we were told we could lift him onto his wheelchair. It took ages.

'Well done,' he said, 'Now how do I get back into the bed?'

He sat looking into space. We wheeled him into the kitchen.

'Isn't this great for you, Daddy?' Greta said to him. She was always trying to look at the bright side.

'If you say so,' he'd say.

'It could have been worse,' she said, 'You could have broken your neck.'

He hated that kind of talk.

'That's like saying to a man who had a leg amputated that he could have lost the other one as well.'

'I know it's horrible. I'm just trying to make you feel better.'

'Well you're not.'

'What do you want me to say?'

'That it's horrible.'

He didn't stay in the wheelchair long at first. Sometimes he tried to throw himself back into the bed without telling us. He usually fell. We'd hear the crash. He'd lie on the floor and growl up at us. It was almost as if he was trying to put himself in pain.

Some days he locked the door of his room. We'd hear him trying to pace the floor using his crutches. Usually he fell then too.

I knew some people in wheelchairs who lived active lives. My father was never going to be like that.

He gave in to his diagnosis as soon as he heard it. If he wasn't going to be able to live his old life he didn't want any one.

Exercises were recommended for him but he wasn't interested. The idea of attending a support group for people in similar predicaments meant nothing to him either.

'What would it consist of?' he said, 'All of us sitting around saying we felt great because our wives died?' I knew what he meant. No matter how bad he felt about being paralysed, losing my mother was ten times worse for him.

At the beginning I thought he was capable of drinking himself to death now that she was gone. He told me once that that's what he'd do if she died before him.

'I killed her,' he said to me one day, 'If I was driving slow it wouldn't have happened.'

That wasn't true. The guards said the man in the other car was speeding.

'There was a moment before we crashed,' he said, 'that my brain went numb. I could have swerved but I didn't. It was like paralysis before the paralysis.'

'It wouldn't have made any difference. He was too close.'

'Don't try to make me feel better. She could have lived.'

'It doesn't do you any good to think like that.'

'I can't help it.'

No matter how many times I tried to console him he wouldn't listen. It was as if he wanted to torture himself.

'Think of all the good times you had,' Greta said to him.

'What good are they to me now?' he said, 'I'm a vegetable.'

'The feeling might come back,' she said.

'I don't believe that. My nerve ends are dead.'

'You don't know what could happen with exercise.'

'I do. Nothing.'

'Do what the doctors say,' she said, 'They know what would be best for you.'

'What would be best for me would be a new pair of legs. Can they organise that?'

'It isn't your legs. It's your spinal cord.'

'Now you're starting to sound like them.'

'Would you consider going to Lourdes?'

'Lourdes? What would that do for me?'

'It could cure you. Miracles have happened there.'

'Don't annoy me with that talk. I'm not like you. I don't believe in fairytales.'

'Would you not even try it?'

'No. I'm like the man who wanted to put his hand in Jesus' wound.'

'Doubting Thomas.'

'That's him.'

He didn't press charges against the man who crashed into him. The man had remorse. The first time he called to the house my father closed the door in his face. He wasn't ready to talk to him at that stage. A few weeks later he called again. This time he brought him in. He'd changed.

'I don't blame you,' he said to him.

The man was on the point of tears. He wanted to give us money but my father wouldn't let him. He told him he'd already got a sum from his insurance company.

We also got a cheque from a life insurance policy my mother had. The two sums helped to pay all the bills that had been mounting up since the accident. They eased the blow a bit but none of us were in the frame of mind to be appreciative of them.

We converted the sitting room into a bedroom for him. The bed had an orthopaedic mattress. We also had a downstairs toilet put in.

The most foolish idea we had was getting a lift installed. It was so he could go upstairs if he wanted to. He never used it. It cost a lot of money but it was for nothing. He couldn't face going back into his old bedroom. There was nothing else upstairs to interest him.

Now and then he wheeled himself out to the kitchen to nibble at scraps of food from the fridge. He only did that when I wasn't there. I'd come in from the farm and find things gone. There would be no other evidence of him having been there. If I passed him in the hallway he said nothing. I shrunk away from asking him any questions. Anytime Betty rang to enquire for him he was abrupt with her. Eventually he started leaving the phone off the hook so he wouldn't have to talk to her.

His arms became muscular from all the wheeling. It was like the way people said that if you lost one sense the rest of them became stronger. By now we had a new car. I suggested getting it adjusted so he could change gears with his hands. I'd seen a programme on television one night that had a car like that.

'Cars are murder machines,' he said, 'Why would I want to go into one?'

Spring arrived. He'd always enjoyed watching the crops grow. That wasn't the case now. We employed labourers to help with the work. He stayed in his room brooding. I'd hear him coughing sometimes as he got out of bed. He kept the wheelchair beside it. He'd lower himself into it and move around for a while before coming into the kitchen. The wheels squeaked as he pushed them. That was the only way I'd know he was up. Suddenly he'd be there in front of me. He was often in his pyjamas. It took him too long to dress and he needed help. I offered to dress him but he didn't want it.

'What's the point?' he'd say, 'I'm going nowhere.'

I'd make him his breakfast and he'd eat it without talking. Then he'd just sit looking out the window.

One day he asked me to make a dinner for him. When he was finished it he put his arms around me. He took the photo of my mother out of his wallet. 'Wasn't she beautiful?' he said, 'Wasn't she the most beautiful woman in the world?

He cried as he looked at it. I cried too. She was full of joy before she met him and full of joy and sadness afterwards. He fulfilled her but he also destroyed her peace of mind.

'She never had a life after she married me,' he said.

'She loved you,' I said, 'That was enough for her.'

'It was her downfall.'

He started to talk about her. I heard things I'd never heard before. He said they'd eloped to get married, that her parents were against it. Her brother was too. Politics was the main problem. They knew about his drinking too. He was also some years older than her.

They arrived at a church one morning at 9 a.m. demanding that the priest perform the service. He refused at first. Then my father said, 'I'm sleeping with her tonight anyway so it's up to you.' After that the ceremony was performed. 'It was the only way to get it done,' he said. My mother had been afraid to challenge the priest.

He talked to me about the problems they had after they got married. Most of them were to do with drink and money.

'That time she took yourself and Greta away,' he said, 'I was terrified she wouldn't come back.' I thought of the rain on the journey to Curracloe, of the house that smelt like the sea, of the car with the slow puncture and the leaking petrol.

'Why didn't you call her?' I asked him.

'I wasn't able to pick up the phone. Something inside me stopped me.' He said he must have written her twenty letters and torn them all up.

'It might have looked like the opposite but I lived in her shadow.'

Summer was upon us before we knew where we were. The long evenings gave him a lift. I found myself growing closer to him. Greta became distant from both of us. She'd taken leave from the convent because of the tragedy. At first I thought it might do her good but then she changed. She didn't talk much to me. When she did we argued. It was like the old days but the stakes were higher now. My mother's death shattered my faith just as it shattered my father's.

'God let it happen to test our faith,' Greta said, 'but it's okay to be mad at him.'

My father didn't want to hear that kind of talk. He said, 'Is it okay to be mad at you too?'

He lost his temper with her a lot. So did I. She thought we were ganging up on her. In the past she had my mother to back her up against my father and me. They thought alike. Now it seemed to her like two against one.

One day without warning she announced she was going back to Belfast. She said she needed to get in touch with her spiritual side more.

'I feel bad leaving you,' she said to my father.

'Don't. You've been here a long time.'

'Mammy is looking down on all of us.'

I drove her to the train the next morning. She was in a bad mood. I didn't know why. A part of me felt she was blaming me for the fact that she was going back earlier than she intended.

She'd done all the heavy lifting for my father. It made her indispensable to him when he couldn't do anything for himself. She'd filled in the paperwork for

46

the hospital and talked to the carers and physiotherapists about what he needed down the road. I'd made myself scarce when these kinds of discussions were going on. I was, as she put it, 'only there for the beer.'

Everyone on the platform had serious expressions on their faces.

'They're looking at us,' I said.

'Relax. You always think that about everyone.'

I asked her a few questions about Belfast. She was measured in her answers. Maybe she felt I was only asking out of duty. I probably was.

'I don't know if I'll ever get over Mammy,' she said.

'I'm sure God will help you.'

'Sometimes I pray and it's as if he isn't there.'

'Don't they say the darkest hour is before the dawn?'

The train pulled in.

'She was such a saint, wasn't she?'

'It was very hard for her.'

'And now it's hard for us.'

I helped her on with her luggage.

'I'll pray for you. Mind Daddy, won't you? I'll be on the phone.'

He went downhill after she was gone. It was almost as if arguing with her took his mind off himself. Now he didn't have her to bounce off.

'What did I do to deserve this cursed predicament?' he said to me one day.

'All we can hope for is that it will get easier with time.'

'Anytime I see people running outside the window I get so angry I feel like putting my fist through it.'

'I'd be the same. Try to focus on what you still have left in your life.'

'Like what?'

'Me for starters.'

'You're great, but nothing can compensate for a pair of legs.'

I must have looked upset.

'I don't mean that the way it sounds,' he said. 'I don't know what I'd do without you.'

'I don't do much.'

He looked vulnerable.

'You wouldn't put me into a home, would you?' he said, 'I mean if I got worse?'

'Never.'

'I couldn't take it with strangers looking after me.
'

'I'd be the same.'

'Maybe you could spend more time with me. I could give you a note to get off school early.'

That sounded attractive to me. He drummed something up that night. I presented it to the Dean the next day. He didn't look too impressed but he didn't contest it.

Betty called up every now and again over the next few days. More often than not he gave her short shrift.

'Why are you so cruel to her?' I said to him, 'She means well.'

'She talks too much. She'd give a headache to an aspirin.'

I got better at taking care of him. There wasn't much to it. I showered him and prepared his meals. Every so often I went into town to get farm supplies. If the day was fine he sat out on the verandah.

In the evenings he listened to music. He pretended to be the conductor of an orchestra as he played his classical tracks. Control was important to him. He was more out of control now than anyone could be but at times it didn't seem like that.

He still had his moods. 'Damn and blast!' he'd say if anything went wrong for him. I watched him making a hash of simple things like making a cup of tea, spilling the water all over himself as he stretched to reach the kettle. He put great effort into household chores. If they went against him he ranted like a child.

I persuaded him to go to a film in town sometimes. He used to enjoy going with my mother after they were married. They went to all the 'Thin Man' films with William Powell and Myrna Loy. Now anything like that was an ordeal for him.

He was too strong for me to lift into a seat on my own. We had to get the manager of the cinema to help. Drawing any kind of attention to himself made him angry. Not all the cinemas had ramps. If they didn't we couldn't even get into the building in the first place.

'What's a cinema but a big television screen when you think of it?' he said.

'If you carried that logic to its conclusion you'd never go anywhere.'

'That's my ambition.'

l became more like a valet to him than a son. He had a bell beside his bed that he rang for anything urgent. If he wanted me to put a bet on a horse I went into town for him. In some ways we became almost like a married couple, our lives untouched by the circumstances most people had to labour under.

I didn't bother much with the farm. It was there in the background but now that we weren't dependent on it financially it was difficult to work up the enthusiasm to cultivate it.

Spending so much time with him changed people's attitude to me in the college. I'd always wanted to be anonymous. Now I was thrust into the forefront of things.

I was only there for half the time I used to be but it felt like double. I sensed people talking about me behind my back. Some of them laughed. I was excluded from activities I'd once have been considered automatically for.

I complained about it to him.

'Would you like to get out of that place altogether?' he said.

I still had almost a year to go.

'Are you serious?'

'What's education anyway? There are a lot of people with half the alphabet after their names who can't get arrested.'

This was music to my ears.

'If you mean it I'm on for it.'

'We have a deal then.'

He spat on his hand. I shook it. The deal was sealed. I didn't even bother to go back and collect my books.

In the following days I spoiled him any way I could to show my gratitude. A weight had been lifted from me.

'I'll never have to worry about anything again,' I said. He laughed.

'In a week you'll be moaning about something else, like we all do.'

He told me that as long as I stayed with him I'd never have to hold down a regular job.

'How will we live?' I asked him.

'Most of the accident fund is still there.'

'It won't last forever.'

'Not forever, but long enough if we stretch it.'

My mother had spent most of her life in terror that we'd end up in the Poor House. Now that she was gone, ironically, money had ceased to be a problem.

'We don't need anyone except ourselves,' he said often. I was sucked into the hypnosis of it. A life with him meant a life without responsibility. The longer I stayed, the more I grew to fear such responsibility.

At the age of nineteen I was able to convince myself that there was nothing abnormal about the way I spent my days with him. We lived in a state of almost clairvoyant communication. Sometimes we sat for hours together without exchanging a word. I seemed to know what he was thinking without him having to say it and he seemed to be the same with me. I got to know the changes in his moods so well I could anticipate them before they took place. I knew what time he'd shave every day, what time he'd read the paper, what time he'd play with Setanta, what time he'd reminisce. I listened to his stories and occasionally chipped in with some of my own.

The months ran by like so many minutes. I catered for his whims, ran his errands and laughed at jokes I'd heard a hundred times before so I'd see the child-like gleam in his eyes as he came to the punchline.

But then something happened that changed everything between us.

I fell in love.

4

The first time I saw Aisling I felt I had to possess her. It was the eyes that did it. They were as iridescent as the sea.

She was from Athlone. Her father was a Sinn Fein counsellor, her mother a kindergarten teacher. She wore dresses that reminded me of Mexico. There were beads hanging round her neck. She parted her hair in the middle like actresses I'd seen in films. She was like a gypsy to me. There was a vacancy about her, an indifference to anything that went wrong for her. She never thought beyond the moment. I loved that in her because it was so different to my own personality.

She was travelling with a group of campers who cruised along the bay. They belonged to an aquatic club in the town. Children went to swimming lessons there. If you were up early enough you'd see them all in the river in their black suits like little walruses.

My father allowed them to dock beside the boathouse. They pitched tents there after mooring the boats, tying them to spikes they hammered into the ground. Aisling tied hers with what she called a sailor's knot. It meant it wouldn't come loose even in high winds.

'It's a sailor's knot,' she explained.

. She put tarpaulin over it to protect it from the weather. The oars were always criss-crossed like a pair of scissors.

After I got to know her better I went down to see her when I finished my work on the farm. She'd usually be in the boathouse with her friends. They stayed there when they were finished their work in the aquatic club or if it was too cold to be in the tents. There were two beds in it. I used to sleep there with Greta during the summer holidays when we were children.

One day I saw her in the town when I was running an errand for my father. Our eyes met. She was on her way to a hostel to register for something. We got talking. I asked her if she'd like to come for a coffee with me. She surprised me by saying yes. As we sat in the restaurant I found myself telling her things about myself that I'd never said to anyone before.

We went to a film. I asked her without planning to. Maybe that's why she said yes. Whenever I planned something I got flustered. Afterwards I walked her back to the boathouse. I asked her if she'd see me the next day. Her quick enthusiasm made my pulse race.

I brought her for a drive. As we sat in a car park beside a mountain she opened up about her past. She told me she was just after getting out of a relationship.

'It could have ended in marriage,' she said.

'What happened?'.

'He had someone else. The old story.'

She told me about the endless excuses he kept making for broken appointments. She followed him to an apartment complex one night and found him with the other woman. It was actually a friend of hers. That made it worse. She wanted to strike out at him with everything in her but then she thought it would be a waste of energy. Instead she just walked away.

We talked to one another like two people who'd known each other all their lives. I felt a kinship with her I couldn't explain.

I spoke too much when I was with her. It was out of nerves. My father told me he'd done that with my mother when he met her. 'I almost lost her,' he said, 'Women like mystery. Don't give away too much.'

I brought her dancing with me one night. In the Town Hall we listened to a band playing Billy Fury's song 'Stairway to Heaven.' I leant my head against hers as the lights went down.

'You're a real romantic, aren't you?' she said.

I didn't want her to see that side of me. Maybe my father was right. It could drive her away from me.

I wasn't much of a dancer. My father had two left feet and I seemed to have inherited them. She was amused by my awkwardness.

I tried to be cool with her but I couldn't. carry it off. My tension was too noticeable. I knew I was getting in too deep with her. If I had anyone to talk to it would have made it easier but I couldn't tell my father for obvious reasons. Neither could I tell her.

'Tell me about the countries you've seen,' I said.

'If you were in them you'd be bored in a day.'

'Maybe, but I'd still like to be there for that day.'

I envied her the stamps on her passport, the stories she regaled me with around the fires we lit at night beside the tents. Every time I met her I felt we were getting into something that might last. I didn't want to hope too much in case it fell apart. She told me she never stayed long in any one place. Would she with me?

Some of her friends were restless to get on to their next pit-stop. They talked about moving on. My father thought of them as squatters. He wanted them to. So did I, but for a different reason. One or two of them drifted off. I was afraid to ask her if she was going to follow them.

Then out of the blue she got a job waitressing in the town. I thought it was a sign she was going to stay.

I made excuses to go in and see her. My father was curious about where I was going. I felt he knew.

One night I told him I was getting serious about her. He acted cool but I could see he was worried. She was annoyed when I told her I'd mentioned her to him.

'I know how possessive he is,' she said.

'I'm not ten years old.'

She started spending more time with the campers who stayed behind. There were less of them now. It meant they could get to know one another better. She went on hiking weekends with them sometimes. They climbed mountains and did some cross country running. She wanted me to go with them but I told her it wasn't my kind of thing.

She sat around the campfires with them talking about the environment, rain forests, the preservation of the planet.

'How are the tree huggers?' my father said.

I was out of my depth with them. They shared anecdotes about their travels in Europe, Russia, even South America.

'I can't compete with all that,' I told her.

'Then don't. They're them and you're you. Just be yourself.'

'I feel I'm too settled for you.

'Maybe you are – a bit.'

'Are you bored with me?' I asked her.

'No, but maybe we should do more adventurous things.'

'Like what?'

She suggested going out in my grandfather's boat. It was as if she was calling my bluff.

'It's in bits,' I said, 'We'd sink.'

'That's just an excuse. When we you in it last?'

'That's the point.'

'Let's give it a go. He built the boathouse. You should honour his memory.'

'I'm not a boat person.'

'What's that?'

'Someone like you.'

'As opposed to?'

'As opposed to someone like me who gets seasick in the bath.'

She wouldn't take no for an answer.

We fished from it. There were old rods in the boathouse. They weren't much use but we tried them anyway. I caught a trout one day but it was so small I threw it back.

Another day we decided to have what she called a 'boat picnic.' Betty made sandwiches for us. Aisling had been down in her house a few times. They got on great. She said she'd do anything for her.

I brought a bottle of wine. Aisling had a transistor. The wine went to her head. At one stage she started dancing to the music. The boat swayed. 'You'll drown the two of us,' I said. She just laughed.

Going out in the boat with her drew us together in a different way than anything else. It was the first time I'd entered her world instead of her entering mine. One night soon afterwards we were sitting on the edge of the bay when she said, 'I think I'm falling in love with you.'

Her words made me tremble. Nobody had ever said they loved me before, not even my parents. I didn't know whether to be excited or afraid. I remembered someone saying once that the phrase 'I love you' wasn't a statement as much as a question. I answered her in the only way I could: 'I think I'm falling in love with you too.'

I didn't know what she saw in me.

'You're the most intense person I ever met,' she said.

'Is that good or bad?'

'You tell me.'

I became almost afraid of my happiness. It was as if nothing this perfect could last.

'Are you going to stay with me?' I asked her. She was bored by the question.

'Don't talk to me about the future,' she said, 'I have a hard enough time getting through each day.'

We went walking in the woods. I pointed out landmarks that had associations with my grandparents.

I didn't think she'd be interested in them but she was. We ran across fields, throwing ourselves into haystacks. I told myself this was the life I should have been having with Greta. I'd done things like that with her but without enjoying it. Because I hadn't got along with her I felt I'd almost grown up as an only child. We'd done everything together but it felt like nothing. With Aisling, nothing felt like everything.

I wanted to carve our names on a tree one day. She found the idea childish.

'That's like something you'd see in a Mills and Boon book.'

'They'd be there forever.'

'I don't care about forever,' she said, 'I only care about now.'

I wondered if her experience with the other man had scarred her. It might have made her distrust all men, me included.

Summer was ending. Would she end with it? The leaves changed colour on the trees. We were surrounded by an ocean of russet.

I joined some of her friends for a meal one night. It was in one of the town's most fashionable eateries They discussed places I was unfamiliar with. It made me feel uncomfortable. She tried to bring me into the conversation but it didn't work. I felt I was being patronised.

She got tipsy as the night went on. I saw her slumping against a wall. One of her friends was chatting to her. He was a jock with tattoos on both arms. I hated jocks. And tattoos.

I thought she was making a play for him.

59

'Don't flirt,' I said, 'It doesn't suit you.'

'What are you talking about?' she said, 'I've known this guy since I was in the cradle.'

She didn't speak to me for the rest of the night. When we were on our own she was cool with me.

'Sorry,' I said, 'I know I'm possessive.'

'Possessive?' she said, 'You mean paranoid. It must run in the family.'

The incident put a distance between us. She went off somewhere to get away from me. It was her way of dealing with things. She didn't need yoga or meditation or argument or religion or anything else, just nature.

She came back the next day. I saw the tarpaulin over the boat and the oars criss-crossed in that way she liked.

'Where did you go?' I said.

'Timbuktu,' she said.

'Sorry. I know you don't like being cross-examined.'

'Don't spoil what we have.'

When it came to the time she was due to leave she let the others go without her. She gave no reason and I asked her for none.

Removed from her connections she became closer to me. She got quiet. I started to see a new side to her, one that was more like me. I wondered if her bohemianism had all been a pose. Maybe we were all the same at base, all us lonely sailors craving a port.

I talked to her about my mother one night, the struggles she'd had to make ends meet with my father's drinking and two children to raise.

'It's as if she was blighted,' she said, 'Just as he was starting to conquer his addiction she died.'

It was a beautiful night. A shower had just ended. The arc of a rainbow hung like a torch in the sky. Rain flooded the trees, weighing the branches down.

'I don't know how you stand it with him,' she said, 'It must be like being in prison.'

It was only when she said it that I began to look at it like that. We live our lives in routines observed by others. When they bring them to our notice it's as if we're seeing them for the first time.

'In another way it's a liberation. He took me out of school.'

The bay gleamed like steel. Waves lashed the coast. As they pounded the rocks I found myself wanting to be enwreathed by them, to taste the surf in my mouth.

'Are you going to stay with him forever?'

'I don't know.'

The sun inched its way down the sky. Clouds massed themselves around it.

'Kiss me,' she said.

I wanted to take her into the tent with me. Was it too soon to ask? Did she want me to?

The lights of the town fluttered in the town like the fairylights of a Christmas tree. I felt I was in a dream world, living a dream life. I didn't want to spoil it by doing anything. But maybe I'd spoil it by doing nothing.

'Let's lie on the grass,' I said.

We looked up at the sky. There were stars sprinkled everywhere. We tried to pick out The Plough.

She saw a shooting star.

'A soul has gone to heaven,' I said.

She puckered up her eyebrows.

'Do you believe that kind of thing?'

'I don't know. My father says it.'

'Do you get all your beliefs from him?'

I told her I was probably conditioned by him, that we get conditioned by most things over time. I'd been with him so long we probably took on some of one another's qualities, like litmus paper.

'How old is he anyway?' she asked me.

'As old as God,' I said. She laughed.

'So does he sit in a big chair and make pronouncements about how the rest of us should live?'

'Yes. If you disobey him he consigns you to eternal damnation.'

I brought her up to him for a meal the following night. She'd only seen him for short periods up to now.

It was a disaster. She dressed in a mini-skirt and a tight-fitting polo-necked jumper. I could see him looking her up and down. It was as if it made her cheap.

'He makes me feel as if he's undressing me with his eyes,' she said to me.

'Don't worry,' I told her, 'He's just X-raying your soul. He does that to everyone.' She put out her tongue at me.

We ordered a pizza but it was stone cold when it arrived. The driver had got lost.

'Typical,' my father said.

'That's what you get for living in the middle of nowhere,' she shot back at him. He took it as an insult.

'I didn't know you came from New York,' he said.

She went out to the kitchen to make tea. I followed her.

'That man,' she said, 'I was just trying to make a joke.'

'So was he. There's a pair of you in it.'

She heated the pizza but it wasn't the same. It tasted soggy.

'I think we can put this down to experience,' he said, handing it back to her. She went out to the kitchen to dump it.

'Her dress is very short, isn't it?' he said to me when we were on our own.

'So what?' I said.

'She's spending most of her time pulling it down. I feel like telling her if she wore a longer one she wouldn't have to.'

'Well don't. Try and curb your tongue.'

'I'm too old for that now.'

'She has nice legs. What's wrong with showing them off?'

'She's not at a disco.'

When she came back he started talking about politics. She had the misfortune to mention she'd been in the Connolly Youth Movement. Anything nationalistic was anathema to him. I knew it was going to drive him up the wall. It led to him launching into a reverie about the time his father used to ride to the hounds, the days when the crown was over the harp, before the debacle of 1916 when some misguided poets fired a few bullets and a way of life he worshipped disappeared forever.

She glared at him after his outburst but she said nothing. He looked triumphalistic. She made some excuse to leave early. I pleaded with her at the door to stay but it was no good. 'He went too far,' she said. I went back inside

'What did you think of her?' I said.

'She's a nice girl but not the type I envisaged for you.'

'What kind would that be?'

'You know what I mean. Don't forget we were a county family once.'

I felt like hitting him.

'And what are we now?' I said, looking out at the wasteland the farm had become.

'It doesn't matter if we're on our uppers. We're thoroughbreds.'

I waited until he was gone to bed before I went down to her.

'That was unforgiveable,' I said.

'To put it mildly.'

'How are you now?'

'Okay. I had a drink to cool me down.'

'How does this affect us?'

'I wish I knew.'

'Were you thinking about us?'

'Obviously.'

'Did you come to any conclusions?'

'No. It's just a bad situation. I hope you realise that if anything ever became of us, my father could never meet him. He wants a united Ireland.'

'I know. You told me that. Don't worry, it'll never happen. I wouldn't want another Civil War.'

'That's exactly what it would be.'

'Thanks for holding your patience with him.'

'It wasn't easy.'

'I could see you ready to explode at one stage.'

'I didn't just have to count to ten. I had to count to a hundred.'

In the following nights I continued to go down to her after he fell asleep, hurling myself down the incline that led to the bayside and meeting her in the boathouse, exchanging the cold of the night for the warmth of her, the suffocation of my father for the freedom she brought me. We pushed the two beds against one another like Greta and myself used to do. When I was lying beside her I forgot all the tension. She said it should never have been there in the first place.

'If Greta stayed at home,' I said to her one night, 'he mightn't be so possessive.'

'Well, hello, she didn't. It's not your fault she left. Or that your mother died.'

She put her head in her hands. I looked out at the silence of the night. The moon descended on the bay.

'Could Betty not move in with him?' she said, 'They'd be company for one another. It would be like killing two birds with one stone.'

'You must be joking. They can't be in a room for five minutes together without skin and hair flying. The killing would be literal. They can't stand one another.'

'They'd get over that if they were together all the time.'

'I don't think so. It would only get worse.'

'What do they argue about?'

'My grandfather mostly. He could do no wrong as far as my father is concerned. Betty saw him as a tyrant.'

'Why was that?'

'He broke up a relationship she had to a man she loved.'

'You never told me that.'

'You never asked me.'

'What happened?'

'He was from the wrong side of the tracks.'

'He sounds a bit like me. I better watch my step. The apple doesn't fall far from the tree.'

'Shut up.'

I made my way back to the house before dawn so he wouldn't suspect anything. When I went into him with his breakfast he eyed me up and down suspiciously. It was as if he knew where I'd been. I made up a story about having gone to meet someone I knew in town. He always knew when I was lying. I felt ashamed of myself, not for the lies but for not being able to stand up to him.

One evening soon afterwards as we lay together in her tent I thought I saw the spokes of his wheelchair glinting in the moonlight.

'Look,' I said, 'He's on the verandah.'

'I don't care where he is,' she said, 'He's welcome to join us for a midnight snack if he wants.'

She could never understand my nervousness with him.

'You might as well be in a straitjacket with the influence he has over you.'

We went down to the boathouse. It was getting on to night. The moon hinted. Anglers examined their catches on the banks of the bay. Worms were tested and discarded. Fishing lines swished through the air, arcing their way across the sky.

The stars shone like diamonds above them.

'I could stay here forever,' she said as she looked up at them.

She thought it was heavenly. It was heavenly for me too but only because she was there. What good would it have been if I didn't have her to share it with? I thought of kings in fairytales courting princesses who didn't love them. Not all fairytales ended happily.

We continued to meet every few days. I walked through the town with her feeling ten feet tall. People who hadn't seen me with a woman before looked twice, wondering if there was a side to me they'd missed. I wondered that myself as well.

In restaurants I acted important. I ordered exotic dishes for her, playing the role of the casual blade. I made a bad job of it but she was lady-like enough not to make that obvious. She went along with the charade, letting me wine and dine her like any other suitor anxious to make an impression.

We went to a hotel for a meal one night. I knew the waitress. She was used to seeing me with my father. I was dressed in his suit.

'Well wear,' she said.

I pretended to be scrutinising the menu.

'You usually have fish and chips, don't you?' she said.

That ruined it for me. Aisling chose something I couldn't pronounce. I said, 'I'll have that too.'

I felt self-conscious as I ate it. When we were finished I asked her if she'd like a bottle of wine.

'Can you afford it?' she said.

'Of course,' I said even though I wasn't sure.

I went out to the toilet to check my wallet. There was just about enough money for everything.

I couldn't get the effect of the wine but she did. She was merry when we got back to the boathouse but I couldn't equal her mood. Even if I drank another full bottle of wine I'd have ended up sober. The night ended with her dancing around the room and me pretending to be drunk.

Another night I bought her a dress the wrong size.

'I don't look good in feminine things,' she said, 'I'm a tomboy, remember? Next time try jeans.'

I did that but I got them in the wrong size too. She squeezed herself into them.

'You must think I'm thinner than I am,' she said, 'Is that meant to be a compliment?'

To another woman it might have been but she had no interest in her figure. That was probably because she never had to worry about it.

I felt I was punching above my weight with her.

'Don't try so hard to impress me,' she said, 'you impress me enough just by being yourself.'

I couldn't accept that. The stories I told on our nights out could never match her ones. When we went to films she tried to act interested but she was more tuned into real life than plots concocted by Hollywood. She'd been too busy living her life to immerse herself in the goings-on of stars.

I wanted to tell my father more about our times together but I couldn't. It would only have increased the tension between us. Meeting her became like sneaking out of a dormitory window. It was unfair to keep him in the dark but I could never confront him with her. I was cool with him as I gave him his meals and he equally cool with me as he ate them. My eyes were almost permanently fixed on the clock. I watched for the moment he'd nod off to sleep so I could be with her.

I read books to kill the time, looking out the window as I waited for the sun to go down. The lights of the bay beckoned to me like an invitation. It always seemed to be on these nights that he wanted an awkward job done. Maybe he sensed my restlessness. I felt he wanted to hold onto me out of a sense of resentment.

When I got down to her on such nights I'd be out of breath. She never understood how he had such power over me when he didn't even have the use of his legs.

'If I'm delaying you will he put you across his knee?' she taunted, making me feel six inches tall, 'Is it past the curfew time yet?'

If the nights were too cool to go walking we stayed in the boathouse. In the mild evenings she dressed in nothing but her bra and shorts. I felt my desire for her growing. It had to be only a matter of time before we became intimate.

That happened after we'd been at a play in the town one night, a play so boring that we left it at the interval. We stopped at an off-licence on the way home to get a bottle of wine. It was a wetter than wet night. The sky was swollen with rain. It pummelled down on the roof.

This time we didn't push the two beds together. I went into her one.

She put her arms around me.

'You're all knotted up because of your father,' she said.

'He didn't do it to me. I did it to myself.'

'Don't beat yourself up for the fact that his mobility was taken from him. If the situation was reversed he'd be living his life without you.'

'You can't say that. What proof have you?'

'I know the way he thinks. He's out for himself.'

He'd said the same thing to me about her. Each of them saw the other as the enemy. Each knew the other could take me away from them.

'Give him the benefit of the doubt,' I said.

'Does he deserve it?'

I woke up the next morning only half-remembering what happened. A hangover from the wine stung my head. The window was open. Light flooded through it. I listened to the sounds of the morning. A tractor in the distance chewed the land.

'We survived the downpour,' she said.

'And one another.'

The sky was as bright as I'd ever seen it. Light burst through it like from a lens.

She looked different without her make-up,

'Am I the first girl you've slept with?' she said. I was too ashamed to admit she was.

'Would you prefer me if I had more experience?'

'Most of the men I've known spent their time playing games with me.' It might have been the truth or maybe she was just being polite.

After that we spent the night together whenever we could. I tried to equal her casualness but there was always some guilt nagging at me, some cold-blooded voice at the back of my mind telling me I didn't deserve her.

My father seemed to know if my bed hadn't been slept in. I wasn't sure how. He said he never went upstairs. Maybe he was using the lift without telling me.

He tried to turn me against her.

'Once a voyager, always a voyager,' he said to me one night, 'She was born under a wandering star. That's not the type of woman I see you settling down with.'

I told her what he said. She said she'd never thought of settling down until she met me. Now she thought she could.

'Are you saying you'd like to marry me?' I said.

'What do you think?'

'You can't just say things like that.'

'Why not? You've told me you love me, haven't you?'

'There's a difference between love and marriage.'

'Is there? Isn't there a song about it? Don't they say it goes together like a horse and carriage?'

'Now you're making fun of me.'

'Maybe I'm trying to get you to face up to what you want.'

'I know what that is.'

'What?'

'You.'

'Then why don't we tie the knot?'

'My situation here is complicated.'

'What situation isn't? Are you telling me you'd go off with me if it wasn't for your father?

'Obviously.'

'You can't stay with him forever.'

'He thinks I will,'

'What do you think?'

'I don't know. This is all happening too fast for me.'

'Too fast after seven months?'

'I don't know if it would work.'

'Why not?'

'Being with you is like trying to hold a moonbeam in your hands. I can't convince myself you'd be content with me after all the things you've seen.'

'Maybe that's exactly why I would be. But I wouldn't be too sure about you.'

'What do you mean by that?'

'I'm a novelty to you. The lustre might wear off. Sometimes I think you want me not so much for myself as that I'm an antidote to the way things used to be for you.'

'That's ridiculous. I need time to adjust, that's all.'

She looked at me with that mischievous expression that suggested she didn't believe a word of what I was saying.

'You know what your problem is?' she said

'What?'

'I create a dependency in you and you like to think you're untouchable.'

The wind came up, weaving patterns in her hair.

'I wish you met my mother,' I said suddenly.

'Where did that come from?'

'I don't know. Maybe she'd have wanted you for me more than he does.'

'One of these days you're going to have to make up your own mind what's good for you.'

'I know.'

'You're always looking at the what-might- have-beens. You have me now. '

I had her and I didn't. The fact that I wasn't able to give her a straight answer made her distance herself from me. She said we were at a crossroads. Either we parted or made a commitment. There was no middle ground.

I couldn't make up my mind. It pulled her spirits down. She went away sometimes. Even when she was with me I noticed her making calls to her friends, arranging meetings with them. It was like emotional blackmail.

The man she'd known for years closed in on her. They went out together a few times. I felt she was playing us off against one another.

'Do you like him?' I asked her.

'Are you afraid to say his name? It's Tony.'

'Okay. Do you like Tony?'

'He's all right.'

'Do you like him as much as me?'

'No.'

'So why do you keep seeing him?'

'Because I don't know where I stand with you."

'I love you. Isn't that enough?'

'There are three people in our relationship. Your father is the third one. As long as he's alive you'll never commit yourself to me.'

'He needs me. I've told you that a hundred times.'

'You're using him as a scapegoat. I've told *you* that a hundred times.'

'Why would I do that?'

'Like most men you see commitment as a dirty word.'

'Not for you I don't.'

'I've seen your fear of me in your eyes. It's almost as great as your fear of him.'

'Now you're being ridiculous.'

'If you don't walk away from him, I will. I can't take your duplicity anymore.'

'You don't mean that.'

'I do.'

She went down to the boat. I watched her loosening the mooring rope from the spike. She sat in.

A moment later she started to move away. The oars went back and forth in her familiar rhythm. I expected her to look back at me but she didn't.

The ripples of the water widened. She went farther and farther out into the water. Eventually she was only a dot. My heart started beating fast. She wasn't bluffing. The game was up.

I approached him that very evening. As I went in the door he looked up at me accusingly from his chair. It was almost as if he knew what I was going to say.

'How would you feel if I moved away for a while?' I said.

I expected him to unleash himself on me but he just sat there.

'I can't stop you if you want to,' he said.

I made him his tea. We talked of trivial things. There was a feature in the news about a rise in the cost of living. It was the kind of thing we discussed every day without thinking twice about it.

That evening, though, I heard him coughing viciously in his room. I rang the doctor. He said he'd call up later.

I went down to Aisling. She was in her tent.

'Well?' she said, 'Did you do it.'

'Yes.'

'And?'

'He said it would be fine.'

'So we're going.'

'Of course. I just need to be sure his health is okay.'

'Has something happened?'

'He's been coughing. I phoned the doctor. He'll be up later.'

She shook her head.

'I knew it.'

Later that night he took a turn. When I went into him with his food I found him lying on the floor. He was reaching frantically for the bell to try and call me. I rang for an ambulance. Aisling was up at the house by the time it arrived. As the orderlies were stretchering him into it she gave me a look that suggested I'd been duped. We followed it to the hospital in the car. She was sullen with me on the journey.

We spent the next few hours going from doctor to doctor. Each opinion contradicted the one before. An intern studied his cardiogram.

'He may have suffered a mild stroke,' he said, 'We'll keep him in for a few days to see what's going on.'

He was like a child in the bed.

'Sorry for putting you through this,' he said.

Aisling walked out of the ward. I followed her to the car.

'Well,' she said.

'Well what?'

'I can see where this is going. Loyal son realises what's truly important in life as gadabout sailor friend gets the heave-ho.'

'I don't know what you're talking about. This changes nothing.'

'It changes everything.'

It was the first night she could have spent with me in the house without having to worry about him disturbing us but she didn't. She went down to the boathouse instead. They let him home the following day. I asked him what happened.

'They said it was a false alarm.'

I wondered if she was right. Had he put it all on?

I went down to her. She was taking her rucksack from the boathouse. The boat lapped in the water at the edge of the slipway.

'Where are you going?' I said.

'Where do you think?'

I felt my life flooding before me the way they say a drowning man's does. I saw the deprivation of life tending an invalid and then the uncertainty of a future under her own power.

I was locked between the two threats. She stood on the edge of the water with a look of sadness in her eyes. I went towards her but she walked away from me. She unloosed the mooring rope from the spike and lassoed it into the boat. The oars were criss-crossed. She threw the rucksack over them.

My heart started to beat fast. I looked into her eyes, the eyes that were like the sea. I felt myself being swallowed up by them.

We were only given one life to live. Could I spend the rest of mine like I was doing, tending a man who denied me the experiences he'd had when he was my age, trying to turn me away from the woman I loved?

'You mean more to me than he ever could,' I said, 'I've been a fool up to now not to see that. Can you forgive me?'

I stared at her. Strength flooded into me from somewhere.

'Don't go,' I said.

She started to cry. I felt a mixture of nervousness and exhilaration. She threw her arms around me. It was as if I was being created into a new essence.

She took her rucksack from the boat and put it on the grass. Then she reached for the mooring rope. She wound it back around the spike.

There was no going back now.

5

My father spent most of the following weeks undergoing tests. They sent him to hospital for a fortnight. He was wheeled into rooms where machines checked what seemed like every inch of his body. Advice about his lifestyle was greeted with groans. In the freedom of his absence I became inseparable from Aisling.

We trekked through the woods that surrounded our land. I showed her paths I'd travelled with my father for decades. She learned them better in the space of as many weeks.

People waved out car windows at me when we were on the road.

'You seem to know everyone,' she said to me one day.

'It's like that in the country. It doesn't mean I have much to do with them.'

'Nobody knows anyone in the places I've lived.'

'Maybe they're better off.'

A tree blew down in a storm. One of her friends had an axe. I chopped wood from some of the branches with it. She taught me how to set fires, how to cook outdoors, how to make slip knots.

'You're becoming quite the camper,' she said. I never thought it would happen.

One day when we were in the woods I said, 'Let's get lost.'

'You mean like Hansel and Gretel?' she said, 'That wouldn't work for me. I'm too practical.' I wanted her to throw her compass away but she wouldn't. She said she was undressed without it.

She taught me how to row as well.

'It's all in the wrist,' she said, 'Glide along the water without making too many ripples and you'll be fine.' She was right. The less strength I used, the faster we moved.

So I was a camper. Would it last? If I turned into her, would she turn into me? Which would be easier?

'Would you ever consider moving in with us?' I said to her one night as we sat in the boat in the middle of the bay.

'Are you mad?' she said, 'With your father the way he is?'

'His bark is worse than his bite. Once you get to know him he's soft.'

'I know he hates me. I can see it in his eyes.'

'He's afraid you'll take me away from him. If you were in the house all the time he wouldn't be. The three of us could be happy.'

'There'd have to be a blue moon for that.'

'Why?'

'He'd resent me with every bone in his body.'

'How do you know until you try?'

She was quiet as we made our way back to the shore. I could see she was thinking about what I said.

'What would I do all day?' she said as he docked.

'You could help with the housework. He'd take to you. I'm sure of it. Maybe you could even nurse him a bit.'

'I know as much about nursing as the man in the moon.'

'It would be mainly for the company. He's lonely. An extra person in the house would prop him up. You might even wean him away from me.'

I was making it up as I went along, latching onto the idea as a lifeline both away from him and towards her at the same time.

'Please say you will. For a few weeks even.'

'I don't know. You never really belong to me when he's there.'

'That's only because he's not involved with you.'

'He doesn't want to be.'

'You're being hard on him. He doesn't have much to live for. I'm all he has.'

'If you had the two of us you'd slip back into your old ways. I'd be like a fifth wheel.'

'I guarantee you I wouldn't. He'd be the fifth wheel.'

'What about the sleeping arrangements?'

'We could pretend you were in Greta's room for a while.'

'Jesus, this gets better and better.'

'It would be only until he gets used to you.'

'And after that?'

'After that I'd tell him we were an official couple.'

She paused.

'You drive a hard bargain,' she said.

'Does that mean you'll do it?'

'I know I'm insane but I'll give it a try.'

My heart beat with excitement.

'Thank you,' I said, 'you won't regret it.'

He was wary of her for a while after he came out of the hospital but then he thawed out. She thawed out with him too. After a bad start they gave one another a second chance. He saw her charm and she saw his. I felt her becoming a part of his life. She was sleeping in in Greta's room as far as he was concerned. After he fell asleep she came into mine. He rarely came upstairs. The lift lay idle.

This was my new life. She replaced Greta as a presence around the house. Or even my mother. She moved like my mother around the kitchen. Both of them had the same casual grace. They say we all marry our mothers. Was this why I'd fallen for her in the first place, to remind me of what I'd lost?

She dressed and fed him. Having her do things like that was a novelty to him. In his demeanour there was a spiritedness I hadn't seen since my mother's death. He enjoyed entertaining her. Sometimes he had her in convulsions. When he told her stories about his past he gave them added twists to entertain her. He'd always liked an audience. Now it was double what it used to be.

His hospital tests came back clear. She didn't pass any comment on that. A month earlier she would have. She was in thrall to him.

I got involved in the farm work again. He gave me a flexible roster of duties to perform. They were shared with the labourers we employed to tie up the loose ends. I wondered what his father would have thought of our system. We were all pulling together for the common gain. Jack was indeed as good as his master.

When I came in from the fields I'd usually find him regaling Aisling with yet another yarn, injecting it with a new-found vigour because of the adrenalin she gave him. Sometimes he even seemed to be flirting with her.

'Am I intruding?' I said once. She was sitting on her knees on the carpet, peering into an old journal.

'If you were a gentleman you'd marry this lady.'

She looked up at me with a big smile on her face. Later that night I asked her how she was finding him.

'He wears me down,' she said, 'He talks ninety to the dozen and you're meant to take it all in.'

'Now you can see how hard it was for me to be with you when he was up here on his own.'

'You should never have let him get a foothold in your life. After you did it wasn't his fault anymore.'

We went out in the car some evenings to get breaks from him. I showed her places that were benchmarks of my youth, places I'd played with Greta when I thought we'd never grow up. One night when we were walking in the woods I heard the siren of an ambulance. It stopped me in my tracks.

'What's wrong?' she said.

'It could be for him.'

'Why would you think that? There are lots of other people living around here.'

'Not that many in his state of health.'

'You'll have to stop thinking the worst. Don't worry about something until it happens.'

'I'll try,' I said, but I couldn't stop fretting.

We'd brought a picnic with us but my heart wasn't in it. As soon as we laid the rug on the ground she noticed that.

'Do you want to go back?' she said.

'Would you mind?'

She said she didn't but there was no mistaking the frustration on her face.

I found myself running to the place where we'd parked the car. She turned on the radio when we sat in. It was a music station that played mostly rock songs. She put it up to full volume. I felt she was trying to spite me.

When we got to the house he was sitting reading the paper.

'More horror in the news,' he said, 'Will it ever stop?'

She gave me a look.

'Nobody ever got rich printing happy things,' I said.

'You can say that again.'

She started to walk upstairs.

'Are you all right?' I said.

She didn't answer. He looked at me with his glasses half way down his nose in that way he had.

'What has you two home so early?' he said.

'We just felt like it.'

'Has Aisling gone to bed?'

'I think so.'

He went over to the drinks cabinet. Sometimes I wondered if he wanted us to argue.

He poured himself a brandy.

'Will you join me in one?' he said, 'I've done some more work on the book.'

'I suppose that means you want to read it to me.'

'Could you suffer another chapter?' He was like a child asking for sweets.

'I love hearing it.'

He made a performance about taking the pages from his drawer, putting them into order over a blanket he kept on his lap.

He cleared his throat the way people did before giving a speech.

'And so it came to pass...'

He launched into it. It was a chapter about land rights, evictions, Catholic Emancipation. He even brought the Famine into it.

'What has this to do with your father?' I said.

He took it badly if I criticised anything. He straightened his glasses, peering at me like a judge.

'Have you ever heard of context?'

He continued reading. I tried to take in what he was saying but my concentration wasn't there. He copped it.

'You're not paying attention. Am I boring you?'

'My mind wandered for a second.'

'No problem. I'll read that bit again.'

Finally he was finished. I over-praised it to take attention away from the fact that I'd only been listening to a fraction of it.

I watched him putting it into a folder, carefully segregating each chapter. He sailed off into the study with it.

It was all hours before I got to bed. My eyes were falling out of my head. I went into her room but she was asleep. There was a writing pad on a tallboy. I tore out a page of it. 'Sorry,' I wrote. I put it on the pillow beside her.

She was still grumpy the following morning.

'You'll have to tell him we're sleeping together,' she said.

'I'm sure he knows. We just haven't talked about it.'

'That's the problem around here. Nothing is ever talked about.'

'What do you want me to say to him?'

'The words don't matter. He just needs to know what's going on.'

'I thought you said he did already.'

'It has to be said.'

'I know. I'm trying to find the best way.'

'No you're not.'

'I can't just say it baldly.'

'Why not? It isn't the fifties.'

One night soon afterwards we were in bed together when we heard the lift being activated. It had hardly been used since the day we had it installed. She jumped up.

'He's upstairs,' she said.

The wheelchair moved down the corridor. He knocked on the door. We looked at one another.

'What in the name of Jesus,' she said.

His voice rang out.

'Are you awake?'

'Come in.'

The handle turned. He was there before us. She pulled the covers around her. He looked at her with a kind of amused malice.

'I heard a noise,' he said, 'I thought it might be an intruder.'

She sank under the clothes.

'Let me check,' I said.

I got out of bed. She was completely under the covers by now.

We went downstairs in the lift. I'd only been in it with him a handful of times. He didn't look worried. I saw an expression of victory on him.

We followed the noise to a window at the back of the house. It was flapping against a rafter in the wind.

'For God's sake,' he said, 'So that's all it was.'

'Did you not check?'

'I was afraid to. Sorry for bothering you.'

'It's no problem. Better safe than sorry. How did you get out of the bed?'

'With great difficulty.'

'You should have rung the bell.'

'I thought it might have given you a fright.'

'You gave us a worse one coming up the way you did.'

I went back to her.

'What was it?' she said.

'A window banging off a rafter.'

She shook her head.

'He gives me the creeps. I think he knew.'

'Why would he come up if that was the case?'

'To find us together.'

'I don't think he's that curious.'

'I do.'

Neither of us slept much that night. She turned away from me in the bed.

'Can I put my arms around you?' I said to her.

'Not now.'

When morning came she said, 'We need to talk.'

'I know this is down to me.'

'We've been through it so much before. I don't know why we're still back at square one.'

'I'll tell him to back off.'

'That's not enough. You'll have to make a clean break.'

The weeks wore on. Winter bit into us. Cows lumbered awkwardly across the fields. The water in the bay was cold and white.

We spent more time away from him. The boathouse was still a bolthole for us. We rowed so far down the bay sometimes the house became little more than a dot in the distance.

'If only it was always that,' she said.

He started to drink more. It was as if he thought he was losing us. He needed something to block that fear. He became merry with it.

'I took a lot of drink in my life,' he'd say as he lifted the brandy glass up in the air, 'but twice as many pledges.' I remembered the way he used to be on a binge, sentimental sometimes and occasionally bitter, inveighing against the people he felt were trying to belittle his father.

He was still up to his tonsils with the book, contacting historical societies for documents every other day. I couldn't figure out why. He said he wanted to list his father's acreage, to document how far the land stretched before we had to sell it off.

I didn't think that would do his reputation any favours. His wealth alienated him from people. When we lost ours we inhabited the world most other people did.

'Why do you want to go back to the other one?' I asked him.

'You don't understand,' he said, 'This is going to be a chronicle. I'm on a different level entirely to what you think.'

He often wrote from his bed. That would be when he was too weak to dress. There was a fire grate in the room. He smoked constantly, throwing cigarette butts into the grate when he was finished with them. Sometimes they didn't reach it. One night he set the bedspread up in flames. I charged across the room with a cloth to try and douse them.

'Let the place go up for all I care,' he chirped, 'We might get another lob from the insurance crowd.'

Aisling thought he was mad. She imagined him scribbling away as the flames engulfed him.

Every night he regaled us with details about his father, the endlessly-repeated phrases coming at us like so many mantras: *You could cut yourself on the crease of his trousers. The bishop was a daily visitor to his house. He gave all his workers twenty shillings to the pound. He drank whiskey every day of his life but was never seen drunk.*

Each time they were trawled out it was like the first time. We tried to look entertained. He was overdosing on a topic we hadn't invited.

'Now I know how your mother must have felt,' Aisling said to me one night as we made our way down to the bay after an exhausting night listening to him.

She took breaks from him to recharge her batteries. One weekend she went to Athlone to see her parents.

'Have I scared her off?' he said.

'She just needed to get away for a while. This is our world, not hers.'

It was back to just having me to listen to him now. His enthusiasm wasn't as great because of that. He didn't bother going into his study to read to me, or even to the living room. We stayed in the bedroom, watching turf crackling up the chimney as he read. Often the readings were flat. An expression came into his face that reminded me of how he used to look when my mother took drink from him. I couldn't concentrate because I hadn't her beside me.

When she came back she seemed different. She started to see more of her friends.

'You should come out with us more,' she said.

I didn't want to go but how could I refuse after all the times she'd been up with my father? Maybe if I made a hit with them, I thought, she might get to like me more.

I tried to be natural with them but it was difficult. They rarely drew me into their conversations. I hovered on the edges of these evenings like an interloper.

When I said this to her she said, 'Now you know how I feel up in your place.'

She met them sometimes without telling me. I'd go into the bedroom and she wouldn't be there. Then I'd find a note. It would have something flippant written on it like, 'Join us in the usual place.' Sometimes I did. I usually came home flat from these nights. She noticed it. I felt guilty, as if I was letting her down. They were her friends after all. She'd known them much longer than she did me.

One night I heard her mentioning the word 'Europe' on a phone call to one of them. After she came off the line I asked her what that was all about.

'Don't eavesdrop,' she said, 'People who eavesdrop generally hear things they don't like.'

'Is it true though? Are you planning to go on a trip there?'

'You're cross-examining me again.'

'You don't tell me things anymore.'

'What don't I tell you?'

'Anything.'

'You know something? Sometimes you drive me up a tree.'

'Sorry. I know it's hard for you here.'

I feel I have no life of my own. Either I'm with you all the time or else he is.'

'I know how demanding he can be.'

'You are too.'

'Why don't you go away for a while and see if it does you any good. You could stay for as long as you wanted.'

'I don't know. I'll think about it.'

Her nerves became frayed over the next few weeks. She forgot meetings we arranged. Sometimes she broke off a train of thought in mid-sentence. If I disagreed with her on something she over-reacted. She went for walks through the woods I told her about when we were seeing one another first, woods she came to know better than me. Back in the house she was distant. Both of us were loth to fill up the silences that welled up around us like judges. In her features there was a lethargy. It was as if this eternally young woman was becoming old without warning. I hated it in her and hated myself for causing it. She didn't even have the energy to pretend now, moving around the house like someone drugged.

She couldn't make up her mind what she wanted. I thought a job outside the house might help. A man I knew ran a business in the town. I asked him if he'd take her on for a while. He said he'd be happy to. She didn't seem to care much either way. It was a secretarial job.

'I'd be useless at it,' she said.

'No you won't. You pick things up fast.'

It got her out of the house but she couldn't adjust to it. She'd never done a nine-to-five before. I felt guilty about pushing her in that direction but I knew it was where she needed to be. If she didn't anchor herself somehow her old wanderlust would surface.

Maybe it never went away. I saw her leafing through old scrapbooks of her travels.

'I'm restless,' she said one day after she came in from the job.

She threw herself into a chair.

'I feel there are two people inside me pulling me in opposite directions,' she said.

'Is one of them towards me?' I asked desperately.

'I don't know anymore.'

We ended, as most of the important things in our lives end, without warning. I was after coming from a cattle mart in Tuam. She usually met me after things like that to ask me how I got on but that day she didn't. The car wasn't there.

I got a bus back to the farm. As soon as I went in the door I knew something was wrong. My father was sitting at the Rayburn. He looked at me strangely.

'Where's Aisling?' I said.

'A man called for her.'

'What do you mean?'

'One of the people from the boating club. She went off with him.'

'Who was he?'

'I don't know his name. He's been up here a few times looking for things.'

'And they went off?'

'She put some things into a case.'

'Did she say anything to you?'

'She hugged me. I asked her if there was anything wrong. She was crying.'

'Did you not ask her where she was going?'

'I could see she didn't want to talk. She looked disturbed.'

I went up to the bedroom. Her clothes were gone from the wardrobe. Everything looked different. The bed was made. She usually didn't do that until night-time. I felt I was in someone else's room. It looked bare. Even the perfume she used to leave on the tallboy was gone.

There was an envelope on the locker beside her bed. I opened it. There was a note inside it. My hands shook as I read it.

'I have to go,' it said, 'Please don't try to follow me. I still love you. I just can't take the way things are anymore. This is for you as much as me.' At the end she said she was leaving me her boat, 'To remember me by.'

I read it a few times, not really seeing the words. They swam before my eyes. I went into the bathroom. My stomach was lurching. I threw up in the sink.

I read the note again. This time my hands weren't shaking.

So she still loved me. But not enough to stay with me. We always kill the thing we love.

A part of me wasn't surprised. I saw it coming even if I didn't admit it to myself.

She told me she'd walk away if I didn't do something about my father. I heard her and yet I didn't hear her. Now she was telling me in a different way.

Who was the man who called for her? Was it Tony? Was she with him now?

It didn't matter. She was gone. That was all that mattered.

I crushed the pages of the note in my fist. Suddenly I hated her. Why was she too cowardly to tell me to my face?

All the months we spent together meant nothing. All the declarations of love, all the shared memories. I would have been an interesting phase to her. A station along the way of her development.

I sat on the bed with my chest heaving. Was I right to hate her? Should I have hated my father more? Maybe I should hate both of them in equal measure. At the end of the day they'd done what suited them. I was the fool caught in the middle.

The dream was over. Now it was back to reality. Sleeping in a bed without her. Marching to the drum of the man who'd caused her to go.

Would I be able to forget her? Maybe anger would help me do that. I'd get on with my life. In time other things would become important. Whatever happened to me in the summer would become as negligible as anything that happened to me at any other time. It would merge into the nothingness of other nothingnesses.

I took a bottle of whiskey out of my father's cabinet. A memory nudged inside me of a time after my mother died when my father did that too. Maybe I'd spend the rest of my life copying his behaviour, the sins of the father being visited upon the son like it said in the Bible.

I went down to the boathouse. How many nights had we spent there? A hundred? A thousand? I looked out at the boat on the slipway. What good was it to me now? I felt like digging up one of the camp spikes and driving it through the ruts so it sank.

I sat there for hours. For a while it seemed as if she'd never existed. Then it was as if she was still there before me. As the night came down I thought I saw her after-image on the water.

Shadows stretched themselves through the branches of the trees. A sheep bleated somewhere. I felt removed from everything.

What would I do now? Continue working on the farm? Being with her every night had made the work bearable. How could I slop out stables without the expectation of her beside me? How could I slink through the mud of a winter evening herding cows at a crossroads? The land owned me and yet it meant nothing to me. Only my circumstances made me a part of it.

I went back to the house. My father was sitting in the kitchen.

He knew what happened. Was he gloating? Was this what he'd wanted all along?

'Where were you?' he said.

'Out.'

I went upstairs. The night was black. I lay on the bed. Setanta sat at the foot of it. He always knew when something was wrong. The whiskey made my eyes droop. It took away the pain as it burned itself inside me. I fell asleep.

When I woke up the next morning it took a few seconds before I remembered what happened. I reached my leg across the bed for her but she wasn't there. I sat up. The whiskey bottle was on the locker. There was only about a quarter of it left.

I looked at her note. Where was she now? Would she have remorse or relief? Had it all been inevitable?

I went downstairs. My father was sitting in the kitchen typing. I felt like wrenching the typewriter away from him and throwing it out the window.

'She's gone, isn't she?' he said.

'Yes.'

'For good?'

'I think so.'

'I'm sorry.'

'Don't be. It was never going to work out.'

'Maybe she'll come back.'

'I doubt it.'

'Will you go after her?'

'No.'

Life without her became bland. In the mornings I worked. After lunch I took care of him. In the evenings I drove the car without a destination in mind, the movement somehow relieving me from thought. Days passed.

After a sufficient amount of time had elapsed I told him I was going to take a break from him. He accepted my decision without arguing. By now we were hardly speaking to one another.

I asked the carer if she'd be interested in coming in every day. She was. We agreed a fee for the extra hours. I didn't want the time to do anything specific. Sometimes I just sat in the boathouse. I drank myself to sleep a lot of nights. My head felt like a fuse about to ignite.

I walked into doors like a blind man. The time crawled by. I missed her the way someone might miss an amputated limb.

Then one day it stopped. She went out of my system like a virus. It was almost as if I trained myself not to want her.

Things had run their course. I had to accept that as I accepted everything else that happened in my life. We had some good times. It was as simple as that. Now the future beckoned. Nobody knew what it held. The secret was not to plan. Not to plan and not to have emotions. If my father's life had taught me anything it was that emotions were what you suffered for. They were the scars that didn't heal. Aisling never had them. That was why she was content with herself.

I decided to model myself on her, to become a kind of non-person.

6

In the following years I settled into a routine with my father that some people saw as unhealthy We shared the house but had little to say to one other that didn't hinge on practical things. I started to go out more often. He said it didn't bother him.

My work on the farm was harmless now. If I could get away from it on any pretext I did. One year I got a job in the town, a white collar one. It involved drawing up advertising programmes for one of its get-rich-quick merchants, a real estate surveyor who thought he was God's gift. I told myself pushing a pen beat driving a plough any day but it was soul-destroying work. Using my mind sometimes took more out of me than using my body.

Snow fell that year. It made me feel young again. I thought of the winters of my childhood where I'd played in it with Greta, making footprints in the ground that were as big as the Abominable Snowman's. Now I just wanted to look out at it.

Another year I converted the attic. It meant I had more space for myself upstairs. I didn't really need it but I made it anyway. Maybe it was therapy for me to get my mind off aisling. I thought the world would stop when she left but that's not what happens. You get on with life. Little things become important again, sometimes even more important than the big things. You forget what traumatised you. It's what people do to survive.

The house was like two houses now. There were days I hardly saw my father. I still cooked his meals for him. Sometimes we watched television together if he wasn't working on his book. In the mornings he did his exercises. He'd once made fun of these. 'The only exercise I ever liked,' he used to say, 'was up, down, one two, three - and then the same for the other eyebrow.' Things were different now. His muscles were getting stronger.

He resented me lifting him in and out of bed even when he couldn't do it himself. The same applied to his carers. They came in as much as he'd let them. He gave out about the money he had to pay them for things I'd done for nothing for so many years. I didn't envy them trying to shower him or even wheel him around. If he got any kind of mobility going he'd elbow them out of his way. They became an encumbrance.

He was able to do a lot of things on his own now. Walking was still out of the question but he could stand without support for longer periods of time.

On the fine days I wheeled him out to the front gate. He liked having the sun in his face. It was somewhat less enjoyable having to engage with the people who passed by on the road. They invariably stopped to ask him how he was. He'd say something like 'Perfect!' before turning away from them. 'This would be a great country,' he said to me one day, 'if we could only get the people out of it.'

Another day a farmer he knew slightly came in the gate and talked the hind legs off him about nothing. He then had the audacity to tell him he was going to bring him down the road to see a trailer he'd just bought. My father was fit to be tied. He told him he didn't want to go anywhere but the man insisted. He started wheeling him down the road. Eventually my father pulled the brake on his wheelchair.

'That's it,' he said, 'You can fuck off now' The man's face was a picture. He'd never been spoke to that way before.

'I was only trying to get you out of yourself,' he said.

'Thank you,' my father said, 'but I prefer being *in* myself.' He said to me later, 'The world is being destroyed by do-gooders.'

Politicians came to the door sometimes to solicit his vote. He usually ran them. Ne stubborn customer wouldn't take no for an answer. He insisted on driving him to the polling booth on voting day. A taxi was even organised for the wheelchair. It had a ramp to get him into it. After he got to the polling station he gave his vote to another candidate.

'That's cruel,' I said to him.

'I don't like being manipulated.'

I brought him into town to buy clothes. He never had much of an interest in his wardrobe. It was really just to pass the time. We went into other shops afterwards. If we ran into anyone the same problem would arise as at the gate. People would ask him how he was. Some of them treated him as if he was totally paralysed. 'I have to stop them from bringing me into toilets to wipe my arse,' he complained.

For a time he developed an interest in painting. That involved buying canvases and paints. He mainly did life drawings. Greta and myself were the first two he tried. Then he did a self-portrait. Betty even posed for a portrait once. He tore it up before finishing it.' She wouldn't sit still,' he said. It was probably just an excuse. There wasn't even one photograph of Betty in the house. Having to look at her in a framed print every day would have driven him barmy.

His favourite paintings were scenes he saw on the farm. He was able to do some of these from the house. They provided one practical advantage of the lift. There was a great view of the land from a window in the spare bedroom. He didn't mind going into that. He painted in an impressionistic style, splashing the colours all over the canvas. It wasn't quite Van Gogh but he had a great gift for making nature come alive.

He made hand carvings for a time. Carpentry was one of his skills. He made a rocking chair from clothes pegs and a windmill from lollipop sticks. There were also more sophisticated carvings verging on sculpture. He gave most of them away. I thought he could have made a business out of it but he had no inclination that way. Neither had he any interest in selling his paintings. They were scattered all over the place. Some he didn't even bother framing.

He became more independent around the house as the years went on. I noticed him being more inclined to use the washing machine and the cooker. His mood was better when he was busy. It meant I could ask him things without him rebuffing me. In the year after the accident he almost always got into bad form if I asked to be out of the house. Later on he didn't seemed to mind as much, at least after Aisling left.

Sometimes I walked into town and met people I knew for coffee. A lot of my classmates had gone to Dublin or overseas. The ones who stayed behind seemed ground down. Maybe I seemed the same to them. Some of them were married and settled in jobs. I didn't envy them. Everything they did seemed to be dictated by their mortgages. The burdens on them became even more pressurising if children arrived.

Most people identified me with my father. If they asked me about him I became uncomfortable. They were circumspect about him because of his snobbish attitudes. I felt I'd been tarred with the same brush.

Sometimes I heard trains passing by in the distance. They gave me a vague urge to travel. It didn't matter to me where they were going. Anywhere would have done me to get away from my routines.

'Life is passing you by,' Betty said to me.

I knew it was but what could I do about it?

I went into Galway as much as I could. There was a great buzz about it. I hung around Eyre Square and the Spanish Arch watching all the action. The bars were electric at night. It wasn't just the energy of youth. Everyone had it. Every time I came back from it I felt ten years younger.

Now and then I went to Dublin for day trips. I left instructions with the carers about what to do. They mostly knew anyway. Betty also looked in on him. He never stopped being grumpy with her. I never knew why. She had the patience of a saint with him.

Now and again I brought girls home with me. There was an unwritten law that they wouldn't stay overnight. He preferred not to be introduced to them. If their paths crossed he more or less ignored them.

He rarely got bad-tempered with me. I wasn't sure if that was because Aisling was gone or a simple question of age. Her name wasn't mentioned.

When he wasn't doing his paintings or his hand carvings he kept himself busy with the book he was writing on his father. I'd hear him on the phone to librarians every hour of the day about some piece of archive material he was looking for.

I didn't think anyone would be interested in reading it. There was a new generation growing up in the town now. People had their eyes fixed on the future rather than the past. They couldn't have cared less if his father had blue blood or if he was born in a dump. You couldn't tell him that. He still carried the newspaper obituary of his father around with him in his wallet.

One day I had the foolishness to tell him he should allow his father's memory to slip away quietly. He turned on me.

'Et tu, Brute,' he said. 'Do you not realise he had half this town on his payroll once? Do you not think that deserves to be remembered?'

'I didn't mean that.'

'You're as bad as the rest of them. It's jealousy, that what it is. Like flies buzzing round a dead lion.'

I drove him to the library every couple of days. Hr attacked the local history section like a man possessed. I usually went for a coffee to give him time to load himself up with his lore. When I got back he'd have the books heaped before him like food on a tray.

The librarian let him have ten books at a go. Six was the usual limit. Behind his back she threw me sympathetic glances. He was known to her. She probably knew I'd be getting the guts of them for tea. Back at the house he went through them with a fine toothcomb. To me they were terminally boring tracts but I couldn't say that. They were keeping him alive.

His excitement acted as the flipside of my own apathy. I watched him burning the midnight oil as the pages of his manuscript mushroomed. The typewriter keys clacked relentlessly into the night. He only used his index fingers. It was like the rat-tat-of a rifle. He hit the keys so hard I thought he'd break them.

He smoked as he read, often going through three packs a day. I'd find the butts in the ashtrays the next morning. He reminded me of a mad inventor, his hair flying wild like Einstein.

I envied him his passion. In some ways I was more paralysed than he was. I had nothing to divert myself, no work or play or even love. He was the focal point of my existence. He'd taken me out of school and he was responsible for Aisling leaving as well. Now I was without an activity and he was drunk on his one.

The book became like another person in the house. He wouldn't allow it out of his sight. Each night he slept beside the pages. They were like substitutes for my mother.

I grew to despise it but in a way it was my saving grace. It meant I could be out of the house without him noticing. I came home some nights and he didn't even ask me where I'd been. All he wanted was for me to serve him his glass of brandy. I was expected to sit there and watch the master at work. He pruned his syllables like a stonemason. The book became his passion.

One night I decided to gamble on that passion for my freedom. It was a night when he was even more frenzied than usual. His eyes burned like coals as he scanned some parochial snippet from a mildewed magazine.

'I was thinking of going away for a while,' I said.

He took off his glasses.

'How long is a while?'

'I don't know.'

'What would you want to go away for? Have you not everything you want here?'

'It's not that.'

'Where were you thinking of going?'

'I don't know yet. I thought I might try London.'

'London? '

'If it's a problem for you I won't go.'

He wheeled himself over to the drinks cabinet.

'London isn't a pretty place.'

'I know.'

'People would walk over you there as soon as look at you.'

'I'd be careful.'

He opened a bottle of brandy.

'Are you bored here?' he said.

'No, it's just that…'

'Go on, say it.'

'Most people my age have been out and about.'

'Hmm.'

'I thought it might do me good to see a bit of life.'

'Oh you'll see life there all right. Maybe more than you bargained for.'

'Are you saying no?'

'How could I do that? I wouldn't want you telling anyone I held you back from things.'

'I'd get people to drop in on you.'

'There'd be no need for that.'

'I might get fed up after a fortnight. If I did I'd be straight back.'

'Thanks.'

'I didn't mean it like that.'

He didn't say anything else. I remembered the way he was the time I was thinking of going off with Aisling. Would he pull another stunt like that?

He stayed up most of the night. After I went to bed I heard him downstairs wheeling himself from one room to the other. He typed for a while. At one stage I thought I heard a glass breaking.

He was distant with me the next morning.

'London,' he said as soon as I walked into the kitchen, 'So our own country isn't good enough for you anymore.'

I thought this was rich coming from such an apologist for the British Empire.

'I don't know why it appeals to me.'

'The grass is always greener.'

He was distant with me over the next few days. Nothing more was said about me going away. It was all in his manner. I didn't lift him right. The dinner tasted bad. The floor was dirty.

He was making me sweat for my suggestion, making me earn it with interest.

His distance turned to aggression. He became the man he'd been before the accident. He drank more. I'd see him flaked out in his chair in the middle of the day. If I wheeled him anywhere he'd give out to me. He winced if I hit a bump on the gravelled path outside the door.

'My back is in agony,' he'd groan.

He didn't read the book to me anymore but he kept working at it. On the day I left he was busier than ever with it. Or maybe he was just pretending to be. He wheeled himself from room to room like a madman, slamming pages into the typewriter and then taking them out a few seconds later. He crushed them up and threw them across the room into the wastepaper basket. I knew he was acting the diva for my benefit. It was hard to grudge it to him.

He got on the phone to a librarian about a report he wanted that had been mislaid. I felt sorry for her. He was like an anti-Christ as he gave her the third degree. She was trying to deal with someone else at the time. I heard her saying, 'I'll be back in a minute' to him. He drummed his fingers along the desk.

She was gone for a while. When she came back he said, 'Did you enjoy your holidays?'

There was a pause. I imagined her trying to contain herself.

'We still can't find the report,' she said.

'Inefficiency!' he roared down the phone, 'That's what has this country like it is. If my father was alive he'd have sacked the lot of you.'

There was a knock at the door.

'It's the taxi driver,' I said.

He hung up.

'Off with you then.'

I went to put my arms around him but he held back.

'We don't need any of that,' he said. 'You might ring me some night to find out if I'm alive or dead. I'd appreciate that.'

I went out. The door was open. He turned the wheelchair around to face me. I blew him a kiss. He gave a half-wave. It was like a gesture you'd use to swat a fly. Then he kicked it shut.

I got into the taxi. We drove over the cobblestones that led to the gate. Setanta was whining. I felt ashamed of myself. What was I doing? It seemed crazy to go now that Aisling was out of my life. I had nothing to gain and everything to lose.

We drove onto the road. I looked back at Setanta. His ears were cocked in curiosity. Was he hoping I'd jump out of the car and come back? I imagined my father sitting in a corner brooding, putting his book aside now that he couldn't fool himself with it anymore. Or me.

We turned the corner. Ahead of me lay the train station, behind me the smatterings of a life I didn't know if I wanted or not.

After I got to Dublin I took the ferry to Holyhead. It was my first time out of Ireland even though I was in my mid-twenties. I had no plans. That was the way I liked it. I didn't want things to have a pattern. If nothing happened I could go back. There was that cushion.

I got the train to London. It was strange listening to the different accents around me. I felt important sitting in my seat, being served tea and sandwiches from a trolley, having my bags carried down a platform by a porter.

We sped through towns I'd never heard of, each looking like the one before. There were telegraph poles, stacks of hay, fields leading to smaller buildings and then larger ones, more fields and occasional pedestrians and cars, bigger buildings, the backs of houses, their clotheslines and unkempt gardens, then bigger houses. A child jumped on a trampoline. A man with a cigarette in his mouth hung washing on a clothesline. More and more people started to appear on the roads. The volume of cars built up. Finally we were in the suburbs of the city.

London was like a new world to me. I arrived close to midnight but there were still people spilling out of the train station. It was like being in a stampede trying to find my way out. Nobody engaged with anyone else. I thought of the words of T.S. Eliot: 'A crowd flowed over London Bridge...'

For the first few days I was in awe of everything. I'd never seen so many people in one place before. They disgorged themselves from buildings, parks, Tube stations. I drifted in and out of shopping complexes and art galleries. Nothing registered with me. It was just sensations.

People bumped into me. Nobody apologised. I thought of my father's words, 'London isn't a pretty place.' But I needed it. Chaos unfolded around me. I drowned myself in it.

I bought a map. The man who sold it to me said he'd lived in the city all his life and still didn't know his way around. When I opened it I felt I was looking at a drawing of the human body with all its arteries.

I found a hostel that was cheap. It was off a side street near Trafalgar Square. I was given a tiny room that looked out onto a car park. There were two other Irish people staying there. They made themselves familiar with me. That always happened with the accent. It was a magnet.

They invited me to an Irish club with them but I said no. I didn't want to turn into the kind of people my father gave out about, people who tried to turn England into Ireland. How could I feel nostalgic for the country when I was only a wet day out of it? I knew people who made for such havens when they were hardly off the boat. That would have defeated the whole purpose of going away for me.

I phoned him.

'I arrived in one piece,' I said.

'Well done. Have you met the Queen yet?'

'That's tomorrow. We're having tea.'

'Tell her I said hello.'

'I will. What's happening there?'

'Nothing, I'm afraid. All quiet on the western front.

'You must have some news for me.'

'Setanta is chewing on a bone. The bins were collected. It rained.'

I wandered around the city. The heat was oppressive. I sat in parks watching life go by. My money ran out. When you were doing nothing it always did. I decided to look for a job.

One of the people in the hostel was working on a building site nearby. He said he'd put in a word for me with his boss. I arrived at the site one morning unshaven. He thought it might help my chances to look rough but it didn't work. The foreman only took one look at me before shaking his head. 'Tenderfoot,' he said.

I registered with an employment agency. They said there was a recession but they'd try their best. After a few days a courier job became available. I didn't fancy it but I was told it was that or nothing. It was a small company in the suburbs. I was told I wouldn't have to worry about knowing my way around. That would have been a problem in the city. I was given a motorbike. All I had to buy was a helmet and some wet gear.

Each day the routine was the same. I went to a destination and collected a package. Then I dropped it off and waited for another call

It was soul-destroying work. I began some days at dawn and was still travelling at nine that night, going round in circles as I searched for some factory annex with a bulldog baying at my heels. The money was good but no job was worth that kind of pressure. I had to run red lights if there was an urgent delivery. The boss barked orders at me until my ears rang. I hauled the bike up on footpaths if there was a traffic jam.

I got about ten minutes for lunch. It was usually eaten when I was on the move. There were wrongly addressed envelopes, streets that had no names, aggressive customers, the clutch that slipped just as the company you were going to was about to close.

Every night when I came back to the hostel my head buzzed with names, numbers, the boss screaming at me through the static. My nerves snapped one night when I swerved to avoid a JCB in a lay-by. I ended up in a ditch. The bike fell on me. I wasn't bleeding but I was sore enough to know I wouldn't be sitting on another one for a while.

I called the boss from the hospital.

'I have a twisted pelvis and two fractures,' I told him.

'Does this mean you won't be in on Monday?' he said.

I hobbled around the hostel on crutches for the next few days. Once again I thought of my father. He'd been on them after his accident. They were harder to use than I thought.

The recession went on. I looked for a job that wouldn't stretch me. One day I saw an ad for a night-watchman job. It was about as much as I could hope for in the economic climate.

I didn't try to sell myself at the interview and maybe that worked. The more you wanted something the less inclined people were to give it to you. I acted cool. That impressed the interviewer.

'Welcome aboard,' he said after I'd given him a bald sketch of my background. He told me the hours were unsociable but the job posed no challenge.

I was based in a warehouse. It was the graveyard shift. There was just me and a family of mice. A machine clicked somewhere in the distance. I managed to find a sofa in an office. It meant I was able to spend most of my time sleeping.

The shift began at 4.30 in the afternoon and went on until 7 the next morning. The pay was an insult. It was all right if you could sleep.

'Don't be a hero,' the foreman told me on the first day, 'If someone breaks in, run. We don't want your brains all over the floor. You're here so we can get the place insured.'

I had only one set of duties to perform. At intervals during the night I had to do clocking. It entailed going around the building every hour or two and turning a key in places that had clocks pinned to walls. It was beyond boring. I decided to dislodge the clocking points from the walls and turn the key in them from the office. At dawn the next morning I put them back so my replacement wouldn't suspect anything.

I brought a sleeping bag into the warehouse with me. Nobody seemed to mind. I had an alarm clock to wake me up for the times I had to turn the keys. I was probably the only nightwatchman in London who came to work with a sleeping bag and an alarm clock.

One night the place was burgled. I slept through it. When I woke up there were two policemen standing above me. I told them I was security. They couldn't resist a smile. The manager arrived afterwards. He saw the set of clocks neatly stacked up in the office beside my sleeping bag. All he could do was smile.

'Were you comfortable?' he said.

I decided it was best not to ask him for the wages I had coming to me. That was the end of my security stint.

I spent the next few days in a blob of inactivity. When I phoned my father he was his usual monosyllabic self.

'How are you feeling?' I asked him.

'Alive,' he said, 'Or at least some days I think so.'

I asked him how he was managing for meals but he ignored the question. When I enquired about his book he was equally offhand, I felt he was punishing me for being away. The only piece of news he had for me was that Greta was working in a hospital now. When I asked him how Setanta was he said, 'Spiffing. He sends his regards.'

I wasn't too pushed about getting a job. You worked because you had to. That was my philosophy. I decided I wouldn't do anything until my money ran out.

I was sitting in a bar one day in Finsbury Park when the barman asked me if I'd be interested in a job there. I hadn't said I was looking for work. I was just sitting there reading a newspaper.

'You're Irish, aren't you?' he said, 'we get a lot of your lot here. We have a vacancy since last night. The head barman knocked the manager out and robbed the till.'

'It sounds like my kind of place,' I said.

I told him I had no experience of bar work. That didn't seem to bother him.

'You're hired,' he said shaking my hand, 'I'm Justin.'

'You mean that's it?'

'The kind of people we get here don't stay long. You won't be mixing fancy cocktails. As long as you can pull a pint you'll do.'

I started a few days later. It was called The Corncrake. In former years it was a hotel. There were still a few people staying in the rooms. I was offered accommodation too. The building had been condemned since the sixties. The walls shook sometimes. 'You'll find it's a bit like being in San Francisco,' Justin informed me.

Sometimes when the Tubes were passing by I felt the floor moving under me. There was a sign above the counter saying, 'Please Do Not Leave Your Seat While The Bar Is In Motion.' I wasn't sure if it was reference to drunkenness or the fact that we were living in London's version of the San Andreas fault.

I worked for dirt pay. Paddy slave labour they called it. They called me Paddy too. Every night after we brought the shutters down they asked me how I felt about the situation in the North of Ireland. It was all anyone could talk about. When I said the whole business bored me they seemed relieved. One of the other barmen said the collective population should be put into banana boats and shipped off to a desert island. The comment was greeted by generous laughter.

We were expected to serve Guinness slops to the customers. This was what overflowed into the tray after you pulled the pint. You could get any sort of disease off it from the germs of the previous drinkers. That didn't bother the manager.

Another hallowed practice was watering down the whiskey when a customer was drunk. You weren't advised to try it with anyone sober. They'd probably have noticed. It was strictly for the closing time quick one. There were lots of watery whiskies flying across the counter coming up to eleven o'clock.

I spent my free days swilling glasses of bitter in the snug with fellow reprobates. I hadn't drunk much in Galway because of my father. Now I was making up for lost time. I drank with people who saw the bar as their home. Before long it became mine too.

The barmen had great personalities. I couldn't keep up with their wit. Justin was the ringleader. He loved showing off. Every night he had us in stitches. Nobody else got a look-in but we didn't mind. He was such an entertainer he should have been on the stage.

The only person who bothered me was Malcolm. He was the manager. Justin told me to be careful with him. 'He likes young barmen,' he said, giving a little whistle to indicate he was gay. 'If you drop your soap in the shower,' he said, 'Don't bend down for it.'

A few weeks after I arrived he put his hand on my thigh. We were stacking barrels in the basement at the time. I told him I wasn't like that.

'We're all like that, darling,' he cooed, 'Some of us just don't know it yet.'

He didn't approach me again that but it was difficult to relax knowing he was sleeping in a room two doors down from me. One night he came into my room after closing time. I feared the worst when he lifted up his shirt. He showed me a scar that ran across his stomach.

'From one of my boyfriends,' he said, 'I was unfaithful to him.' Apparently he'd lunged at him with a Stanley knife.

Another one of his stories concerned the night he threw up after making love to a woman.

'Everyone should try it once,' he said, 'for the experience.'

In his room he had a miniature white coffin. It had 'Welcome to the Clap' inscribed on it. He said it was a present from an Arabian he'd slept with in Corfu the previous summer.

He made life difficult for me after I rebuffed his advance. If I made a mistake he pounced on it. He ran me off my feet when we were busy, trying to trip me up with complicated orders. 'Get to know the customers,' he said, 'This job is about more than serving drink.' But if he saw me in conversation with one of them he pushed me away from them

'Just get the lolly,' he'd say after they had left. 'There's no need to hear their life stories. While you're talking to a customer, two others have come and gone.'

He gave me lectures on how to clean glasses.

'They have to be so clear you can see your face in them,' he'd say, 'like a mirror.' These were the same glasses we were expected to serve slops in.

'He likes messing with our heads,' Justin said, 'That's how he keeps control of us.'

Every now and then he'd call these emergency meetings. At one of them he told us he'd have to lay a few of us off if things didn't pick up.

'Is that a threat or a promise?' Justin said.

Malcolm told him to shut up. He hated his levity. That was especially the case if there were new recruits listening. He preferred to get people on their own so he could manipulate them.

'His policy is divide and conquer,' Justin said, 'It'll never work as long as I'm here.'

Malcolm knew that. It cut into his lust for power. There was a war of attrition between them. It led to tension if they were serving at the same time. One day Justin was mistaken by a customer for 'The Guv'nor.' He was wearing a suit at the time. Malcolm was in a jumper. It drove him mad to be undermined like that.

He wanted to sack Justin but he couldn't. His union was strong. Malcolm couldn't have run the place without him anyway. He drank too much. And he had emotional problems. He got clingy to his boyfriends. Some of them turned on him, like the one who stabbed him. When he was on a binge or in the throes of a doomed romance he needed someone to keep the place ticking over.

Justin often came into my room after closing time. 'To protect you from the queer fella,' he'd say, 'Think of my as your bodyguard.' Sometimes he'd have a naggin of whiskey that he filched from behind the counter. He regarded it as compensation for the poor wages we were getting.

When there was just the two of us he didn't perform with me. I saw the real person. One night he told me all about his upbringing. There were beatings at the hands of his father. His mother was an alcoholic. She died young from cancer. 'I grew up on the streets,' he said. He ran away from home at seventeen and was only back once since.

He was cynical about life. Maybe he had a right to be. He hadn't been given much. His attitude was, 'Do it to him before he does it to you.'

'My only ambition in this world is to get rich,' he told me one night, 'If it means going outside the law, so be it.'

I could identify with him running away from home but I wasn't that bothered about getting rich. We were the most incompatible pair you could imagine and yet for some weird reason we clicked.

I told him Malcolm was doing my head in.

'Tell him to take a flying fuck for himself,' he said.

'That's easier said than done. I need the job.'

'What's the main problem?'

'Bullying.'

'He does it with all the new lads. The ones that survive are the ones who stand up to him. If you don't it gets worse. I had to put some manners on him after I came here.'

'What happened?'

'He was trying all that luvvie luvvie stuff with me. I didn't respond so he started intimidating me instead. I took it for a day or two. Then I asked him outside. I won't tell you what I did but after our little altercation his boudoir performances were a bit diminished, if you know what I mean. He knew if he ever looked sideways at me again he wouldn't be looking for boyfriends anymore, he'd be looking for an undertaker.'

'How was he with you afterwards?'

'A week later he promoted me.'

'You're joking.'

'He knows I'm more intelligent than he is. I also dress better. And I know what the customers want.'

'Would you like his job?'

'Let's put it this way. If I took over from him I'd double the turnover in a month.'

'How?'

'For starters we need to get into the food game. That's where the money is nowadays. Get them in to eat and it acts like advertising for the booze.'

'Did you ever suggest that to him?'

'I mentioned it to him after I started.'

'And?'

'He looked at me as if I was from Mars. His idea of pub grub is two Comish pasties and a bap.'

'I don't know how he ever got to be manager.'

'Have you ever seen him try to pull a pint?'

'You'd make the dinner quicker.'

'He doesn't know how to deal with the customers either.'

'So I've noticed.'

'He gets ikey with them if they're drunk. That doesn't work. The customer is always right. That's the first law of any business.'

'I don't think you'd get very far on it with some of the ones I've seen.'

'That's the problem. A good half of them shouldn't be allowed in in the first place. We should have a door policy to weed them out. If we did we'd do ten times better business. He lets all the scumbags in and then he gives out when they act the maggot. What does he expect? He's let Jack the Ripper in if he had the dosh.'

I knew what he meant. I'd got so used to rough diamonds I'd started to accept them as the norm. There were customers who insulted me for my accent, my country, even the way I dressed.

'Where's the cloth cap?' one of them said to me one day, 'Have you cleaned the sheep shit off your shoes yet?' Knowing I was a farmer's son gave them an added advantage over me. Being Irish was bad enough. Coming from the bogs meant I was doubly cursed.

'He thinks he's being clever by letting in the bad eggs,' Justin said, 'but he's really cutting off his nose to spite his face. The word is out on this place. It's the dumping ground for every deadbeat within a ten mile radius. That's why we never grew. He gets frustrated about that and then he goes to the other extreme, coming down heavy on people who wouldn't say boo to a goose. The whole thing is crazy.'

'Why don't you leave?'

'I'm hoping he will first.'

'That could take forever.'

'I know. That's why I don't think about it. I'm just filling in time here like yourself. If anything better came up you wouldn't see my heels for the dust.'

'And if it doesn't?'

'The longer you stay here the more the place takes you over. That's what he feeds off. It's why he gets away with paying buttons. He takes a lot of people like yourself who just got off the boat. They don't know their arse from their elbow if you don't mind me saying so. They're content to say, "Yes sir, no sir, three bags full sir."'

'What do you think I should I do?

'Fuck off to the West End and have a good time.'

'On what I'm earning?'

'There's more than one way to skin a cat.' He winked towards the till. 'Everyone helps themselves to a few quid sooner or later. Malcolm knows that.'

'Was anyone ever caught?'

'Once or twice. I don't think he pressed charges. Just be careful the customers don't notice. If they do he has to make an issue of it. Let justice be seen to be done. All that crap.'

I didn't have to resort to this. A few days after our conversation Malcolm was arrested. It was after midnight. I was lying in bed when I heard a siren blaring. A few minutes later a gang of police charged up the stairs. They burst into his room. I could hear him screaming as they led him away.

I asked Justin what happened.

'I don't know the details. I imagine he put his hand down the trousers of one too many blue-eyed boys.'

123

'So it's happened before.'

'More times than I care to mention.'

'Has he been in jail?'

'A few times.'

'Why didn't you tell me?.'

'I didn't want to worry you after him coming on to you.'

'I'd prefer to have known.'

'Sorry.'

'Will they throw the book at him this time?'

'Never mind the book. They'll throw the key away.'

I was more relaxed after he was gone. Justin gave me more responsibilities. The days passed faster because I was busy. It was easy to lose yourself in the daily routines – changing barrels, mixing cocktails for the upmarket clientele, preparing the occasional meal. I threw myself into it as if it mattered and eventually it started to.

I drank with the other barmen. Some of them had left their wives back in Ireland. They were sending home cheques. There wasn't much left over for themselves afterwards. I pitied them on Friday nights as I watched them going up to their rooms with their little brown envelope tucked in their pockets and a Chinese takeaway under their arms. Time off meant little more than time to kill for them, not time in which to live.

In some ways they were better off than I was. I took my comforts for granted. When every night was action-packed, how could you appreciate any of it? I saw myself becoming like them one day myself, going through the motions for the twelve pieces of silver, doing my forty hours not because I wanted to but because I had no choice.

They were wary of me at first. As far as they were concerned I was only there for the *craic*. When I got to know them better they dropped their defences.

I became friendly with the customers. Everyone had a different story. One man who came in every day was running away from a bad marriage. Another one was in trouble with the law. Both sought solace in the haven of the snug. That was where the real stories of their lives were unleashed. Whispered confessions replaced the cacophony of chatter when the customers were gone home.

Some of them had trouble with drink, some with relationships. Nearly all of them worried about money. It made nonsense of my father's idea of emigrants finding gold at the end of the rainbow and coming back to the old sod to splurge it around.

They bought whatever possessions they had from shady characters who appeared every now and then to 'have a word.' I took these people to be loan sharks. They didn't ask for credit references like the banks did. Your word was your bond but God help you if you broke it. One man I heard of was kneecapped when he welshed on a debt. I don't think he was ever able to walk properly again, having had the misfortune to get in hock to someone who knew the Kray twins.

Others were more careful. We were usually able to tell them if a creditor walked in. They'd disappear without leaving a forwarding address. If we were asked abut them we'd go, 'Who?' We were like the

Mafia. Or as Justin put it, the Murphia. We knew who to cosset and who to cajole, who to rush with their drink and who to take slowly, who to engage in political debate and who was liable to pull a dagger on you if you did.

Guinness was both food and drink for many of the clientele. Justin joked about a seven-course Irish meal being a six-pack and a potato. It wasn't too far from the truth for some of the customers. I watched them drinking themselves into stupors and then starting from scratch again the next day, interrupting their binges only to collect welfare cheques or stop in the bookies down the road. They'd do a Yankee on some allegedly hot tips that invariably came in down the field. As they engaged in their *ochóning* about the what-might-have-beens I thought how happy my father would have been to sit listening to them licking their wounds as they railed against the cruel world outdoors.

I had two hours off in the middle of the day but they weren't much good to me. Where could you go at three o'clock when you had to be back at five? I usually just slept. After tea we were into the home stretch. The night revellers arrived. They expected you to join them in their jocularity simply because they were throwing money in your direction.

On Saturday afternoons I watched Arsenal at Highbury. The perfect pitch was a bit different to the scraggly fields of home that we trudged through. The players made goal-scoring look so easy. They could thread their way from one end of the pitch to the other almost untouched. I saw them assuperstars. People crowded around them at the ends of matches looking for autographs. I imagined them owning Rolls Royces in luxurious homes in the country.

Afterwards in the West End with Justin I'd see them in the fashionable clubs surrounded by different kinds of fans, a scrum of idolators hanging on their every word. Many of them were Irish. At such times it didn't matter what nationality you were. Genius did away with all borders. Later in the night we hit the Irish clubs in Kilburn or Kentish Town, spending the night listening to emigrants singing songs of love and war. Often it was hard to know the difference.

Getting up the next morning to serve the Hard Contingent was a killer. How could you make conversation with anyone when your head felt like it had just been blown off? I just wanted to dawdle over the Sunday papers. If I did something wrong there was the possibility of a fight. A senseless comment could lead to a punch-up.

Justin was quick to bar people. I usually fell for it when they apologised. That wasn't clever. A small fight often led to a bigger one a few nights later.

We got a new manager after Malcolm. His name was Rodney. He was one of those small people who liked throwing their weight around. He didn't drink. When I came home from the West end one Saturday night the worse for wear he told me I wouldn't be fit for work the next day.

'If the customers smell booze off you it isn't good.'

'Would it not act as an advertisement for it?'

'Don't be cheeky. I'm not allowing the staff to leave the building on work days anymore.'

'That's entrapment.'

'Call it what you want. It's the way it's going to be from now on.'

He took my key from me. If I wanted to go out after work I had to climb out the window of my bedroom and shinny down a drainpipe. It reminded me of the times I met Aisling in the boathouse after my father fell asleep. I kept meaning to get a copy cut but I never got around to it.

Forbidden fruit tasted sweet. There was nothing to compare to those nights on the West End, meeting people I'd never seen before and would probably never would again, going to parties that ended only with daylight. I used to taxi it back to Seven Sisters Road afterwards. Justin would be waiting for me on the roof with his set of keys. He'd throw them down to me. I'd creep up the stairs quietly so I wouldn't wake Rodney. After a few black coffees I'd be behind the counter again. He always looked suspiciously at me but he could never prove anything. I'd take orders from people I only half-recognised, my pockets full of phone numbers of the women I'd met the night before. Somehow I'd get through the morning.

At the eleven o'clock break I'd hook up with Justin. I'd lash back glasses of water to hydrate myself as I tried to remember how I behaved – or rather misbehaved – the night before.

'You didn't say that, did you?' he'd ask, his eyes widening as I told him about my adventures.

'I might have. I can't remember.'

'Oh Jesus.'

My confidence increased with the alcohol. It was like buying temporary insanity. I got to a situation of not caring what I did. I spent many mornings making calls to people I'd insulted the night before. Some of them accepted my apologies. Others slammed down the phone on me.

I often wondered what my father would have thought of me living this kind of life. I was a far cry from the boy who promised he'd never drink anything stronger than Club Orange. There was a time when three pints could make me drunk. Now I could take up to a dozen and hold them. It was a dubious rite of passage into acceptance by those who worked with me.

It wasn't all about alcohol. One day I went to a garden party with Justin and some of the other barmen. As we sat outside a house in Charing Cross singing songs from the old movies and eating barbecued steak I felt a sudden burst of happiness inside me that I couldn't explain.

This was my new family. People who'd been strangers to me until so recently. I decided I wanted nothing else in life but to be sitting with them, singing these songs and eating this food. It was all here, passing a lazy Sunday with these people under a baking sun in a suburb.

We played a game of football on the lawn afterwards. It hardly measured more than the size of a large kitchen but we still managed to make a pitch from it. My legs were kicked more than the ball but I was so involved I felt no pain. It ended up being more like rugby than soccer. The final score was 73 goals to 39. Justin's team won. Part of the reason was because he tied up the star forward from our side with a tow rope and dumped him in the garage. It was that kind of a day.

Later in the evening he organised a meal for us with two women he knew. After we got to the restaurant I found myself talking the hind legs off the one he paired me with.

'You'll get lockjaw from over-exertion,' he told me.

She was amused by my accent.

'It makes you sexy,' she told me.

I found English women more assertive than Irish ones. Back home they tended to be reticent if they didn't know you. Here they were up for anything. Things developed faster with them. And probably ended faster as well.

Justin watched me chatting them up. He watched me writing their phone numbers on beer-mats and the backs of cigarette packs. It wasn't me. I was trying to copy him, to get as far as possible from anything I knew before.

One of the women I went out with was originally from Galway. That turned me off her.

'I think my father knew your mother,' she said to me one night. That was the last thing I wanted to hear.

Rodney employed a barmaid in the pub. It was all men until then. He thought it would improve trade. I went out with her for a while, relaxing into the easy comfort her company provided. Neither of us was interested in anything lasting. We were mutually convenient. She kept telling me I was 'sweet.' I took that as a kind of insult. It was the kind of thing a woman said to a man when she was about to break it off with him.

'All the Irish are mad,' she kept saying. I tried to live down to her expectations. At parties I played the role of the resident begorrah clown. On one of our dates we went to a fancy dress party. I was Saint Patrick and she was a snake.

Her mother had died when she was seven so she grew up fast. Her father beat her. She didn't like to talk about her past and I didn't pry. It suited me for her to be like that. She didn't want me to talk about my own past either.

She was staying with her sister in a two-room flat in Islington but we spent most of our time in my room. She was easier to be with than anyone I ever knew before, even Aisling. All that mattered to her was to dredge the maximum amount of enjoyment from a night. She felt life owed it to her. Justin thought that way too. She was like a female version of him.

The three of us used to take the Tube into the city on our days off. We browsed around the flea markets. Justin usually helped himself to anything he could when the dealers' backs were turned. In toilet cubicles he'd show me what he lifted. They were often useless items he took purely for the buzz of it. Sometimes he even left them behind him in the cubicle.

He flirted with her in front of me. It was probably to annoy me. He liked winding me up. One night he told me he slept with her. I didn't know whether to believe him or not. It didn't matter. We weren't going anywhere.

I didn't break up with her. We just stopped going out together. Shortly afterwards she left the pub. I understood why. It was awkward working with someone that used to be your boyfriend. Maybe I'd have left if she hadn't.

Justin now had me back to himself. That suited him. He saw himself as my Svengali, my baptism by fire into the ways of the world. I was happy to go along with that.

When I was serving pints with him I joined him in the kind of banter every barman develops with time. It was important to sound jaded even if you weren't. We were dealing with people whose lives had let them down. The last thing they wanted to be confronted with was a positive thinker.

There was an undeclared assumption that life was a disease and drink the cure. In our repository of shop-soiled dreams, imbibers could get a temporary reprieve from it. People in a bar listened to you. They gave you a carte blanche to misbehave. Over-indulging in your favourite tipple became a boast rather than a confession. The people who jacked it in were cowards. They were the ones who didn't have the courage to confront their demons. Such was the logic of the alcoholic.

Whether the booze was a crutch or a blindfold didn't matter to us. All we knew was that it got us through the night. There was a pact between all of us that we wouldn't go straight. That applied to the barmen as much as the customers. We all believed a life lived on the tear was a heroic one. It didn't seem to register with us that an hour or so after closing-time some of us would be found hugging lamp-posts in back streets as we struggled to find our way home.

Everything went back to square one the next morning. The Pearly Gates would open at the appointed time as Justin shouted out, 'Abandon hope all ye who enter here' in his cockney drawl. The regulars would slouch in for another day's revelry. These were the serious drinkers, the patrons of the early houses, unshaven men who may have even slept rough the night before. Most of them had the DTs. Our humble establishment would tell them this was no problem. A few glasses of Guinness would quell their shakes.

Justin told me once that he wanted to marry Arthur Guinness. Arthur, he said, didn't talk back. He didn't ask you how it was for you. He didn't ask you to hold his hand after making love or to take him out to dinner. He didn't ask you to take out the bins or tidy yourself up or to get a decent job or mind the kids or go to church on Sunday. Above all he didn't ask you who you slept with last night.

Long relationships terrified him. He thought they made him lose his edge. Some of them even led to that ugly word, marriage. Marriage meant the end of life for him. It meant having a cat in the window, putting an extension onto the back porch, joining the Resident's Association and Neighbourhood Watch and spending 49 weeks of the year in a sweatshop so you could afford the other three in Blackpool.

He thought his ideas rubbed off on me. Sometimes I pretended they did. I didn't want to be a stick-in-the-mud. He could turn on you if he saw you losing interest.

I drank more when I was out with him than I did with anyone else. If he was in my room I probably took double what I did in the Corncrake.

It was a while before I realised I had a problem. The only symptom I noticed was a heaving of the heart. Then the memory lapses started. I'd come down to work trying to remember where I'd been the night before. I was still drunk. Even Justin would be surprised. 'What are you *on*?' he'd say.

I remembered the days when one drink would knock me off my head. It was like your first cigarette, the one you threw up after. I was throwing up now too, but for a different reason.

'You'll be dead before you're thirty,' a customer said to me one night. The comment shook me. Was I like my father? Would I admit it to myself if I was? I told myself Justin put me up to it, that he made me feel guilty if I didn't indulge. It was a convenient excuse.

Like every drinker I drank because I wanted to. My father was the same. Now history was repeating itself. I had more temptations than him because I was surrounded by the stuff every minute of the day.

I was supping with the devil. But I didn't use a long spoon.

Justin made me perform for him every night. He wound me up until I either made a fool of myself or of him. The next day I had to repeat the trick. No matter how entertaining I was on Saturday I had to do it again on Sunday and then again on Monday. For Justin you were only as good as your last excess. He observed me from the sidelines, not half as drunk as he pretended he was.

I vowed to myself that one day I'd turn the tables on him but deep down I knew he had too much power over me for that. Some nights I prayed he'd leave the bar. In another part of me I felt I was nothing without him. He played on that, taking me under his wing like a puppet.

The women we shared fed into his lust for power. He stole some of them off me and I let him. The other barmen told me he was bullying me. I didn't care.

I never had so many women making me feel they wanted me. At home it was just Aisling or some sporadic crush that went nowhere. It was different here, different because I didn't care.

'You're a dark horse,' he said to me, 'The quiet ones are always the worst.'

He asked me what my secret was. I said I didn't have one.

'Then why do women like you so much?'

'I don't know. I'm awkward with them.'

'Maybe that's it. I wish I could be awkward. Does it take a lot of practice?'

'Years. In fact there are courses on it. I could refer you to them.'

'Fuck you.'

Whether they said yes or no to my advances I felt others would follow. The bigger a selection you had, the more rejections you could deal with. It was like a

135

lottery. You got to know yourself better every time you played it. The only rule was to be cool. If you were, everything started to happen. Almost without you being aware of it or even wanting it.

Beer increased my confidence but a time came when I became immune to it. I started on the shorts afterwards. My father told me he'd gone down the same road as a young man. Was I turning into him? Would I one day have.to dress up in a woman's clothes to get a drink?

Justin saw it happening. One night he saw me trying to get a buzz from the beer and getting nowhere. He produced a pill. I didn't know what it was.

'Take it,' he said, 'It'll make you feel sweet sixteen again.'

I swallowed it. It made me feel good. I asked him for a second one. That made me feel even better.

'Let's conquer London,' I said.

The other barmen joined us on our trips across the city sometimes. I was usually the one commissioned to do the driving. The reason given was that everyone else was 'out of it.' That was nonsense. I was usually more out of it than any of them. I drew the short straw because I was Irish. It meant if we were pulled up by the law I'd take the rap.

I don't know how I made it in one piece on all those nights when I wouldn't have even known the roads sober. Justin rarely helped me. He was usually splayed out over the back seat singing country and western songs, drinking vodka neat from the bottle.

The women we used to meet in the posh bars were more refined than the ones who came into the Corncrake. A lot of them had notions about themselves. They made me conscious of my accent. Sometimes I felt like I was speaking a foreign language with them. Justin said everyone spoke the same language after midnight.

A lot of the women I knew in Ireland hid their sexuality. Here it was screaming out at us. It made me self-conscious with them.

'Relax,' Justin said, 'They're all the same in the Jeyes Fluid.' He said his ideal woman was a barmaid who lived above a racecourse and turned into a pizza after sex.

After a couple of weeks we became tired of the treks across the city. After a gruelling day behind the bar it was difficult to gear yourself up for what was in many ways like another day's work. I told Justin I wanted out.

After that we stayed in the bar when closing time came. We helped ourselves to whatever drinks we wanted as we re-lived the night's events. Justin fought with me if the drink went down the wrong way with him. One night he attacked me for a reason I can't remember. The two of us went tumbling across the counter and into a row of liqueur glasses. I told him if he was a customer I'd have had to bar him.

I knew I was living a dissolute life but I was trapped in it. The going up was worth the coming down. I learned to live with the hangovers, the dark night depressions, the sense of aimlessness. The longer I stayed, the more contented I became even during the bad times. I rarely thought of Ireland. It was different from the beginning where I'd phoned my father every other night. I felt like a chrysalis breaking out of a shell, being born into a new identity.

The party stopped for me the night a builder's labourer decided he didn't like the look of me. It was a night when my defences were down. Maybe that's why it happened. I'd just won some money on a horse and was feeling light-headed. Usually the banter I exchanged with the customers was jovial but sometimes I crossed a line. Over the months I'd established a rapport with the ones who sat at the counter doing crosswords and eating pasties. In the evenings different laws applied. The noise threatened to break the sound barrier then. More pints were spilled than drunk.

It was on one such night just before closing-time that I happened to say the wrong thing to the wrong man. I didn't know him by name. He worked on a building site down the road. You could set your watch by him. He came in religiously for shots of whiskey after each shift.

He drank from the bottle like someone out of a cowboy film. We knew better than to stop him. Nobody else was allowed to do that. He'd never been troublesome before. That was the mistake I made. I thought such a pattern would continue.

As he sat guzzling the whiskey I had the misfortune to say to him that maybe he'd had enough. Even as I spoke I knew I'd made a mistake. He looked up at me the way drunk people sometimes do, their expression conveying the fact that you've just walked into a lion's den.

'What did you say?' he said through half-closed eyes. I told him that I didn't mean any offence but that I had had a long day and it was getting on towards the last orders anyway.

'Are you saying I'm drunk?' he said.

He grabbed me by the collar. Suddenly I saw the side of him that everyone told me was as much his reality as the quiet man who always sat alone sipping his drink.

He threw a punch at me. I ducked it. He grabbed the bottle he was drinking from. It was almost empty. He hit me a glancing blow to my head. The bottle crashed to the floor. Someone screamed.

He produced a knife. The bar became quiet. He lashed out at me with it but his movement was sluggish. I was able to get out of the way.

He kept swiping at me. Then he toppled over onto a bar stool. He hadn't seen it in front of him. He fell to the floor. I listened to him cursing. Everyone looked at him as he picked himself up. Nobody said anything. He pointed his finger at me.

'You...you,' The words wouldn't come out.

Someone started laughing then. He looked at them. The knife was still in his hand. Some of the customers ran out the door. That seemed to sober him. He looked around the bar as if only now aware he was the focus of attention.

'I'm goin' to *do* you,' he said to me. Then he stumbled out.

Nobody moved for a few seconds after he was gone. It was like the calm after the storm. Then everyone moved.

Justin came over to me. He asked me if I was all right. My head was lifting. Blood was spilling down my forehead. He wiped it.

He carried me over to a chair. I sat down.

'Drink this,' he said.

'What is it?'

'Don't mind that.'

He handed me a glass of something. I slugged it back.

'Is he gone?' I said.

'Yes.'

He carried me up to my room. A few of the other barmen came up after us. They wanted to know what happened. I tried to tell them but I couldn't. Every time I started to speak the pain got too bad.

'Let him rest,' Justin said.

One of my teeth came loose. It swam around my mouth with the blood.

He handed me a mug.

'Spit it into that,' he said.

Blood came out with it.

He spilled it down the sink. My head started to feel woozy.

He wanted me to call a doctor but I wouldn't let him.

'Just let me sleep,' I said.

They all left the room. Then everything went black.

It was hours before I woke up. Everything ached. The room was quiet. I got out of bed. My mouth felt funny with the missing tooth. I examined myself in the mirror. My face looked as if it had been mashed in a grinder.

I went over to the window. The street was dark. All I could see was a chip shop across the road. It was a place I went to sometimes after the bar closed. I decided to do that again now. Would I be able to eat with the pain in my mouth?

I went out to the corridor. Someone was snoring in one of the rooms. I wondered what time it was. How long had I been asleep?

Somehow I managed to haul myself down the stairs. The steps creaked. I hoped Justin wouldn't hear them. He'd only drag me back to the bedroom.

I looked through the frosted glass of the door that led to the bar. A few hours ago it had been chaotic. It was as quiet as a graveyard now.

I went out the front door, the door Rodney never let me do that after business hours. I tried to leave it ajar but a wind came up and slammed it shut behind me.

There was no traffic on the road. The wind knifed through me. I lurched across the street. My head throbbed.

I went into the chip shop. The glare of it stung my eyes. It made it look like morning.

The man who ran it knew me.

'What happened to you?' he said.

'I cut myself shaving,' I said.

He laughed.

'Chips, I presume?' he said.

'What else.'

He shovelled them into a bag. I threw some coins onto the counter.

'Keep the change,' I said. He winked at me.

'Mind that face.'

I went outside. Everywhere was still quiet.

I was only gone a few steps when I saw someone in front of me. It was the man who hit me with the bottle. He was with a few other people. One of them had a plank of wood in his hands.

'Look who's here,' he said.

He'd sobered up. It made him look meaner.

'Remember me?' he said. 'I promised you I'd be in touch. My mother always told me to keep my promises.'

There was an alleyway to my right. I wondered how far I'd get before he caught me.

'Aren't chips lovely at this time of night?' he said.

He knocked the bag out of my hand. I tried to run but he tripped me. He punched me in the face. It felt sorer than when he did it in the bar.

I fell down. He kicked me in the chest. Then his friends started on me. I vomited blood.

They kept kicking me but I didn't feel too much pain. Maybe what Justin gave me numbed it. I lay there taking it all. I tried to hit back once but it was only token resistance. My hands felt paralysed.

I must have fainted then. The next thing I knew I was lying in a pool of blood. It seemed much later. There was still no traffic on the road. The chipper was

142

closed. There was a hint of light in the sky. Was morning coming?

I started to crawl across the road. When I was in the middle of it I heard the screech of a car. It stopped just before it hit me. A man got out. He started shouting at me. Then he saw I was injured.

'Oh my God,' he said.

He carried me over to the kerb.

'I nearly knocked you down,' he said, 'I thought you were drunk.'

He asked me what happened. I tried to answer him but the words wouldn't come out. I was gurgling blood.

The feeling came back to my hands. I lifted my finger to indicate the pub. He linked me across the road. When we got to it he banged on the door. A light went on. Justin came out. He was in his pyjamas.

'Jesus H. Christ,' he said, 'What the fuck.'

'I found him on the road,' the man said, 'He's lucky I didn't run over him.'

'Are you sure you didn't?'

He went off. Justin carried me inside. Blood was dribbling out of my mouth. I tried to walk but my legs felt like they weren't there.

He brought me up the stairs. When we got to my room he put me on the bed.

'I smell chips off you,' he said.

'Sorry I can't give you any.'

'I always knew you were bonkers.'

He dried the blood with a cloth. Then he put some plasters on me.

'You look a sight,' he said.

143

'You should have seen the other fellow.'

He went outside. A few minutes later he came back with a bag in his hand. He put it on my forehead. The coldness of it soothed the pain.

'What's in that?' I said.

'Peas from the fridge. Don't eat them. We need them for the tea.'

He gave me a tablet. I felt myself getting woozy again.

'Time for little boys to go to sleep,' he said.

The next thing I knew it was morning. A few barmen were standing around the bed.

'He looks better, doesn't he?' Justin said. They laughed.

'Our resident mummy,' he said.

I tried to move but I couldn't. The pain started to get bad again.

'I don't think you'll die this time,' he said, 'Unfortunately.'

I spent the day in bed. Justin brought meals up to my room.

'Dinner is served,' he said at lunchtime, putting on a posh accent. I couldn't eat it. My mouth was swollen. I wondered how many teeth I'd lost.

'How's the head?' he said.

'Like a bad hangover.'

'Then it'll be nothing new to you.'

I got out of the bed. Every limb ached. I could have done with my father's wheelchair.

I looked out the window. The chip shop was barely visible.

'You bloody fool,' Justin said, 'Walking into a trap like that.'

'How was I to know it was a trap?'

'He has a screw loose. You know that, don't you?'

'Do you think he'll come back for me?'

'I doubt it. Do you want to go to the cops?'

'Hardly. I like living too much.'

I didn't work in the bar again but I hung around it. Rodney let me stay in the room until I was back to myself.

I wore my scars like badges of honour. Every night when I went downstairs I was greeted like someone who'd returned from the wars. I milked the attention.

There's nothing like a beating to get people interested in you. One night under the influence of the better part of a bottle of Southern Comfort I started to talk about my past. Nobody knew much about me until then. I don't know why I did it. There was nobody forcing me to. I'd always been the mystery man of the pub. People accepted me for that. Now I turned into my opposite.

The bar had just closed. Justin was doing the washing up. There were a few of us sitting at the counter getting sozzled. Suddenly it all started to come out of me in a flood. I told them about my mother, about Greta, about life with my father after his accident, how he'd stopped me doing the things every other person of my age was doing.

I watched their eyes becoming wider the more I went on but I couldn't stop myself. It was as if there

145

was a stranger inside me saying the words. They gathered round me in a ring, seducing me with their attention. I even told them the story of my father going out drinking dressed in Greta's jeans. And I told them about Aisling, the woman who stole my soul from me before disappearing from my life.

When I was finished, Justin said, 'You know something? You're even more certifiable than I thought you were.'

When I woke up the next morning I felt disgusted with myself. I felt I'd betrayed anyone who'd ever been important to me, especially my father.

I was as shabby as the man who wrote the obituary of my grandfather in the newspaper after he died, as shabby as anyone who tried to impress strangers with some tatty stories from his past for the cheap buzz.

The old bastard deserved better of me.

7

I didn't go back to my father until my scars healed up. There would have been too many questions from him about them. Instead I hung around the Corncrake until Rodney got fed up of me. There was nothing to do but drink. I started to put on weight. Up to now I'd got away with my over-indulgences. I was on painkillers now too. They made me put on even more.

I phoned him to say I was coming home.

'Be careful crossing the sea,' he said, 'There are still a few snakes under it.'

'The ones Saint Patrick forgot, presumably.'

I lied about the reason, telling him the bar was going through a slack time and they were allowing me leave of absence.

'I always knew it was only boredom that would bring you back to me.'

He met me at the train station. That was a surprise to me. The mountain had to come to Mohammad before.

'That's a fine big belly you have there,' he said.

'It took a lot of money to get it to that size. Don't knock it.'

I wheeled him to a taxi. He didn't let me help him in, pushing me away when I tried to lift him from the chair. The driver folded it and put it in the boot. He didn't talk on the way to the house. The driver was slightly known to him. He was conscious of things he said being repeated. I wasn't allowed ask him even the slightest personal question. He put his hand over his lips every time I put one to him.

When we got to the house I saw a meal on the table. It was some foreign concoction.

'Sit down and get that into you,' he said, 'You're probably hungry after the journey.'

'I had something on the train.'

'It's a change for me to be feeding you.'

I wondered if Betty had a hand in it. I remembered the time the meal was prepared for me after we got back from Curracloe.

'I hope it didn't tire you preparing it,' I said.

'Most of it came in packets. I just slopped it onto a plate.'

It was stale but I didn't like to say anything. I tried to force it down as he stared at me.

'You can give me all your news now,' he said.

I told him as much as I could think of without mentioning the beating. He took everything in. His mind had always been razor sharp. It was only in the year after the accident he let it go to seed.

Setanta came in. He almost knocked me over in his excitement.

'Do I not matter at all?' my father said to him, 'after all I do for you?'

He crawled under a chair.

'See?' he said, 'He knows I'm annoyed with him.'

'You should apologise.'

'Sorry, Setanta. I didn't mean it.'

He wagged his tail.

'He's my legs now,' he said, 'He opens the door with his paws when I want to go out. Sometimes I think he knows what I want even before I do.'

I made tea.

'How have you been?' I asked him.

'The same, only moreso. Nothing changes around here. You'd get more excitement in a graveyard.'

'How is the book going?'

'I'm not bothered with it much these days.'

'Why not?'

'Who cares about how my father lived? You said that yourself once.'

'*You* care. Isn't that enough?'

'Not anymore.'

He gave out about his health, about Betty, anything he could think of.

'What's wrong with Betty?'

'What's right with her?'

I didn't think he disliked her. He'd got himself trapped into a position of making light of her no matter what she did for him. I could never understand how she took it.

He wheeled himself over to the coat-stand. Setanta's lead was hanging on it. He started yelping at him, tugging at the sleeve of his jumper.

'What's up with him?' I said.

'He saw me looking at the lead. It makes him go mad.'

'Didn't Pavlov say something about that?'

'Who?'

He twirled the lead off the loop.

'Walkie time,' he said to Setanta. He wagged his tail.

'Fancy a look at the grounds?'

'Why not.'

'I'll alert the groundsmen.'

I wheeled him outside. He didn't bother putting the lead on Setanta after all.

'Off you go, dog,' he said, hooshing him away. He raced into the distance.

The grass was high in the fields. Wind ruffled the leaves of the trees. The sun was blinding. It felt good to be looking at the sky instead of buildings, to smell the salt of the sea in the air.

There was a shovel standing at a wall beside one of the outhouses. I started to dig with it. My hands were soft after all the months pulling pints. He watched me amusedly.

'A few days ploughing will sort you out,' he said.

I looked around me. Everything seemed different. All I could see of the stock was a handful of heifers tethered to a post beside an out-house. They were as scrawny as Setanta the first day I set eyes on him.

'Why do you keep them?' I said to him, 'They'll never make a profit for you.'

'They keep the grass down.'

He could never let anything go even after it outlived its usefulness. It was like the way he was with his book, with his father, everything.

I wanted to lift him out of his chair to take a few steps with his crutches but he said no. He looked out over the land like a king.

I saw his father in him. He had the eyes of power, power even in powerlessness. He affected an air of defeatism but there was something unquenchable in his spirit.

'This will all be yours one day,' he said. It reminded me of the day in the bar when he said I'd be heir to all his millions.

'I don't want it.'

'I know. We're birds of a feather that way.'

He wheeled himself away from me. Setanta barked at us from the top of a hill.

'Come on, dog,' he said, 'We're going home.'

He raced towards us.

'Good boy,' he said rubbing his ears. I could see his mood lifting even after the short spell outside.

Back in the house he opened a bottle of brandy. Anytime after lunch was fair game for this.

'You'd feel better if you didn't drink so much,' I said.

'No I wouldn't. It's the only thing I have to look forward to.'

It loosened his tongue. He told me stories about the neighbours – who married, who died, who left the area. For someone who professed not to care about it he knew a lot.

He said Betty called a few times to keep an eye on him. She wanted him to get more exercise. Everyone did. She tried to stop him smoking. Everyone did that too.

'I don't know how they don't get tired listening to their own voices,' he said, 'If I didn't have my smokes I'd pull the plug.'

At teatime I went upstairs to unpack my luggage. As I was looking through it I remembered I had a gift for him. It was a statue of a man on a horse. I took it out of the bubblewrap. It had reminded me of his grandfather when I saw it in the shop.

When I brought it down to him he looked at it strangely. After a few moments I realised it couldn't have been a worse choice. His eyes filled up. Why had I risked bringing the past back to him?

'Thank you,' he said formally.

He put it back inside the packaging. Then he left the room. I waited for him to come back but he didn't. I played with Setanta for a while. When I went looking for him I found him asleep in the living-room. He had a bottle of brandy cradled in his arms. The statue was on the chiffonier.

I brought Setanta for a walk. When he was off the lead he roamed free. He barked at me to follow him but I was too tired.

I went down to the boathouse. It had deteriorated even in the relatively short time since I'd been there last. The cladding was corroded, the roof eaten away with rust. It smelt of decay.

I had trouble opening the door. All I could see inside was dust. I threw the curtains open. It was obvious nobody had been there for ages. Why should they have been? The bed I used to sleep in lay on top of Greta's one. The little ladder that used to be between them was gone.

I sat looking out the window remembering the palm trees, the swans on the water, the way the lights came on in the surrounding cottages when it got dark.

The moon shone down on the bay like a presiding goddess. A magpie skeetered across it. Dim stars blinked invitingly.

I started thinking of Aisling. Where was she? A part of me wanted to seek her out. Maybe it was just curiosity. After a while I got bored.

My father was still asleep when I got back to the house. He slept in the chair a lot of the time. Maybe he was better off. It took him so long to undress.

I played records for a while and then I went to bed. Nothing had really changed since the old days. I could have been the child I always was, the deluded child trying to recapture a dream.

When I woke up the next day I heard voices downstairs. It was a few minutes before I remembered where I was. I looked out at the fields. They shone like rivers in the morning light, snaking their way across the landscape. Their roughness was attractive to me after the billiard table tidiness of London.

The barks of the trees looked gnarled, like wrinkled fingers. Setanta sat under one of them, a bored gun-dog waiting for the day to begin.

There was a nurse attending to my father when I got down to the kitchen. He didn't look up at me. Was he still upset about the statue?

'I'm Lynn,' she said.

I shook her hand.

'You must be the man of the house,' she said, 'I've heard a lot about you.'

'I plead innocent of all charges.'

'Your father has been looking forward to you coming home.'

153

He didn't react. She asked him to put up his arm.

'Blood pressure,' she said.

'Not that again.'

She whooshed it up.

'We go through this rigmarole every morning,' he said to me, 'The excitement kills me.'

'It's keeping you alive,' I said.

'That's debatable.'

She threw her eyes to heaven.

'I see his nibs is his usual charming self,' she said to me.

'It'd be time to worry if he changed.'

'Right!'

'Where did you go last night?' he said to me.

'Down to the boathouse.'

'Ask a stupid question.'

'That's the kind of thing you're missing in London,' Lynn said.

'Don't I know it.'

'I believe you're living the high life over there,' she said.

'He's at the wrong end of it,' my father said.

He had a welt on his leg. Lynn took out some ointment to put on it.

'I think you've done enough for one morning,' he said.

'God love you,' she said, 'you'd die of gangrene if you didn't have someone to look after you.'

'Leave me alone.'

'And let it get septic? Not likely.'

She wheeled him out to his bed. I helped her lift him onto it.

'Up's a daisy,' she said.

He shouted out in pain.

'Don't mind him,' I said, 'He's just looking for attention.'

'It took me a while to cop on to that.'

'I'm in agony. You'll break my leg yet. Then I'd be in a nice condition.'

'Hold your whist and let me deal with it.

She put the ointment on.

'Fuck this for a game of cowboys,' he said.

I went out to the kitchen. She came in a few minutes later.

'Did you manage it?' I asked her.

'Just about. He makes such a big deal out of everything.'

'It's the way he's always been. Sorry.'

'Don't worry. I enjoy him. Children make the best patients.'

She collected her things.

'I'll be off now,' she said.

'Thanks for all you're doing for him.'

She called goodbye in to him.

'You're good for another 24 hours anyway,' she said.'

'Is that all you're giving me?'

'Maybe it's all you deserve.'

She zipped up her anorak.

'Nice to have met you,' she said to me.

'And me you.'

'See you tomorrow,' she said to my father.

'Not if I see you first.'

She shook her fist at him. I walked her to the door.

'Thanks again,' I said.

She walked across the cobblestones to her car. It was a SUV. She was about to get in when she turned back.

'I nearly forgot the most important thing,' she said.

She reached into the glove compartment.

'Voila!'

She took out a package.

'It's some salad,' she said. I bring it to him whenever I can. He pretends he eats the right food but I know he's on a junk diet. Betty tells me he rings out for deliveries anytime she's not with him. He's able to cook for himself but he'd prefer to order junk food. She finds the empty cartons when she calls up. He acts the innocent if she says anything.'

'It's the way he's been all his life.'

'I can imagine. Anyway, do your best to get him to take it.'

'I will. You're very good to go to the trouble.'

'I'd do anything for him. Any of us would if he'd let us.'

She drove off. I went back inside. He was looking into space.

'You should be nicer to her,' I said to him, 'She cares about you.'

'Does she? Surely the government pays her to do all that stuff. I'm sure she's on an expense account with her big car.'

'Maybe you don't know who your friends are.'

I handed him the salad. He took it grumpily.

'It's probably one of those macrobiotic things.'

'It's got all the vitamins you need.'

'Vitamins be damned. She gave me one of them another time and it nearly finished me off. If that's health food, give me poison any day of the week.'

I put it on a plate for him. He took a bite of it before throwing it in the bin.

He asked me to cook a fry for him instead. I turned on the cooker.

As we were waiting for the ring to heat up he put on that look of his, the one that always preceded some pronouncement.

'I'm thinking of selling the farm,' he said.

He said it in the tone in which he might have said he was thinking of buying a loaf of bread.

'That's a bit of a bombshell.'

'What's the point of keeping it on?'

'I thought you liked the activity.'

'What activity? I've been doing nothing but supervising since I got crocked up.'

I wasn't sure if he was serious or not. You never knew with him.

'So you'd be moving out.'

'Obviously.'

'Where would you go?'

'I was thinking of Dublin. Isn't that where everyone ends up?'

'You know nobody up there.'

'I know nobody here either. All my friends are dead – if I ever had any.'

'It would be a big move for you. You've been in Galway all your life.'

'The place doesn't do anything for me anymore. Dublin might be nicer - for the two of us.'

Was this why he was thinking of it, I wondered, to get me back to him?

'Dublin is over-rated.'

'It couldn't be worse than this dump.'

He picked up a newspaper.

'Look at that,' he said,

There was a headline on it about a murder in the area.

'That's another thing about living down here. I'm a sitting duck if anyone decides they want to break in.'

'What about Setanta?

He grunted.

'He'd lick a burglar's hand instead of biting him.'

'We could get a bigger dog.'

'Even if he was a Doberman it wouldn't make any difference. There are people round here that had their guard-dogs chloroformed.'

'Maybe we need to get an alarm in.'

'I heard of an 88 year-old woman the other day who was murdered for £10. I think they raped her as well. They're calling it "anti-social behaviour" now. Anti-social for me is someone who doesn't want to go to a party.'

'Most of them are on drugs. It makes them insane.'

'What kind of a world are we living in? Sometimes I think it's a sin to bring a child into it. If I

158

had my life to live over again I'd probably be celibate.'

'Where would that leave me?'

'You might have been better off never to have seen the light of day. Or me either.'

'Don't talk like that.'

'Why not? Isn't it the truth?'

'You have a lot more than some people have.'

'Like what, for instance?'

'Do you not get enjoyment out of your book?'

'I'll be lucky if six people in Ireland read it. They'd as soon buy a bus timetable.'

Despite what he said I saw him working on it over the next few nights. I learned to take his rants with a grain of salt. Complaining was so much a part of him he hardly knew he was doing it.

He drank as he wrote. He'd ask for a glass of brandy to be brought in to him on a tray as he waited for his muse to descend. Each night it had to be the same glass filled to the same height. It was like a superstition to him, a religious ritual. He felt the inspiration wouldn't come otherwise.

If he had just two or three glasses it gave him the concentration he needed. Any more and he wrote balderdash. He was capable of lowering half a bottle a night. I often had to pretend we were out of it when I saw him having too much.

'I could have been rich if it wasn't for this stuff,' he said to me one night.

'I know the feeling.'

'Don't turn out like me.'

'Now you're beginning to sound like Greta.'

'Does she give out to you about it?'

'She read me the Riot Act one night in London.'

'The men drink and the women watch them. It was always the way. If I had a penny for every time your mother gave out to me about it I'd be a millionaire.'

'Did you ever take her out for one?'

'It wasn't the done thing in those days. Not like today where the women would drink you under the table. You'd get funny looks in a bar if you had a woman with you.'

'Even your wife?'

'Sadly.'

'I don't think I ever saw her having a drink.'

'It was a waste of money buying her one. She was happier with a cup of tea.'

'Did she tell you that?'

'She didn't have to. On the odd occasion that we were in a bar together Her mind never left the kitchen. She was capable of spending the whole night worrying if she left the cooker on. You could count on the fingers of one hand the nights she enjoyed a glass of wine.'

'I suppose it was on one of those nights that l was conceived.'

I was surprised to see him blush.

'I think we'll talk about something else now.'

'What would you say about the two of us going out for a drink tonight?'

'Tonight?'

'Why not? It would do you good to see people.'

'They'd only make a laugh of me.'

'I don't know why you say that. You have a lot of respect around here.'

'In my hat. Maybe at one time I did. Not anymore. I'm just "Yer man" now. It's a long time since anyone doffed their cap to me when they saw me.'

'Do you need them to do that? Are you still dependent on that injection to your ego?'

'You love impaling me on that particular stake, don't you? All I'm looking for is respect. That isn't there now. Most of the people who live around here now are the *nouveaus riches*. If they get a promotion in their job they want to buy the biggest house in the town.'

'Would you grudge them that? We all have to start somewhere.'

'You don't realise what I'm saying to you. The monied people today don't know how to handle their wealth. It sits uneasily on their shoulders.'

'Money is money. Either it pays the bills or it doesn't. I can't see how it makes any difference whether you handle it well or not.'

'I'm a bad example. You should have seen my father.'

'Let's leave your father out of this. I asked you if you'd come out for a drink. I didn't intend to get a speech. Is the answer yes or no?'

'I'm not dressed for it.'

He had a tattered old jumper on him. He wore it day in day out.

'You don't need to be. Who'll be looking at you?'

'With these legs, everyone.'

161

He wheeled himself over to the drinks cabinet.

'Let's just have another one here.'

He poured a glass of brandy for himself. As he drank it he looked at a picture of my mother that was on the mantelpiece.

'It must be an evil God,' he said, 'who let me survive when I had nothing to live for and took her away from a life she loved.'

'Has time not helped you to come to terms with that?'

He buried his head in his hands.

'She must have been insane to stay married to me. I shiver when I think of what I put her through.'

'Maybe it fulfilled her to have you to look out for.'

'You've been reading too many psychology books.'

I asked him if he thought about her much.

'I look forward to being with her.'

He talked about 'coming up the straight' like one of the horses he backed. He often quoted the lines of Omar Khayyam, 'The moving finger writes, and having writ moves on, nor all thy piety nor wit can lure it back to cancel half a line, nor all thy tears wash out one word of it.'

He looked old.

'I won't be around much longer,' he said.

'Don't talk like that.'

'Why not? Every time I pick up the paper, someone else I know has kicked the bucket.'

'Then don't pick up the paper.'

'That's not the answer.'

'You need to stop thinking about things like that.'

'How do I do that?'

'By keeping yourself active.'

'How can I? I don't have hobbies.'

'You have the book. Your art.'

'Art? I'd be better off painting the house.'

The easel had been stashed in the garage for many years now, alongside most of his paintings. Like so many other things in his life, he'd cast it aside when he got fed up of it.

'A good day for me is a day without pain,' he said, 'That's all I have to look forward to now. I was watching a programme on television the other night. It was about a man who kept hitting himself on the head with a hammer. Someone asked him why he did it. He said, "It's lovely when you stop."'

'We need Greta here to get you to think positive,' I said.

'Positive thinkers always depressed me. I prefer negative ones.'

He said he thought it was time to settle his accounts with 'the man upstairs.' At least if that's where he was going. He might have more fun in the other place. Heaven for the climate, as the old saying went, and hell for the company.'

There was no point arguing with him. I fell in with his train of thought.

'I'm sure you're going up,' I said.

'If I am I'm going to put the head man in the witness-box when I see him. I want to cross-examine him about the lousy life he put us in. What's the point of it all? It's just apple pie in the sky when you die.'

When he got going on religion there was no stopping him. I was more of a soundboard than anything else. Eventually he wore himself out.

The next morning he insisted on making breakfast for me. When he was in good form he could wheel himself around the kitchen like a child. I heard him fumbling with matches as he tried to light the gas. He started swearing as they fell all over the place. It was a miracle he hadn't torched the house so far. He'd reached over a jet of flame that many times with his shirt cuff hanging down.

After we'd eaten our breakfast I saw a look coming into his eyes. It was the look that said he was going to ask me a favour.

'I added a few bits onto the book. Would you like to hear them?'

What choice had I? It was his life.

He put on his glasses. A sheaf of pages was taken from a drawer. He started to read.

It was impressive. He'd drawn an interesting picture of the past, how things changed after 1916. I made some comments that he liked. He purred with pride as he listened to me. It was so easy to please him I should have done it all the time.

It was stupid to tell the truth about anything, be it what was in store for us on the Day of Judgement or the stock his father came from. He got high talking about a book that would probably never be published. Or, if it were, never read.

He repeated stories I'd heard a hundred times before. Reiterating the tried and trusted excited him.

The same events wound up to the same conclusions like an old movie or a sentimental song.

One day when I came home from the town I saw him talking to his solicitor. He was someone I'd only seen in the house one or two times before, a ferrety little man in a crumpled suit.

'Is something up?' I said.

'I'm making my will.'

I was surprised. He often told me he wasn't going to bother.

After the solicitor left I said, 'I thought you told me once that you'd be as well off writing it on the back of a racing sheet as paying someone.'

'I probably would. That's where most of my money went anyway. Or maybe a beer mat. That would be even better.'

'So what came over you?'

'I don't know. There was something on the television about it. You better be nice to me now or I'll leave everything to Setanta.'

'Would you like a cup of tea?' I said, 'I'll even throw in two biscuits with it this time.'

Shortly before I was due to go back to London he told me Aisling phoned one night. The news shook me. I was surprised he mentioned it in view of everything that happened between them. There was no reason for him to bring her name up. We hadn't been talking about her. I took it as a sign that she didn't represent a threat to him anymore.

'She only stayed on a minute when I said you weren't living here anymore,' he said.

'Why didn't you tell me before now?'

'I didn't want to upset you.'

'You wouldn't have.'

'She left a phone number in case you want to contact her.'

'They always come after you when you don't need them.'

She was out of my system now. It was like getting over an infection. I wasn't good enough for her when she was living in the house and if she came back now she wouldn't be good enough for me. That was the way life worked. It was like a pendulum. The more you wanted something the more it drifted away from you. If you were stronger than it you could have it any time you wanted. It would be sitting there waiting for you like a reward for the fact that you'd burned the need for it out of yourself.

I went into the town the following night. It had grown bigger since my childhood. Most of the people I knew were gone to Dublin to work. Those who remained behind either lived with their parents or invested in the cramped little semi-detached houses that were springing up like mushrooms in the open spaces I used to play in as a child. They were now the property of businessmen who'd moved in from abroad with their vulture funds.

There were a lot of fast food places, computer centres. One of the cinemas I used to go to had become a bingo hall. The other was cut in half and made into two. Most of the small businesses I remembered were gone. The area where my father bought and sold cattle had been turned into a shopping centre. It was the pattern of probably every little town in the country. I wasn't surprised. What did surprise me was how everything looked so wrong.

I thought of a child who was trying to grow up too fast. The town had created an image of itself that it wasn't able to live up to. It was like a man trying on a suit of clothes that were too big for him.

I walked down the main street. Most of the traders were gone home for the evening. I crossed the river that led to the church and the college. Every building brought back a memory. I was going to call in on Betty but decided not to. She'd only try and persuade me to stay. It would be easier to ring her from London.

I recognised few of the people who passed by me. Most of those I thought I knew looked through me. Did they know who I was or had too much time elapsed? Maybe they thought I'd got ideas about myself when I set off for 'the big smoke.' Some people were like that. They assumed you'd change because the place you lived changed. These were often the very people who'd have accused me of living a wasted life if I spent it caring for my father.

I came to the bridge where my mother died. It always gave me butterflies. We never found out how long she lived after the collision, how much pain she suffered. My father never talked about such things. I didn't blame him. Who would want to know that?

There was a broken wing mirror in a ditch. Was it from our car? I didn't want to think about that either.

I stood at the end of the avenue leading to the college. It wasn't the place it used to be. There were cracked bricks, broken windows. I thought back to the days when it had so much power over me. It was just a run-down building now. Many of the priests inside it were retired. It was no longer a boarding school. The number of day pupils had trailed off as well. In a few years it would probably be pulled down.

A priest rambled down the avenue. It was Fr McGinty. He'd always been friendly to me. I remembered him as one of the few teachers of his time who didn't use corporal punishment. He got pupils to do what he wanted by the force of his personality.

'What has you back in the land of ghosts?' he said.

'I'm surprised you recognised me.'

'Teachers and elephants never forget. How have you been?'

'Well enough. And you?'

'At my age being alive is a bonus.'

'You look well anyway.'

'They tell me I have a leaking valve in my heart.'

'I'm sorry to hear that. Hopefully they'll sort it out.'

'I said I didn't want to hear the details. Thinking about things like that will kill you sooner than the condition itself.'

'I agree.'

'How is your father?'

'I wish he had your attitude.'

'Don't be too hard on him. He never recovered from the accident.'

'I know.'

'I think of your mother a lot.'

'So do I.'

'I pray for her. Maybe I should be asking her to pray for me.'

'I'm sure it works both ways.'

He looked me up and down.

'We lost you after the accident. It was a pity. You were a good student.'

'Not many of you thought that.'

'It was a different time. If you were with us now you'd be happy.'

'School was never for me. I needed to get out into the world.'

'Most young people are like that. Then they realise it isn't all it's cracked up to be.'

'Even at its worst it's better than school.'

'Thanks for the compliment!'

'I didn't mean it that way.'

'Your father told me you went to England.'

'I was in London.'

'Ah! The pagan city.'

'You could say that.'

'What were you at?'

'Just some odd jobs. Nothing of any consequence.'

'I believe there are only grey heads in the churches now.'

'I'm afraid so.'

'Anyway, we can't change that. Time marches on. What can't be cured has to be endured.'

He looked old in the night air.

So what's next for you?' he said.

'I'll stay here a while and then go off.'

169

'I admire you. So many people put their parents into homes.'

'He wouldn't last a week in one of those places. Either that or he'd drive the staff round the bend.'

'Does he drain you?'

'I give him a hard time myself sometimes.'

'I'm sure you're just saying that.'

'He's a sheep in wolf's clothing, or whatever the expression is.'

'I prefer to think of him as a bull in a china shop.'

'I'm sure you've had your moments with him.'

'When I came here first I thought he was going to murder me. It was my first parish. I thought it was going to be my last.'

'He does that with everyone.'

'I know that now. People with tough appearances are often the softest inside.'

'My father keeps his soft side pretty well hidden!'

He gave me a card with his number on it. It made me feel strange. Suddenly he was like a friend to me rather than a figure of authority. The years between us didn't seem to be as unfathomable as they once were.

'If that doesn't work I'm in the book,' he said.

'Are there still phone books?'

'For a few anachronisms like me.'

'I'll be in touch one way or another.'

'Call down to see me anytime. Or I'll drop in to you.'

'Bring your bullet proof vest if himself is around.'

He laughed.

'God bless you,' he said.

I watched him going down the road, his cassock flying in the wind. He was a happy man. I remembered him in the classroom with a smile on his face. He taught us Maths. He'd sit on our benches explaining some theorem, asking us what films we'd seen recently. He had the gift of child psychology, getting the most out of us by his casualness.

It amazed me how men like him could be jolly when they seemed to have so little in their lives. Did their faith make up for it?

I stood on the bank of the river looking up at the sky. An arabesque of clouds closed in on the sun as another day ended. Everything seemed so serene. Could I one day live here for good? Would it be enough for me now that I'd sowed my wild oats?

I was on my way home when another familiar face appeared. He was almost past me when he said, 'Is it yourself?' I had to look twice. Even then I wasn't sure.

'You wouldn't be Sean Glynn by any chance,' I said.

'I certainly would.'

He'd put on weight since I saw him last. His hair was practically gone. But it was the aura of wealth he exuded that amazed me most. Was this the same person who sweated over the memory of dates in history on wet Monday mornings?

'You've grown a bit taller,' he said, 'but I'd recognise that ugly mug anywhere.'

He put his arms around me. I hadn't particularly liked him in school. He was a teacher's pet. I remembered him being fascinated by cars. His father owned a garage.

There was a woman with him.

'This is Nicola,' he said, 'The eighth wonder of the world.'

She smiled at me through perfect teeth.

'Pleased to meet you,' I said.

She was pretty in a kind of forgettable way. I shook her hand.

'Nic is from Frisco,' he said, 'I kidnapped her.'

'It was a midnight flit,' she said.

'You're a long way from home.'

'I had to see this cute town Sean keeps talking about.'

'It's a bit smaller than San Francisco.'

'You could say that!'

'Nic and myself are going to jump the broom in the fall,' Sean said.

'The fall?'

'She has me Americanised already.'

I asked him what he was working at.

'I'm based in an airport in Denver. If a plane crashes, they blame me.'

'I don't like the sound of that.'

'I'm what they call a flight coordinator. Translated into English it means I make squiggles behind a screen and pretend I know what they mean.'

'Don't mind him,' Nicola said, 'He's a genius.'

'What about yourself?' he said, 'I hear you're over in Thatcher Land.'

'For my sins.'

'Bartending?'

'Yes.'

'Is it not more fun being at the other side of the counter?'

'It's a job.'

'How's your father?'

'Chugging along '

'I don't see him out much since the accident.'

'We try not to talk about that.'

'Sorry.'

'He was never very sociable.'

'I suppose not.'

'Do you come home much?'

'Now and again.'

'Was that Fr McGinty I saw you talking to?'

'It was.'

'I always liked him.'

'He was one of the good ones.'

'I never heard anyone saying a bad word about him.'

'Do you keep in touch with anyone from the class?'

'A few of them.'

'What are they up to?'

'Let me see. John Melvin married a teacher. Paul Hanley became a guard.'

'What about Liam Byrne?' The name came out of me from some forgotten part of my brain. He used to get the best marks in all the exams. I hated him. He was just a mouth.

'The last I heard of him he was panel-beating cars in Slough.'

'Jesus. I thought he'd do better than that.'

'So did we all. It's like the hare and the tortoise. Some of the quiet ones are going a bomb.'

'There's probably a lesson in that for us.'

'We meet up every time we get a chance. You should join us.'

'Let me know if something is happening. I'll try to be there.'

He produced a business card with his phone number on it.

'My details,' he said.

It looked very elaborate. There was a photograph of a plane descending on a landing strip.

'Wow.'

'It's bullshit. The company drafts up these things to make us look good.'

'I'm impressed.'

'We have a new client already,' he said to Nicola. She laughed.

'Call me,' he said.

I shook Nicola's hand again.

'Lovely to meet you,' I said.

'Likewise.'

He went to go.

'Oh,' he said, 'I nearly forgot.'

He took a photograph out of his wallet. It had Nicola and himself in it. They were standing in front of the house they planned to live in after they 'jumped the broom.' It was built in the middle of a wood in Colorado Springs.

It struck me as the epitome of boredom.

'Is that heaven or is that heaven?' he said.

'You've got it made.'

'It'll do for the first year,' Nicola said.

I could imagine his life with her, commuting between two continents but belonging properly to neither, being more in love with Ireland maybe than he could ever be if he lived in it, going from promotion to promotion as Nicola made him move to bigger and bigger houses.

'We're in Scotland next week,' he said, 'Nic's mom is originally from Dunoon. We're under orders to find out everything about her DNA. You'll get me after that.'

He put his arm around me again.

'Great to have run into you, old buddy.'

'And you.'

He put his fingers into a 'V for victory' sign. Nicola blew me a kiss. Then they were gone.

It was coming on to night. I loved the way the sky became burnished at this time every evening, how it painted the sky blood red. In the distance the mountains brooded.

I walked down by the river. It always relaxed me to do that. How many nights had I sat here as a child watching the fishermen taking in their catches? There were no fishermen there now but I still sat there soaking in the atmosphere.

The water was as clear as glass. A salmon leaped up for a fly.

I thought of how life would be if I stayed here forever. Could I go back to this life or had I been blooded into a different one? We know ourselves only through the things we do, the people we meet. If I never sampled London I'd never have missed it. Now

175

that I had I had to go back to it even if it was the wrong place for me. That was what growing up did. It turned you into someone you didn't want to be.

When I got back to the farm my father was asleep. He was lying on the bed in his clothes. In former times I'd have woken him up to tell him my news.

I brought Setanta up to the bedroom with me. He gazed at me with his ears up. His head was tilted sideways. It was the way he always looked when he was curious. He lay down beside me.

I couldn't sleep. My mind was racing too much. I saw so few people that when anything at all happened I over-reacted to it. I started to wonder if I'd be happier if I was like Sean, meeting all the old classmates every time I came home. I'd left the college so suddenly I didn't really get a chance to say goodbye to them. Seeing them around town afterwards wasn't the same. There was a bond that came from sharing things with people, even painful things. Or especially those. I'd sacrificed that by living with my father. Could I have been Sean Glynn if things worked out differently? Maybe the solitary life was as addictive as that one. We were all locked into our routines.

I was so late waking up the next morning my time was short for making it to the bus.

Should I wake my father? I wasn't sure if it was a good idea.

I went into his room. He looked small under the sheets.

'Goodbye,' I whispered.

He opened his eyes.

'I wasn't sure to wake you or not.'

'I'm always half awake. Never don't wake me.'

'I overslept myself. I'll have to go soon.'

'Give me a minute. I'll see you in the kitchen.'

He never liked me watching him dressing. It embarrassed him because it took him so long.

I brought my case into the kitchen. He appeared after a few minutes.

'Sorry I missed you last night,' I said.

'I waited up till all hours. What happened you?'

'I ran into Fr McGinty.'

'Fr McGinty? Is he retired from teaching yet?'

'More or less. I think he's doing more parish work now.'

'He comes up to see me every once in a while. Your mother adored him.'

'I met Sean Glynn too.'

He screwed up his face.

'That name rings a bell.'

'He was in my class.'

'What's happening with him?'

'He got a job in the States. There was an American girl with him. They're getting married soon.'

'He has my sympathies. What kind of job has he?'

'Something to do with planes.'

He put the kettle on.

'Cup of cha?'

'I can't. I'm dead late.'

'Not even a quick cup?'

'I'd miss the bus.'

He went over to the dresser. There was a biscuit tin on one of the shelves. It was where he kept his money. He took out a wad of notes. There was a few hundred pounds in it. He shoved it into my hand.

'I can't take that,' I said.

'Shut up and put it in your pocket.'

'Are you leaving yourself short?'

'I'd only waste it on the nags.'

There was never any talking to him when he'd made his mind up.

'Thank you. I really mean that.'

'Take care of yourself. And come back again soon.'

'I will.'

I put on my coat. Setanta looked up at me. He scraped the ground with his paw.

'Don't be in a hurry to go back to that bar either,' he said, 'You'll get the same thanks for it in the end.'

'I know.'

He looked lost sitting there in front of me.

'Ring Betty for me, will you?' I said, 'I should have spent more time with her.'

'I'm sure she's spent nights lying awake pining for you.'

I took up my case.

'Behave yourself in that den of iniquity,' he said.

'I'll try.'

I didn't want to leave him again. There was no sense of an adventure this time. The novelty value was gone for me now. I was going back not because of a need but because it seemed the only option available to me.

He sat hunched in his chair as I went out.

'Don't do anything I wouldn't do,' he said.

'If I do I'll name him after you.'

He gave a dry chuckle.

'The old ones are the best.'

I felt a lump in my throat. Either I was already lonely for him or I was thinking of his maxim, 'In every parting there's the image of death.'

The wind was blowing as I stepped outside. There were leaves all over the gravel. A jet plane slashed through the sky, leaving plumes of smoke like a tapeworm.

He looked unusually frail as he sat there. The sun was starting to come out as I walked down the road.

He had the door already closed when I looked back to wave goodbye.

8

When I got to London I moved back into the hostel I'd been in before. I was too lazy to look for an apartment. When I rang Justin to say I'd arrived he nearly went through the phone with excitement.

'How's the war hero?' he said, 'Did the old lad lick your wounds for you?'

'He wrapped me up in cotton wool for the whole time.'

'So what's next for the wandering boy?'

'I haven't thought ahead.'

'There's a job here if you want it. I'm running the show now.'

'That must mean things are even more degenerate than usual.'

'For sure.'

'Are you drinking much?'

'Is the bear a Catholic? Does the Pope shit in the woods?'

'I presume Rodney is still there.'

'He's gone too. That's why I'm in charge.'

'Rodney gone? That surprises me.'

'It surprised him too. He had his eyes on buying the place eventually.'

'What happened?'

'I don't know the details. One day he was there and the next he wasn't. He obviously got the bum's rush.'

'I hope it wasn't because of my little escapade.'

'If it was, I thank you from the bottom of my heart. He was a cunt. And that's being disrespectful to all the other cunts in the world. I wouldn't piss on him if he was on fire.'

'Now tell me what you really think of him.'

'Very funny. So are you coming back?'

'Not yet.'

'You're probably worried about the guy who beat you up.'

'Sort of.'

'There's no need to be. He upped sticks.'

'How do you know?'

'I hear he's running guns in Belfast these days.'

'Great. So instead of being hit with a bottle, next time I'll be shot.'

'Don't be so negative. He might just kneecap you.'

He kept at me to go back to the bar.

'You wouldn't even have to work in it. There'd be no charge for the room. For old time's sake.'

'I think I'll stay here for the moment if you don't mind. I'll come back to you when I'm ready.'

"Is that a definite?'

'It's a definite probably.'

'That sounds like an Irish answer.'

I knew if I went back to the Corncrake the whole merry-go-round would begin again, the drinking and the late nights and the wild dates.

'I have a few women lined up for you that'll knock your socks off,' he said.

I wasn't interested. We'd both got that particular T-shirt. What would it wind up to in the end except a drunken fling with someone I wouldn't have two words to exchange with if I met her again when I was sober.

I told him I'd call him when I felt back to myself. It was a lie. I didn't want to contact him at all. Being beaten up ended that phase of my life.

I moved out of the hostel a few days later. I didn't want him to put pressure on me to meet so I didn't tell him. The money my father gave me came in handy now. I didn't need to look for a job.

I rented a small apartment in the area. It wasn't much but it did me. I decided I was going to spoil myself for a while. The days passed in a pleasant lethargy. I got up when I felt like it. There was a park nearby that I strolled around after lunch. It was pleasant sitting there doing nothing. I let the apartment get manky. Dishes piled up in the sink.

It was a relief not to have to mix with anyone. I came and went as I pleased. It was like being at home except without my father to contend with.

I felt I was becoming more like him in my ways. My mind was all over the place. I didn't mind that. When I was too relaxed I got bored. I told myself I owed nothing to anyone. My only responsibility was to myself. Some days I didn't even bother dressing, becoming like him that way too. I read the papers from cover to cover and watched all the dumb shows on the television.

Aisling came into my mind now and again. I thought I'd got her out of my system until my father brought her name up. All the things we'd done came back to me then. Something was drawing me back to her.

I dialled her number one day but it just rang out. I started thinking about how close we were for a while. How was it that things changed so suddenly? I was still angry about how it ended.

Justin called around. I didn't know how he got my address.

'How is Hamlet?' he said when I answered the door. I was in my pyjamas.

'I thought you'd fallen off the planet or something.'

'Sorry for being such a bore.'

'That ends tonight,' he said, 'I'm driving you to the Corncrake.'

I couldn't say no. He still had that power over me.

'Grab whatever you need and we're off.'

He drove like a madman across the city, crashing all the red lights. He grinned at me like an adolescent every time he went through one.

'I have so much to tell you, you won't believe it,' he said. I tried to revive my old enthusiasm.

When we got to the bar he sat me down in a corner. I was presented with a glass of cider.

'This is my latest poison,' he said. Because it was his, it had to be mine too.

He knocked one after the other back as he filled me in on what was happening since I left. He'd lost a lot of money on the stock market. His brother died. He had a heart scare.

I tried to feign interest. It was like being with my father. Both of them told me I was a good listener. It wasn't true. I was able to turn my mind off and look like I was listening. Maybe I should have been an actor. I was like someone appearing in a play he couldn't get out of, mouthing the lines until curtain call. He gave me my cues and I reciprocated but the lines felt as flat as my own mood. I watched him laughing himself senseless at his trite quips and it was as if it was happening to someone outside me. I was a ventriloquist's dummy mouthing a prepared script to satisfy a man I didn't care about anymore.

'What's up with you?' he said to me one night. The drink had gone down the wrong way for him. A woman he was trying to get off with had just dumped him.

'What do you mean?' I said, 'I'm just sitting here.'

'That's the problem,' he said, 'You're just fucking sitting there. Get up off your arse and do something.'

I stood up.

'Are you happy now?' I said.

'Ecstatic, fuckhead.'

I went to hit him then but I missed. He fell off his chair trying to avoid the punch. When he got up he was laughing.

He stood up on his chair and started singing 'I don't know why I love you but I do.' Everyone in the bar was looking at us.

He loved embarrassing me like that. I was the straight man for his gags, the person he slapped on the back when he wanted a bellylaugh. Whenever I told him to lay off he got worse.

Anytime he was going into the West End he still gave me a call. I didn't want to go anymore but he wouldn't take no for an answer.

I tried to make the best of it. He had a book where he kept the phone numbers of old flames. They dwindled as time went on. Some of them got married. Others said they didn't want to see him anymore. I told him it was time he thought of settling down. He said he'd die first. 'Vive le coq!' he'd say with his hand up in a military salute, his heels snapping together.

I phoned my father every now and then. He sounded as if he was glad to hear from me. I pretended I was still in the Corncrake.

He went on about local news. There were a few friends from the old days who called in to see him, 'Fossils like myself' as he put it. Together they mourned the state of the world.

The only enjoyment he had in life, he said, was the occasional flutter on a horse. Sometimes he backed them simply because he liked the sound of their name. Most of them lost. He had a joke he liked to tell: 'I put a bet on a horse at twenty to one yesterday. He came in at a quarter past three.' It was closer to the truth than he might have liked to believe. He had an unhappy knack of backing donkeys.

I asked him if he saw Betty much.

'She rings me when she feels like it. In other words the same way as she does everything else in life.'

She brought him out for a drive one day, he said.

'I was made to feel as if I was getting the Crown Jewels but I'd have preferred to stay in reading a book.'

Well-meaning neighbours were as bad. They poked their nose in the door asking him how he was. He tried to put on a plastic smile for them.

'Has Greta been on?' I asked.

'She never goes too long without checking in on the state of my soul.'

'Welcome to the club.'

'The last time I talked to her she told me that those the Lord loveth he chastiseth. In that case, I said, I'll just bid him a cautious hello from the other side of the street.'

She visited me once. It was when she was on the way to one of her medical get-togethers. Justin was with me at the time. We were both drunk.

'Meet my sister,' I said, 'She's a personal friend of Jesus so if you want anything, now is the time to ask.'

'I'd like a blow-up rubber doll of Pamela Anderson,' he said.

She looked at me.

'Well,' I said, 'Can you organise it?'

'If this is going to continue I'm not staying,' she said.

'Sorry,' I said. 'Justin, behave yourself.'

He did his military salute again.

'Yessir!'

I started talking to her about her conference. Justin flopped onto the sofa. He lay there scrunched up like a baby.

'Is he asleep?' she said.

'What does it look like?'

'Are all your friends like that?'

'What's wrong with him?'

'No comment.'

'Try and be patient with him. He had a rough childhood.'

'What's that got to do with it?'

I put on the kettle.

'I can see what's happening,' she said, 'You're trying to make up for the years you think you wasted with Daddy.'

'Is that what it is? I often wondered what was at the back of it.'

'You're not cut out for this kind of life. Don't you see that?'

'Of course.'

I was smoking a cigarette. She grabbed it out of my mouth.

'Do you realise the damage these things are doing to you? The people I nurse are so sick, some of them would give everything belonging to them to be able to take a breath without effort. Most of that is from smoking.'

'I'll cut down if it makes you happy.'

'It isn't me I'm thinking about. It's you.'

The kettle boiled.

'Sorry for preaching,' she said.

'Don't worry. It goes in one ear and out the other. Sometimes it doesn't even get to the second ear.'

She said she heard my romance with Aisling had broken up.

'I was sorry to hear about it. I liked her.'

She asked me how long I intended to stay at the bar work. I said that as soon as I could get out of it and live off her Majesty you wouldn't see my heels for the dust.

'So that's your only ambition, to live off the government?'

'Can you give me a better one?'

She sighed. I was hoping she'd leave. She looked at the dishes in the sink.

'This place is unbelievable,' she said, 'What would Mammy think?'

'Never mind about Mammy. It's me that has to live in it.'

'How could anyone be happy here?'

'I am.'

'It's a pigsty.'

'Then I must be a pig.'

She sighed again.

'You should go home and live with him.'

'Why?'

'He needs you.'

'What gives you that impression?'

'It's blindingly obvious anytime I ring.'

'If you're that concerned about him why don't you go home yourself?'

'You know that's not on.'

We went back and forth with the same old arguments. It could have been ten years ago. We'd never change.

I brought her over a cup of tea.

'It's too strong,' she said.

We were even different that way. I added some water.

'How is it now?'

'Much better thanks.'

She looked at the sink.

'I suppose it's out of the question for you to allow me wash the dishes.'

I imagined her in the hospital bustling around. Was that what her vocation was about – control?

'I like them as they are.'

She started breathing heavily. She did that when she was tense.

'I suppose the next time I visit you you'll have a safety pin through your nose.'

For some reason I started laughing.

'Where did you get that idea?'

'I see them on the street.'

'You crack me up,' I said.

'And you drive me up the walls.'

She put down her cup.

'If you don't mind I won't finish the tea,' she said.

'Why not?'

'I just don't feel like it.'

'Is there anything else I can get you?'

'No.' She looked at her watch. 'In fact I'll probably just go.

'What's your hurry?'

'I have to prepare for the conference. I told you about that, didn't I?'

'I vaguely remember hearing something about it from you.'

'I'm giving a speech.'

'Good for you.'

She took up her handbag.

'I might drop in again on my way back from Brighton.'

'So you're leaving from Heathrow?'

'I always do.'

'Goodbye,' she said.

'Goodbye.'

She gave me a kind of hug at the door.

'You know Mammy would turn in her grave if she saw the way you were living,' she said.

'Maybe the exercise would do her good.'

'Please don't say things like that. You think you're clever when you come out with that kind of nonsense, don't you?'

'You drive me to it.'

'This stuff isn't you,' she said, 'It's an image you've created.'

'Good insight.'

'I beg you,' she said as she went out, 'Clean up this place before you catch some disease.'

'I will,' I said, 'Enjoy your conference.'

She went out. I heard her feet trundling down the corridor.

Justin sat up.

'I thought you were asleep,' I said.

190

'When you live the kind of life I do,' he said, 'you learn to sleep with one eye open.'

'So you heard all that.'

'Most of it. Now I know why you left home. Phoar!'

'I call her Hitler in knickers.'

'Attila the hen?'

'That's even better.'

He kept needling me about her over the next few days. I was sorry I introduced him to her. I knew there'd be no end of religious cracks from now on.

'Sister Greta,' he said, 'The woman who's going to save the church from extinction.'

She rang me one night from Brighton. I was drinking again.

'I don't believe this,' she said when I started slurring my words.

I could hear her drawing in her breath.

'You're killing yourself with that stuff,' she said.

'Really? Thanks for telling me.'

Why do you do it?'

'There's nothing else to do around here.'

'I wouldn't mind if you were good company with it but you're not. You just talk nonsense.'

'That's probably true but then you always told me I talked nonsense even when I'm sober.'

'Alcohol robs your system of its nutrients. It'll kill you if you keep going the way you are. You'll turn into Daddy.'

'I can envisage worse fates,' I said, 'I could turn into you.'

She hung up on me. When I told Justin he said, 'Good on you. Keep those killjoys down.'

Maybe her words had some kind of an impact on me. The following week I re-joined the employment agency. They put me in temporary jobs here and there. Work got me out of bed early in the morning. I didn't ask for anything else from it. My concentration was poor. Moving from place to place suited me.

In between jobs I lounged around Piccadilly. I liked seeing life going on without having to be a part of it. It was like the way I felt when I went into Galway. I preferred being the watcher rather than the watched.

Justin joined me sometimes. One night we sat on a park bench with some down-and-outs drinking wine from plastic cups. As it got to midnight he said, 'I have something to tell you.'

'Go on.'

'I'm a junkie.'

I wasn't sure if he was joking or not. No more than with my father, you never knew with him. Then he showed me the needle marks on his arms.

'You're serious,' I said.

'You better believe it.'

'I never had you down for this.'

He told me how it happened. He'd been offered money to stash some cocaine in the Corncrake one night. The money he was offered was unreal.

'I didn't have to do anything with it. Just hold it. There was even a little extra for myself. A sort of "Thank you." That was what did the damage.

I wondered how many people had got in on drugs from dealers giving them "Thank Yous."

'Now I'm hooked,' he said, 'Scary, isn't it?'

If I had any sense I'd have parted company with him after that but I didn't. Maybe a part of me was attracted to danger.

He introduced me to his dealers. Their names were Aldo and Denis. They were two brothers I'd seen him with in the Corncrake now and then. They seemed to be just casual acquaintances of his as they sat at the bar drinking with him. I now realised they were his suppliers. He was up to his neck in debt to them.

Their names were Aldo and Denis. Aldo had a Greek background. His people had got rich in the olive industry. Denis grew up in Stoke Newington.

They were big into cars. Aldo had a Maserati and Denis a Skoda. Both of them had been involved in petty crime since their teens. They'd been in corrective institutions on and off for most of their youth. In adulthood they'd kept a clean slate as far as the law was concerned.

They lived in an apartment in Maida Vale. It had more locks than Fort Knox. When I went there first it was after dark. It looked like nothing outside but inside it was like a mansion. It was a penthouse apartment with a jacuzzi. There were mounted televisions in the rooms. A balcony gave a view of the city.

There was Irish blood somewhere along the line with Denis. It made him feel he could be familiar with me. 'We're family!' he said to me one night. I wasn't impressed. Maybe I gave him a smart answer. Justin dragged me into the kitchen. He whispered to me, 'Be very careful what you say.' He told me to humour them or I might wake up somewhere with a crowd around me.

We visited them every other weekend. They loved showing off. Denis spent most of his time shouting at the television. It was on a wall above the fireplace. Justin said he was a maniac but I felt he was just putting it on.

Aldo was quieter. It was obvious he was the brains of the outfit. When he spoke it seemed to be in coded language. He was always having these intense conversations with people on the phone. I presumed he was organising drug deliveries.

When we got to know them better we were invited to stay over. This was the ultimate honour. I tried to look appreciative.

Justin enjoyed the aura of danger Aldo exuded. Aldo liked him because he licked up to him. He didn't quite trust me. I was an unknown quantity in his eyes.

'Why are we getting the royal treatment from them?' I asked Justin one night. He put on a face.

'Because we're nice people,' he said.

'Don't be funny.'

'Okay. Every few months I hold a million quid's worth of gear for their top man until he comes and collects it. Now are you happy?'

'Are you serious.'

'There are no free lunches in life, kiddo.'

'Walk away, Justin. I mean it.'

He gestured the balcony, the jacuzzi.

'I'm earmarked for some of this down the road. Aldo told me.'

'You're earmarked for Wormwood Scrubs.'

'No shit, Sherlock.'

Sometimes we went gambling with them in the fashionable clubs. The kind of money they spent on these nights would have exceeded my annual earnings in the Corncrake.

One night I woke up in the middle of the night. I heard Aldo talking to a man with a foreign accent in the next room. He was either threatening him or being warned not to do something. There was a scuffle between them. After a few minutes I heard a door slamming. Someone was stumbling around the room.

I went over to Justin's bed.

'Wake up,' I said.

I shook him but it was no good. He was out cold on whatever substance Aldo had given him.

The next morning I told him what I'd heard. He didn't want to know.

'Don't be so observant the next time,' he said. 'In fact if somebody comes into the bedroom and sticks a Luger up your left nostril, just say, "Excuse me, can I help you?"'

The next time I saw Aldo he had a cut on his forehead. He didn't make anything of it and neither did I. His mood seemed good. He pottered around the apartment making breakfast. I noticed that he was limping.

'Are you all right?' I asked him.

'Never better!'

He put something up his nose.

195

'Like some blow?' he said. I shook my head.

'Why don't you get out of that kip in Finsbury and work for me?'

I told him I was content where I was but Justin pricked up his ears. He wanted to hear more details. Aldo started to throw around some figures. The higher they went, the more Justin got interested. I started to leave the room.

'Stay put,' he said, 'This could be our future.'

'Maybe yours,' I said, 'not mine.'

'Do you want to grow old serving slops?' he said.

Aldo laughed at that. He came over and started mussing my hair.

After a while it became clear to me that Aldo was the deal-maker and Denis the one who liked a good time. Aldo was also the more dangerous of the two. From his room sometimes I heard moaning sounds. If his girlfriend was with him I was never sure if he was making love to her or beating her up. Neither did I know if she was part of his operation or just light relief.

I didn't even know what the operation was. All I knew was that he was gone for a few days every month. The rest of his time he devoted to making phone calls. Whenever he got one he had to move fast. We wouldn't see him for a while. In his absence Denis started throwing his weight around with Justin and me, trying to look important. After a week or so Aldo would come back. He'd be all spruced up and maybe with a new girl. He was always friendly to me at these times. I didn't take it seriously. He was higher than high. He'd spoil me with attention. And, now and again, 'presents.' You didn't have to be Einstein to know where they came from.

Justin told me not to question anything.

'These are the good times,' he said.

It didn't look that way to me. I felt I was being bought. There had to be retribution somewhere along the line. We could just as easily be left to rot as wined and dined. Justin said that was a miserable way of looking at it.

'With you the glass is always half empty,' he said.

'Maybe, but empty or full it's a glass of poisoned water.'

'Fuck you and your high ground,' he said. He thought I needed a few hour's therapy with Aldo's girlfriend in a sauna to sort me out.

Maybe he repeated my comments back to them. They were different with me afterwards. I stopped being asked round. If I met them in company they were cold with me. One night in a disco toilet Aldo took me into one of the cubicles. He said he wanted to show me his latest 'toy.' I knew it was going to be a gun even before he took it out. He pressed it against my face.

'Do you like the feel of that?' he said.

Then he took he outside and bought me a drink. Justin was dancing at the time. It was with one of the many beautiful women they presented us with. After the dance he came over to the table we were at. He knew something was up.

'I've been getting to know your friend,' Aldo said.

The police raided the apartment the following week. They said they were acting on a tip. I don't think they found anything except some syringes but that was enough to make them want to bale out. They got nervous.

Everything happened fast after that. The women disappeared. A house they had in the suburbs went up for sale. I even saw Aldo trying to sell a yacht one day. Policemen patrolled the streets around us. Justin never said anything to me but I knew I was suspected of being a snitch. It was the last thing I would have done. Not from honour but fear. They had no evidence against me but I was still suspected. I was last in. what else would they think?

My weekends were quieter now that I didn't have them to go to anymore. Justin started avoiding me as well. He took up with some new friends. They seemed to be in the drug trade as well. People with sharp suits, wads of money to splash around, sexy women hanging out of them with legs up to their shoulders and more silicon than you could shake a stick at.

I worried about him. What new consignment was he holding for them? What new debt had he incurred?

He didn't introduce me to them. I'd dirtied my bib.

My life ground to a halt. There was nothing happening. I wondered where I'd go now. My father's money was running out. Greta kept nagging me about going back to him.

I sat in cinemas watching films over and over again. Then I went home and cooked instant dinners. I slept a lot of the time, even in the day. My nerves were shot. It was as if my brain was atrophying. London felt like a surreal world to me, a night-time hell of excess and boredom. The old guilt came back to me: guilt over my father, over Aisling, over the way I was sleepwalking through my days.

One morning as I was having my breakfast I heard a letter coming through the box. My father's writing was on the envelope but when I opened it I saw it was from Greta. She'd sent it to Galway. My father forwarded it to me. She must have forgotten my address. The envelope was sellotaped. He must have opened it and sealed it again. That made me smile. At least he hadn't lost his curiosity.

She started off by saying she'd left hospital work and was back in the convent again. Then came the reason for the letter. She said she'd been on the phone to my father a few times and it seemed to her that he was seriously depressed, even suicidal. At the end she said he'd die of loneliness if I didn't go back to him.

I rang him.

'What's up with Greta?' I said.

'She thinks I'm depressed. What could have given her that impression? Has she not noticed the sun shines out of me? That I wake up every day singing "Oh what a beautiful morning"?"

'She wants me to leave London so I can be with you all the time.'

'So I gather. What are your own feelings on the subject?'

'I hope to do that soon.'

'Don't let me rush you.'

A few weeks later another letter came. It was the same bullshit. I rang him again.

'What's going on?' I said.

'I'm no wiser than you are. Lynn is getting a bit fed up going to the post office. She'll be looking for extra wages yet.'

I rang Greta.

'What's with the letters?' I said.

'Did you not read them?'

'Sort of.'

'He needs you.'

'Why don't you go back to him yourself if you're that worried?'

'I'm 4000 miles away, in case you hadn't noticed.'

'I thought you were gone from the hospital.'

'What's that got to do with it?'

'You're not dealing with seriously ill people anymore, right?'

'I'm dealing with their souls.'

'Ah. So a bunch of contemplatives down on their knees are more important to you than a geriatric old man on the arsehole of Europe.'

'Don't talk like that. You demean yourself.'

'Thank you.'

'Do you know how many times I had to write that letter to get it right?'

'No, but I have a strange feeling you're going to tell me.'

'Eight. I threw away the first seven attempts.'

'It's a pity you didn't throw the eighth one away as well.'

'What was wrong with it?'

'Nothing, except for the fact that it was written at all.'

'What's that supposed to mean?'

'You're trying to ruin my life by remote control. Was it not enough that you ruined it when you were living with me?'

'I can see you haven't changed.'

'And I can see you haven't.'

'Would you not go back to him even for a visit?'

'Why?'

'He's not well. Any fool can see that.'

'This fool can't'

'He won't live forever.'

'Yes he will.'

Life has a strange way of punishing us for comments made on the spur of the moment. It was only a couple of weeks after our conversation that I got a phone call from him to say he had a shadow on his lung. His tone was light but I could see that he was worried.

Two years had passed since I left him. I was just starting to feel independent of him. Now this.

'What do you mean a shadow on the lung?' I said. As if there could be more than one kind.

'It's the cigarettes. I can't give the bloody things up.'

All my life I'd watched him lighting them off one another. He did it in the way another person might look at his watch or scratch his head. It was as natural to him as breathing. Even at Mass he sat near the door. He'd drop out during the sermon for a few puffs.

'It might be nothing.'

'That's not the message I'm getting from the doctors.'

'What would they know?' I was using his own kind of language now.

'It's probably the bug,' he said. He meant cancer.

'Most of these things are benign.'

'Sure I'm only held together by sticky tape anyway. The accident buggered me rightly. If I was a horse they'd have to shoot me.'

After I put the phone down I rang Greta. She said she'd been on to the doctors. The tumour was malignant.

'It's the cigarettes,' she said, echoing himself, 'I call them coffin nails.'

But he'd have been in his coffin long ago if it wasn't for the same coffin nails. They were even more of an addiction to him than the drink.

I flew home a few days later. As I sat into the plane I wondered if would be for good. I felt like a salmon swimming upriver to the stream where he was spawned. No matter how many times I broke away from him there was always something dragging me back.

9

It was raining when the train pulled into the station. In a way it comforted me. I associated it with most of the memories of my youth. I thought of the sheen it gave to the fields, the way it seemed to wash all the dirt off the roads.

I decided not to get a taxi. My case was light. I trudged through the rain without bothering to put up the hood on my anorak. When I got to the farm my clothes were sticking to me. It was coming down in sheets.

The house looked unrecognisable. Paint was flaking off the walls. The grass at the front of it must have been near enough my own height.

There were six bottles of milk outside the door. The tops of them had been pecked by birds. The milkman only came every second day. That meant my father must have been in hospital for at least two weeks. He probably hadn't phoned me until the results of his tests were in. That would have been his style.

I tried to turn the handle of the door but it was locked. In my hurry to pack I'd forgotten my key. He usually left a spare one under the mat but when I looked there was nothing there.

After a few seconds I heard Setanta barking. He pawed at the door. When I called his name he didn't seem to know my voice. It was only when I looked through the letterbox that he recognised me.

I tried to pick the lock with a piece of wire but it wouldn't give. Setanta barked louder. I was about to break a window when I got an idea. Maybe I could get in through the loft. There was a staircase leading from it into the kitchen.

I climbed the tree that stood beside the gable of the house. There was a piece of rope hanging from a branch near the crook. I swung myself from it to the loft. It was something I used to do as a child.

The window was broken. I was able to slide the latch across.

I jumped down onto the ledge. There were cobwebs everywhere. I drew the curtains open. It made everything a bit clearer.

The old wickerwork chair with the twisted legs was still there. So was the table where we played push penny.

I sat for a few minutes just looking around me. How many years was it since I'd been up here? It was our hideaway, our secret place. Adults weren't permitted. Greta and myself held high level political meetings up here, meetings that were sure to change the course of the world. She pounded the table with a gavel when I was talking too much. I pulled her hair when she was.

There was a Moses basket under the table. I started to look through it out of a vague curiosity. There were any number of football stickers there. Also my old school copy books. The red marks on them left me in little doubt that I was as poor a student as I'd remembered.

Under the copies there was a photograph album. I blew the dust off it. There were photos of myself and Greta. She stood in front of me with her chest out.

Even then she had to dominate. I wasn't allowed my half of the frame.

Other photos showed the farm as it used to be. There were people working in the fields, hay being saved, cows calving. I imagined my father looking at these scenes, cursing the life he lost after his accident.

I lowered myself into the kitchen. It was a smaller leap than I expected. That jump of some four feet was once an Everest to me.

I landed on the floor with a thud. Setanta ran over to me. He nearly took the legs off me in his excitement.

I went over to the window. The blinds were half-drawn. Shafts of light came through them. In the sink there were dishes piled half way up to the ceiling. They reminded me of my flat. It was something else I shared with my father. He only washed a cup when he was down to his last one.

Betty had left some food for Setanta. My father must have given her a spare key. I put it in a bowl for him.

There was a note from her on the table.

'Don't look too close at the mess,' she wrote, 'I didn't have time to clean up. And don't get a fright if you see a light coming on. Your father told me to put timers in a few of the rooms.'

I went into his study. The typewriter was on the table. There was a piece of paper stuck in it. 'Chapter 7,' it said, 'The Tide Turns.' It could have been a novel.

There were papers scattered all over the place, cuttings from turn-of-the-century newspapers, sepia-tinged photographs of my grandfather. They were stacked on the floor beside his desk. His familiarly illegible handwriting was on other scraps of paper, so many notes about vaguely historical occasions to adorn his masterpiece.

Stern men in frock coats stared out at me, men who were important once, so many pillars of the community when Adam was a boy. Looking at them made me feel as if time had stood still since I moved out. How many nights had he pored over such papers in search of inspiration? How many relics from the past had he resurrected? It had been an ambition for him once to recreate the past in his book. That ambition was gone now. I hadn't heard him talking about it for a long time. It was as dead to him as it had always been to me. In the last few years the getting through of a day was fulfilment enough for him.

His smell was in the room. It was the smell of drink and cigarettes and dark, midnight depressions. The walls were yellow from the smoke. Here and there pictures hung lopsided from them.

I went upstairs. His bedroom was as badly cared for as everywhere else. On his locker there were bottles of pills, a half-drunk bottle of whiskey. I felt I was invading his privacy by being there without him.

His jumper had been thrown onto a chair. There was a Walter Macken book on top of it. On the floor was the biscuit tin where he kept whatever few pounds he had left. There was a picture of my mother beside it in an old frame.

I started thinking about her, about how I'd beg her to let me have a day off school, the way her tired voice would say, 'I can't, it's for your own good,' as she packed my lunchbox. I thought about how she was with my father, her patience with him when he came home with drink, the way he'd tell her he loved her and would never drink again, how she'd nod her head sadly knowing he would. I'd be lying awake listening to these conversations, stopping myself sleeping because I knew that if I did, the next thing would be morning and I didn't want it to come soon.

I'd listen to her putting on the kettle for a cup of tea or a hot water bottle. He'd come up the stairs soon afterwards. He might be singing a song if the drink went down the right way. Sometimes he looked in on us to kiss us goodnight. I'd keep my eyes closed if he did that, pretending to be asleep. Greta would be lying in the bed opposite, a book or a teddy bear in her hands. She usually slept through it all. I remembered chasing her around the bedroom, forever at her about some childish thing, or she at me, neither of us imagining for a moment that anything could ever change, that we'd always be these people in this room.

Was youth something you grew out of, like clothes? I was the returned emigrant now rather than the Galway child. Which was the real me? Was there a real anyone? Maybe the only realities were phases, phases that became you when they were happening and then stopped being anything to do with you when they ended.

I went back down to his bedroom. The wheelchair was in the corner, a bone of Setanta's on the seat. He probably used it as a bed. There was no one to shoo him off it anymore. It would be his way of keeping in touch with his master. It was electric now. I remembered him mentioning it over the phone to me. He said it could do everything but cook the dinner. 'Do I need a license to drive it?' he asked.

I wondered what the past two years would have been like for him, living twenty-four hours a day in one room, seven days a week. Watching inane television programmes, getting high on his anachronisms, not answering the door on the odd occasion that someone might call.

He was keeping himself as well as he could. So I told Greta. The cliché saved me from any responsibility towards him. It kept me safe in my decadent life. Maybe we were all in our prisons, be they a ramshackle farmhouse or a tatty bedsit in London or even a Nebraska hospital spreading sweetness and light.

I'd always boasted about my freedom. He spent most of his life bemoaning its absence. Neither of us had it. Some of us imagined we had. I'd acted like I was on a mission by leaving him, a mission towards fulfilment. It was the hippie goal of finding yourself. But what had I found? Indulgence? Self-delusion? I'd strayed off the main highway of life and made the detour my new destination. I cossetted myself with illusions, surrounding myself with people who told me the emperor still had all his clothes.

My head was spinning. I decided to go down to the bay. It usually helped me clear it of tension.

It was a bright night. Stars speckled the sky. A wind came up. The palm trees shook as I threaded my way through them. There were swans on the bay. The water was shiny. It was as clear as a skating rink, the circle of the moon visible on its surface.

Aisling's old boat was tethered to a tree beside the water. It lapped back and forth like an old log. Beside it were discarded pieces of wood from the tree I cut down all those years ago. We lit fires with it as we exchanged stories about what we'd done with our lives and plans for what we were going to do with the rest of them. How many conversations were embellished by the anticipation of love in this place, or what passed for it to an impressionable adolescent.

Lights came on in the surrounding cottages. A triangle of roads scythed their way down the hill in front of me, so many tributaries looking for the sea. The cars travelling on them were like toys. Everything seemed unreal, a dream within a dream.

The sun crawled down the brow of a hill. The sky was golden now. It was like a circle of paint. In the distance I heard the sound of children's voices. From what I could tell it was the last stages of a football game. Their screams brought back the days when I played these more-important-than-life matches, when I resented my father for calling me away from them.

I looked up at the house. Its air of decay reminding me of him. They said husbands and wives began to resemble one another as they grew older. I imagined people and houses did too. It stood there insolently in the night air, defying you to cast aspersions on it.

I rang him to the hospital. Betty had bought him a mobile phone. I was able to speak to him directly without going through the nurses.

He was crabby. I thought that was a good sign. It was only when he sounded optimistic that I felt he was putting up a front. He said Betty was driving him to distraction with her visits.

'I'm speaking to you from her latest bright idea. You're lucky I was able to answer it.'

He always looked ridiculous with any kind of modern device. I imagined him struggling with it as he strained to hear my voice. He said he thought it was the remote from the television when she gave it to him. They were about the same size.

'I suppose Setanta lost his reason when he saw you,' he said.

'He didn't know who I was at first.'

'It's been a while since you were home.'

'Why didn't you leave a key for me?'

'I told Betty to put her one under the mat.'

'She must have forgot.'

'How did you get in?'

'Through the loft.'

'Good thinking, Robin. How does the place look?'

'It puts Buckingham Palace in the shade.'

'I can well believe it.'

'I told the butler he could take the rest of the day off.'

'How are things going with yourself?'

'They tell me nothing in here. It's like talking to the Secret Police.'

'They don't like committing themselves. There are so many legal actions these days.'

'Is that what it is? I thought they were just stupid.'

'Give them time.'

'That's something I don't have too much of.'

He gave out about the food, the early morning calls, anything he could think of. Eventually he ran out of things to complain about. That was usually a sign he wanted to go.

'I'll be in to see you in no time,' I said.

'Will you be driving?'

'Hopefully.'

'Don't trust the car.'

I gave Setanta the food Betty left for him. He didn't show much interest in it. It was as if he sensed there was something wrong. He sat beside the wheelchair like a sentry.

I went out to the car. It looked like it hadn't moved in an age. Nothing happened when I turned the ignition. I couldn't remember when I'd been in it last. Betty used to give it a run down the road to keep it tuned up. I wasn't sure if she was still doing that. I kept gunning the engine. Each time it sounded weaker.

I was walking down the road when a driver beeped his horn at me. It was Ger Dempsey, the local Nosey Parker. My father couldn't stand him. He lived a bit down the road.

'Was that you trying to start a car?'

'It was. I got nowhere.'

'I'll drop you into town if you like.'

'That'd be great.'

211

I sat into the car. I could see him taking in my appearance, the suit I was wearing.

'I heard your father isn't well. I hope it's nothing serious.'

'I'm going in to see him now.'

'It's not cancer, is it?'

'I'm afraid so.'

'I' sorry to hear that.'

'He's in the right place anyway.'

'Aye. And he's a great battler.'

'None better.'

'I notice he's still puffing away. We see him out on the verandah some nights with the dog.'

'That doesn't surprise me.'

'Isn't he right? We'll be dead long enough.'

The road was wet. We drove in silence. His eyes darted forward and back curiously.

'What about yourself? I believe you're across the pond now. Are we not good enough for you anymore?'

'I thought I'd give it a go for a while.'

'You're not the type of fella that'd be bothered with a steady job I'd say.'

'We all wind up that way sooner or later, don't we?'

'Maybe, maybe.'

I could see him trying to think of more questions.

'Are jobs hard to come by over there?'

'I'm taking anything I can get at the moment. It's not like it used to be.'

'So I believe. It's the same everywhere. My own lad has more degrees then you could shake a stick at and he's working in some kind of pea factory in Pittsburgh. What would you think of that?'

'It's better than sitting at the side of the road scratching your arse.'

'Too true! Greta is over there too, isn't she?'

'She is indeed. She wouldn't be too far from your son.'

'Where is she?'

'Nebraska.'

'Begod. They have so many places over there.'

'It's a big country.'

'She's a lovely girl. I always knew she'd get the call.'

We reached the town. I told him he could let me out.

'I'll drive you to the hospital if you want. It's no trouble.'

'No thanks. The walk will do me good.'

He was capable of inviting himself into the ward.

'Are you sure?'

'I am. Thanks for the lift.'

'It was my pleasure. I felt sorry for you when I saw you trying to start the car.'

'I'll have to get rid of it one of these days. It's outlived its usefulness.'

I got out. He revved up his engine.

'Tell your father I was asking for him.'

'I will. Thanks again.'

He gave me a thumbs up. I walked up the road towards the hospital. He didn't move for a while. I was almost at the gate when I heard him driving off.

I went inside. There was a heavy-set woman behind the counter. I gave her my father's name.

'You're his son, aren't you?' she said.

She started prattling about him. As she spoke I remembered why I'd gone away from the town in the first place. It would always be like this everywhere I went, the endless rambling about nothing.

'He's in St. Malachy's. It's on the first floor. They're taking good care of him.'

I took the lift up. When I got to the ward I saw him at the end of it. There were tubes coming out of him.

I got to the bed.

'They have you well connected,' I said.

He looked up.

'Jesus. Yourself.'

I reached down to hug him. He'd lost a lot of weight. His cheeks were sunken into his face. He held onto the hug for longer than usual.

'How are you?' I said

'Bloody awful if you must know. They do nothing in here but jab me with needles. What about yourself?'

'Not too bad.'

I sat on the edge of the bed.

'Did you give the dog something to eat?'

'Betty left something for him.'

'Sorry about the key.'

'It was no problem.'

He asked me about London. I told him I'd left the Corncrake. He was surprised to hear that.

'How are you filling in the time?'

214

'Spending your money mostly.'

'You won't get far on that. I believe the cost of living is fierce over there.'

'I don't go out much.'

'If that's the case you should come home.'

'I know.'

'Have you been back to the pub?'

'A few times.'

'What about that bastard who punched you up?'

'He's gone off somewhere.'

'I'd sort him out if I got my hands on him. Are you drinking much?'

'There isn't much else to do.'

'I never trusted a man who didn't like his drink. Nine out of ten of them have something worse wrong with them.'

A nurse came over. She put something into his ear.

'What are you doing to me?' he said.

'Taking your temperature.'

'Do you not use thermometers anymore?'

She laughed.

'Thermometers? They went out with the Indians.'

She went off.

'Is there anything that stays the same in this bloody world?' he said.

I asked him if he had any results from his tests but he didn't answer me. Instead he started to talk about how bad the food was in the hospital, how boring the days.

'It's like being in prison here.'

The way he spoke it was as if he was leading a super-active life outside. The reality was that he'd probably had more activity in the last fortnight than in the year preceding it.

'How did you get in here?' he said.

'Ger Dempsey. He saw me trying to start the car.'

'That fellow would see the grass grow. I suppose he wanted to know about me.'

'I didn't tell him much.'

'Good on you. He'd have it all over the place before it was out of your mouth.'

'So I suspected.'

'Does he know what I was in for?'

'Unfortunately.'

'He's probably organising Mass cards as we speak.'

'I remember him growing up. Isn't he almost a permanent fixture in the church?'

'It's like a home from home to him. Did he ask about Greta?'

'Just in passing.'

'Has she been on to you?'

'Once or twice.'

'She has me plagued with calls. The doctors tell me she's quizzing them too. She's getting worse than Betty.'

'She'll be here tomorrow.'

'I get nervous when people come to see me from far away places. Does it mean I'm on the way out?'

'You'll be around to torture us all for a while yet.'

He started to cough. I handed him a handkerchief. He spat something into it.

'Can I keep this?'

'I certainly hope so.'

He produced a packet of cigarettes from under his pillow.

'They haven't spotted these yet,' he said, a twinkle in his eye.

'You're hardly intending to smoke them, are you?'

'What harm can the blackguards do me now? It's a bit late for going off them at this stage.'

As I looked at him surrounded by all his medication I saw him as an invalid for the first time. I'd never regarded him that way before no matter how many years he spent in the wheelchair.

He lay back on the pillow.

'Don't let me keep you if you have something else to do,' he said.

'This is where I want to be.'

'The matron is looking at us. I think visiting time is over.'

'Are you trying to get rid of me?'

'Don't be ridiculous.'

'I'll be back later.'

'Leave it till tomorrow. I'm a bit tired.'

'Are you sure?'

'Bring Greta in with you. Didn't you say she'd be here then?'

'Hopefully. You'd never know with the flights.'

'Play it by ear. I'm not going anywhere anyway.'

She got in the next day. I met her at the train station. She'd put on weight since I saw her in London.

'Don't say anything,' she said, 'I see you looking at me.'

'I wasn't going to.'

'I've been eating like a horse. It's from worry.'

She waddled her way towards me.

'What's happening with Daddy?'

'I haven't much news for you.'

She looked well apart from the weight. It seemed to take her over, throwing her features out of proportion. I offered to carry her case but she wouldn't let me.

We sat into the car. She was breathing heavily.

'How was the flight?' I asked her.

'A nightmare. There was turbulence all the way. I presume you've been in to see him.'

'Just once.'

'How is he?'

'He's lost weight.'

A tear came into her eye.

'I'm not sure if I want to see him.'

'He's in good spirits.'

'I can't bear the thought of him lying there with all those strangers around him. I hope he won't be like he was after the accident.'

'I don't think there's any danger of that.'

She was quiet back at the farm. I asked her about her work but she didn't want to talk about it. All she could think about was his health. She said she'd been on to the doctors a few times, that they weren't sure what they'd find when they opened him up.

'They said the X-rays were ambiguous.'

'How can an X-ray be ambiguous?'

'Don't ask me. I'm just telling you what they said.'

She went up to her room. I heard her bustling around. She spent a long time unpacking. When she came down she was cranky.

'There are no hangers in the wardrobe,' she said, 'I had to leave all my clothes on the bed.'

I brought her to the hospital later. She kept picking her lip on the way. She always did that when she was thinking. I imagined her rehearsing questions to ask the doctors.

She made me stop at a petrol station to buy him a bunch of flowers.

'Are you sure that's a good idea?' I said.

'Why not?'

'You know how he thinks about flowers.' He had a saying, 'Pansies are for pansies.'

'I can't go in with one arm as long as the other.'

It took us a long time to find parking at the hospital. I could see her getting frustrated. When I finally found a spot she grabbed the flowers and started walking towards the entrance.

'Hold on,' I said, 'I have to get some coins for the meter.'

'Forget the blessed meter,' she said.

I caught up on her. We came to a revolving door. The flowers got stuck in it as she tried to make her way through. I thought I heard her swearing.

We climbed the stairs. She had to stop twice to catch her breath. Eventually we got to the ward.

She broke down crying when she saw him.

'How are things in the land of opportunity?' he said.

I gave her a tissue.

'How are you feeling, Daddy?' she said.

'Rumours of my death have been exaggerated.'

He was on a drip.

'Look at this crack,' he said, lifting his arm up.

'They're putting all the good stuff into you,' she said.

'I don't want the good stuff. I want the bad stuff.'

'I know. That's why you're in here in the first place.'

He looked at the flowers.

'You can put those where the monkey put the nuts,' he said.

'I thought they'd brighten up the room.'

'A ball of malt would brighten it up better.'

He indicated the matron.

'Maybe you could organise one when Nurse Ratched isn't looking,' he said to me. She was sitting behind a desk filling in a form.

'I'll see what I can do.'

A doctor came in. He stood by one of the other beds looking at a chart. Greta ran over to him. I heard her muttering. He looked frustrated.

She came back.

'Wrong doctor,' she said.

'It was the wrong doctor.'

'Thank God,' my father said, ''I'm not in the mood for hearing bad news.'

She quizzed him about himself. He kept fobbing off her questions as he'd done to me. Looking at her

220

serious face and his frivolous one it was as if she was the patient and he the visitor.

'What's the bottom line?' she kept saying, 'What's the bottom line?'

I wanted to tell her there was none, that his condition could never be as black and white as her religion. Or anything else in her life.

His eyelids started to droop. The matron came over.

'I think he needs to sleep,' she said.

'But we've only got here.'

She was almost at panic point.

'The team will be here soon. We'll have more news then. Why don't you come back later?'

We stood up. She put her arms around him again.

'sorry, Daddy, we wanted to stay longer.'

'Don't worry about it pet. Get yourself some rest. You're probably jet-lagged.'

'I hate leaving you.'

'Send me a postcard from the farm.'

'Don't be funny, Daddy. I'm too upset.'

'Take care of that girl,' he said to me.

'I will.'

'You'll be fine, Daddy,' she said, 'Don't worry about anything.'

'You look a bit pale,' he said to her. 'Maybe you should report in for a few tests.'

'Let's go,' she said to me.

She was irritable as we walked down the corridor.

'He's making fun of the whole thing,' she said, 'It's all wrong. I think he knows something we don't.'

On the way home in the car she was quiet. When we were stopped at a red light she said, 'Would you be prepared for the worst if it happened?'

He hadn't even been opened up yet and she was counting him out.

'What are you talking about?'

'Could you take it if Daddy died?'

I pulled the car over to the kerb.

'My father died the day I left Ireland,' I said.

'That's a bit dramatic.'

'You're one to talk about drama after what you just said.'

For the next few nights we were thrown together in a house both of us hardly recognised, united only by our uncertainty. Betty kept ringing for updates. I let Greta deal with her. She went down to the church every few hours, trying to batter down the gates of heaven with her entreaties. I sat outside waiting for her in the car.

'I don't suppose you'd come with me,' she asked me once.

'I doubt my prayers would hit the target,' I said, 'considering the condition of my soul.'

'The prayers of a sinner sometimes travel the fastest.'

We went in to him every day. He continued to act jovial. We didn't know if it was an act or not. Greta collared the doctors any time she could to try and get information out of them. They'd done some CAT scans but they weren't conclusive. Everything would be clearer after the operation.

We staggered our visits to him, relieving one another like sentries. Betty stepped in now and again. Ger Dempsey called once as well, bringing a box of sweets with him and a drunken brother. I liked his brother better. When we were on our own in the house we talked of simple things like who'd get the dinner or take Setanta for a walk.

I asked him how he felt about the doctors.

'I don't think they have the foggiest what they're at,' he said. 'They sound fancy when they use the Latin words but I'm too long in the tooth to fall for that. They've done all the tests under the sun on me but they're still saying nothing. They should be in politics.'

'Don't be too hard on them. It might take them a while to sort you out.'

'That's what they're paid for.'

'I'm sure they're trying their best.'

'One genius has me on pills to speed up my heartbeat. Another one is trying to slow it down. They'll meet themselves coming back yet. I asked the second fellow why he was so concerned about my ticker when it's the lung the shadow is on. He said, "That's my department." I ask you. You'd think you were in Clery's.'

The days dragged for him. There was nothing to do. A tiny television screen propped up on a height at the end of the ward showed sport all the time.

'The screen is too small for you to see,' I said.

'Be thankful for small mercies.'

During one visit I noticed he had a scapular in his hand. It surprised me. I asked Greta if she'd given it to him.

'He was glad to get it,' she said, 'He's changed.'

I asked her what she meant. She said he'd started asking her about his soul, about what was ahead of him. I was stunned. Was this my father we were talking about?

Maybe there were no atheists in the trenches. Religion used to be his soapbox. Now it was a raft he clung on to so he could get to the shore.

'I'm frightened,' he said to me one day out of the blue. I didn't know how to react. It was a comment that didn't seem to belong to him. It didn't come from anywhere in his past. Maybe he wasn't even saying it to me. Maybe he was saying it out loud to himself.

How do you react when somebody who's spent his life hiding behind their pride confronts you with such a statement? Do you tell them that they have every reason to be? Or that the Lord will temper the wind for the shorn lamb?

'I know,' I said, 'I'm frightened for you too.'

In the days afterwards he was a different person. I watched him lying there, coughing his guts out in a congested ward because he hadn't enough money to go private. He'd lived his life in isolation. Was he going to end it in the glare of the public?

My visits grew repetitive. He usually told me to go before the time was up. After we chatted about the farm there was little more to be said. It was strange, I thought, how he could spend hours talking to me about a negligible horse race when I was young. Now that things were down to life and death, all we had was the silence of a 45-minute visit.

Greta started to go into him more than me. They prayed together. I mostly stayed at the farm now. After tea most evenings I walked through the fields like the gentleman farmer he once wanted to be himself. There was something pristine in the landscape, I thought, something you had to leave behind to appreciate fully. As I looked at the fields I remembered how he was in his heyday, giving orders to Greta and myself as he supervised the saving of the hay, relishing the authority he exuded. How often had I cursed these self-same fields when I had to leave a game of football to work in them? How often had I seen them as an albatross around my neck?

I doubted I'd ever have to farm them again. They weren't much more than scutch now. The sheep had even deserted them to graze on the neighbouring pastures.

I sat with Greta on the verandah one evening watching the sun go down. Each of us was lost in our thoughts. Setanta was sleeping beside us. I sucked in the smell of cut grass. The sun was like a ball in the sky. Clouds gathered around it like pieces of fluff. I wanted to sit forever in this unreal peace where no danger lurked, where there was nothing to threaten the silence. It surrounded us like an angel, enwreathing us in the bubble our childhood had been. I found myself wanting to be ten years old again, to be frozen in that time warp.

The wind whipped around us. It fluttered the clothes on the line. A farmer in a nearby field was leaning on a pitchfork. He took a cigarette from behind his ear. I watched him getting into his tractor. It wobbled across the ruts of the field. He could have been my father.

'Can you imagine anyone else owning this place?' Greta said to me.

The thought nagged at me. I tossed and turned in my bed that night with threatening visions of him never setting foot on his turf again, her words approximating to the authority of fact.

10

I woke with a lump in my stomach on the day of his operation. Breakfast was a glass of whiskey. Greta threaded rosary beads through her fingers as I drank it. For once she didn't give out to me.

Morning crept across the sky. We waited for a phone call from the hospital but it didn't come.

'We're going to have to go down there,' she said to me, 'I'll go out of my mind sitting here.'

As we drove to it I felt my heart beating fast. When fear was a distance away you could inure yourself to it. You could even pretend it wasn't there. Now that we were reaching the point of no return my natural pessimism made me envisage the worst.

She must have sensed as much because she put her arm around me after I parked.

'He'll come through this,' she said, 'God is good.'

But how could He be good to have given him the cancer in the first place? If we got good news she'd tell me it was His intercession but if things went wrong she'd say the same God worked in mysterious ways. It was the fail-safe mechanism buried in all her theology.

As we walked from the car park I avoided the cracks in the pavement out of some vague superstition. I remembered a day in my childhood when I was having my appendix out. The same hollow was in the pit of my stomach then. My father had come to visit me. Now the situation was reversed.

We sat in a waiting-room outside the operating theatre. A nurse offered us tea. She spoke gently to us. I always got worried when people spoke gently to me in a hospital. It was as if they were doing it for a reason.

The clock on the wall said 9.47. His operation had been scheduled for 9. It ticked noisily or maybe I was just hearing it that way. There was a notice on the wall advertising a basketball tournament for trainee nurses. I found myself looking at it.

We didn't talk. Greta prayed. I bit my nails until they bled. At a few minutes past 10 I saw the surgeon coming out of the theatre. He had a mask in his hand.

His face said it all even before he started to speak.

'It's bad,' he said, 'very bad.'

Blood drained from Greta's face. She held my hand.

'So it was bigger than the X-ray showed,' I said.

'I've never seen anything like it.'

He tapped the table.

'It was as hard as that. I couldn't go near it.'

I wasn't surprised. There was almost relief in the freedom from hope. I became strangely relaxed.

'So there was no operation,' I said.

He shook his head.

'There would have been no point. He'd have died on the table.'

How many people had he given such news to after his expert hands could do nothing, how many had he watched crumble in front of him?

The clock ticked even louder. But time was irrelevant now.

'Is he awake?' Greta said.

'Not yet.'

'How long has he got?' I asked. It was like a line from a film.

'I can't say. A few months, maybe a year. I've counted people out in the past and they're still walking around.'

I watched his face lighten. The worst was over for him.

'He could outlast the lot of us,' he said, the gentle cushioner that followed the doomsday scenario.

He put the mask into his gown. It had a small blood mark on it, the only evidence of where he'd been.

Greta lay back in her seat. She was beaten. Her rosary beads fell to the floor.

'I know how you must feel,' he said, putting his hand on her, 'I had great hopes for the operation. I've failed you both.'

'You did everything you could,' she said, 'I know your reputation.'

He was very well thought of in medical circles, a miracle worker according to some. He'd pulled people back from the brink.

'None of us can live forever,' he said, 'He hasn't done too badly. 74 is a good age to reach. I'd be happy to get to it myself.'

I didn't want to hear that. How had anyone the right to say your time was up at any age, be it 74 or 104?

'Thank you for all you did,' I said.

He shook my hand.

229

'We've grown very fond of him. You're not the only ones that are upset.'

It seemed to be true. I saw a nurse coming out of the theatre in tears. She was the one who'd taken his temperature with the probe that day.

I picked up Greta's beads. She put them into her pocket.

'We'll go,' she said.

'Take care of yourselves,' the surgeon said. He went back towards the operating theatre.

We walked down the corridor. I felt the eyes of the nurses on me. One of them pretended to be looking at a clipboard. I saw tears in her eyes too.

Greta leant on me. She was having trouble walking. Her breath came in heaves.

We reached the car park. I didn't have to worry about avoiding the cracks on the pavement now. I didn't have to worry about phone calls or letters or tests or anything where there was a chance something could be salvaged. Life had attained a simplicity. The simplicity of being or not being.

She gripped my hand.

'I feel weak,' she said, 'I need a brandy.'

It was the first time I'd ever heard her asking for a drink in my life.

There was a bar across the road. It was one my father frequented. A place I used to collect him from when he was at his worst. Fishermen went there.

Everyone looked at us as we went in. It was a man's bar. There was a picture of a pike over the counter. An old man was drinking a pint of Guinness in the comer.

I sat down. The barman came over to us.

'I heard about your father,' he said, 'How is he?'

'Two brandies please,' I said.

I didn't want to talk. He went away. I saw him going out a door.

'Where is he going?' she said.

'How do I know?'

A few minutes passed without him re-appearing. People were looking at us. She started to wheeze.

'My asthma is acting up,' she said, 'I forgot the inhaler.'

I remembered her having it as a child.

'It isn't usually as bad as this.'

'Doesn't stress make it worse?'

'Probably. I'll have a seizure if he doesn't come soon with the drink.'

'I'll go and look for him.'

'Give him another minute.'

He appeared just as I was about to get up.

'Two brandies, sir,' he said, propping them down in front of us.

I paid him. She took a swig of hers.

'Oh my God,' she said, 'The relief.'

'We might get you in on it yet.'

'Please. One is enough in the family.'

I watched the colour come back into her cheeks.

'You can have mine if you want,' I said, 'I'm not thirsty.'

'No. Two would make me sick.'

'Are you feeling any better?'

'A bit.'

It was the first time I'd ever sat with her in a bar. I felt strange.

'How is the asthma?'

'A bit better now, thanks.'

I thought of my father waking up from an operation he never had. Would we tell him? Would he guess? I imagined her thinking the same things. There was no point in talking about it. What would be would be.

She finished her drink. I knocked mine back.

'Will we go?' she said.

We went out to the street. The air was sharp. A bell tolled somewhere. I felt cold. We sat into the car.

'I had a bad feeling about him from the start,' she said.

'I know. You told me.'

'I shouldn't have. What good was it worrying you any more than you were?'

'I was only clutching at straws.'

'It was important for you to do that. To deaden the shock.'

'Maybe it was more important for you to prepare me for what happened.'

'You're good to see it like that.'

We got to the house.

'What now?' I said.

'I don't know.'

'Would you like a drink?'

'Not now. How are you feeling?'

'Numb.'

I phoned Betty.

'I was fearing the worst and hoping for the best,' she said, 'I've been praying for him all day. And for you two as well.'

Greta rang her convent. She said she didn't know when she'd be going back. I sensed some kind of disapproval on the other end of the line. Her voice sounded strained.

'They said they need me back within the month,' she said.

'Why? What can be so urgent over there?'

'It's Sister Immaculata. She has some strange ways about her.'

'Tell her what to do with herself.'

'Sometimes you can be very naïve.'

She gave a sigh.

'I'm falling asleep,' she said, 'I'm going to bed.'

. I'm going to go up.'

I told her I'd join her soon but I didn't. My mind was too alert. I stayed downstairs thinking of him.

Setanta cowered under the table. He seemed to know. The phone rang a few times. I didn't answer it. Upstairs I heard her snoring. Setanta whimpered. He sounded as if a bone was caught in his throat. I slept in my clothes on the sofa.

We went in to him again the next day. His eyes told me he knew I knew. Greta was too distraught to speak. I decided to go straight into it.

'The doctor told me you'll be coming home,' I said.

'So I believe.' There was no life in his voice now, not even the old sarcasm.

'They didn't operate,' he said.

'It was the right decision.'

'They can do nothing for me.'

'At your age the metabolism is slow. It won't spread quickly.'

'It's a stay of execution. I'm fucked.'

'He said you could outlive the lot of us.'

'Have you any more jokes?'

He was a different man in the next few days, barely rousing himself to speak to us anytime we went in to see him. I watched his frame becoming thinner. His wedding-ring slipped off his finger.

He stopped eating. I wasn't sure if it was because he didn't want to or because he couldn't. The doctors said his body was like a traffic jam. Nothing was going anywhere.

Nurses brought meals into him that he ignored. When we asked them about him they just shook their heads. His strength ebbed. We sat by his bed doing little but watching him sleep. When he woke he was often confused. In sleep he groaned quietly in his dreams, murmuring words that had no meaning. He was lapsing into oblivion.

We were sitting in the kitchen the night they rang to say he was sinking. There was little reason to hope for anything else now.

I took the call.

'It's the hospital,' I said to Greta.

'I'm ready.'

We went out to the car. She usually spent some time making herself up before she went anywhere. Not this time. Her hair was tousled. She'd buttoned her blouse the wrong way. A bit of it hung down over her skirt.

We didn't talk on the way in. Ten minutes later we sat by his bedside. There was a mask over his face. I wanted to tell him to fight it, to rage against the dying of the light, but I knew it was too late for that.

I whispered in his ear that I loved him but he didn't react. When I tried to hold his hand there was no grasp in it.

We sat with him all night, taking turns to watch for any change. There was a drinks machine in the corridor. Every so often one or other of us went out to it. I drank so much coffee my heart started to palpitate. The hours passed. Nurses came and went. A machine pipped beside his bed.

I didn't want to be there at the end. Greta was saying the rosary beside him. I went out to an ante-room. A nurse gave me a cup of tea. I tried to sip at it. Greta's voice came through the partition like the chant of some medieval ritual. A few minutes later I heard a machine being switched off. It was over.

I didn't feel anything. I'd stopped hoping since the operation. The moving finger wrote. That was all there was to be said. 'We kill time until time kills us,' he used to say. Now it had done that.

She was shaking when she came out.

'There was no pain,' she said, 'Thank God for that.'

We sat watching dawn nudge along the horizon. I wanted to cry but I couldn't.

'Now he's with Mammy,' she said.

She sat down beside me.

'Do you want to go in and see him?' she said.

'No. I want to go home.'

'We can't. We have to talk to the doctors about what's to be done.'

'Not tonight.'

We stood up. The room was as quiet as a crypt. I looked into the room where he died. A dull light shone down onto his bed. Everything else was switched off.

We walked down the corridor. She was limping.

'Take my hand,' she said.

I linked her.

'He'll have no Purgatory,' she said going home in the car, 'He did it all in this life.'

'Maybe that's the only Purgatory there is,' I said. Was it the only Hell as well?

We got to the farm. Setanta was waiting at the door. He crooned beside me.

'Your master is gone,' I said to him. He looked up at me with his big eyes. His paw scratched the floor.

'My heart is going a hundred miles an hour,' Greta said to me.

'Take a tranquilliser. I'm going to.'

'Should we ring Betty?'

I'm going to bed.'

I tossed and turned for most of the night. I could hear her doing the same next door. It was nearly dawn when I fell asleep.

I dreamt of him. He was a young man in the dream. We were at a beach. He was throwing a stick for Setanta to chase. My mother was walking beside him. They were in the dawn of their lives, the wind blowing in their faces as the waves of the sea rolled into the coast.

I woke early the following morning. For a few seconds I forgot what had happened. Then I remembered. I went into Greta's room but she was still asleep. Her clothes were on the floor.

I rang Betty.

'Please don't give me bad news,' she said.

'He's gone, Betty,' I said, 'I'm sorry to be the one that had to tell you.'

I could hear her crying on the other end of the line. She wasn't able to speak for a few minutes.

'God rest him,' she said.

She asked me how it happened. I told her as much as I could think of.

'It looked bad from the beginning,' she said, 'We were all trying to hold it together.'

'He's better off.'

'How is Greta?'

'She's not awake yet. She wanted to ring you last night.'

'I had a sense something was wrong. It was like clairvoyance.'

She said she'd been in to see him a few times in recent days. They'd made their peace with one another.

'It's a small consolation,' she said.

Greta spent most of the next day liaising with the hospital and the funeral parlour. She knew I couldn't do things like that. I was grateful to her for taking the weight off me.

She came home from the hospital with his clothes in a bag.

'They're all we have of him now,' she said, 'What will we do with them?'

The funeral was the following day. Fr McGinty said the Mass. The church was thronged.

He gave a eulogy.

'Today we've lost a man who's been a legend in this area for many years,' he said. 'He experienced a terrible shock many years ago when his wife died. The blow to his health was almost as bad. He could be a difficult man to deal with at times but I never one who was straighter. He didn't suffer fools gladly but if he gave you his word on anything it was as solid as a rock. I loved him like a brother.'

He wanted me to say a few words but I wouldn't have known where to start. How could you put a person's life into ten minutes? Or even ten years?

Greta gave one instead. I thought she was going to break down a few times but she didn't. She spoke of his kindness, his wit, his love of the past. At the end she said, 'Anyone who knew him saw him as being larger than life. They also knew about the tragedy that robbed us of our mother. He didn't deal with it well at first. That made him even more heroic to me in his later years.' There was applause from the congregation as she stepped down.

Betty spoke then. Her speech was shorter.

'We fought like cats and dogs all our life.' she said. 'There were times I could have strangled the oul' divil but I loved him to bits.'

Everyone erupted into laughter at that. It was always the way at funerals. The slightest levity got a much stronger reaction than it would have outside the church. Maybe it the release of tension.

There were crowds outside the church as the coffin came out. They milled around me shaking my hand and offering their condolences. How did so many people know he died? I remembered similar crowds from other funerals. People from everywhere around turned up to pay their respects. News went from one to the other of them in a heartbeat. It was almost as if it was carried on the wind. I wasn't sure how well many of them knew him. Most of his real friends had died years ago.

'If anyone comes to my funeral,' he said to me once, 'it won't be for the love of me as much as to make sure I'm safely down.' He toyed with the idea of composing a fake obituary once, of putting a dummy corpse in a coffin to see how many people would turn up at the obsequies.

I wondered where he was now. He used to speak of sneaking into heaven by the back door when St. Peter wasn't looking. I preferred the image of him whooping it up downstairs with all of the renegades from his past.

He had a joke about a man who died and found himself facing St. Peter at the Pearly Gates. 'What good things did you do on earth to deserve getting in here?' he asked him. The man racked his brains but he couldn't come up with anything. Then he snapped his fingers. 'I remember something,' he said, 'I gave £5 to a tinker in 1958.' St. Peter thought for a minute. Then he said to one of his angels, 'Give this man his fiver and send him down to hell.'

The coffin was put in the hearse. I drove to the graveyard with Greta and Betty. Greta cried when we passed the farmhouse. Setanta was sitting at the front gate with his ears up.

'Look at him,' Betty said, 'He wants to be with us.'

Rain started to fall. People got out of their cars. They walked behind us to the graveside.

Two men in overalls nodded at me. They had cigarettes in their mouths. I presumed they were the gravediggers. A hole had been dug.

They lifted the coffin from the hearse. I helped them carry it to the grave. They lowered it into the ground on ropes. I threw the first sods of clay over it.

Fr. McGinty said a prayer. We blessed ourselves. The grave continued to be filled. I held Greta with one hand and Betty with the other.

Suddenly everything went quiet. All you could hear was the rain. People started to shuffle away.

My mother's brother came over to me. I'd seen him in the church. He hadn't approached me there. I'd only seen him a handful of times over the years. I remembered the time in Curracloe when we stayed in his house after my mother left my father.

'He was a great man,' he said to me.

I knew he didn't believe that.

'Not great enough for you to visit him when he needed you,' I said. It was cruel of me. My father often told me he'd have given him his marching papers if he ever darkened his door. Maybe I needed someone to lash out at.

Back in the car Betty asked me what I'd said to him.

'I told him to fuck off,' I said.

'Don't use language like that,' Greta said, 'on a day like this.'

'The worst is over now,' Betty said. She clenched my hand.

People came back to the house. Greta and Betty made sandwiches. Bottles of Guinness were produced.

Sean Glynn was there. Nicola wasn't with him.

Ger Dempsey put his hand on my shoulder.

'I didn't see much of him in the last year,' he said, 'but he knew I was there if he needed me.'

A group of old men drank Guinness in the corner of the kitchen. Their wives had tea. There were one or two young people. They were respectful in their silence.

'He was larger than life,' a man with a lived-in face said to me, 'a presence even when he wasn't there.' I felt embarrassed not knowing who he was. How many others were there like him around us, people who watched me going about my life without me being aware of them?

I normally wouldn't have wanted to see anyone but these people were a comfort to me now. They saved me from my thoughts.

I told Greta I felt bad for spending so much time in London.

'You had to do what you did,' she said to me.

She had to do what she did too. It was life. We ranted and raged when things were happening. When they were over we stopped. By then it was usually too late. But in another way it wasn't. We understood why things happened. They happened because we were flawed. We had to forgive ourselves because of that. Greta called it Original Sin. I had no name for it.

I watched her shaking the hands of people I knew better than she did. They were people who'd come to the house to see him over the years, people I met along the road, in the town, acquaintances from his past that he'd either disowned or forgotten about, drinking friends from the good old days, farmers he shared fields or cattle with. Friends, enemies, neutrals.

She spent a long time talking to Fr McGinty. When she left the room he came over to me. I told him I felt bad about not being home more.

'You never lost touch with him,' he said, 'That was what was important. He lived for your phone calls. You were here even when you weren't here.'

I thanked him for saying that. He knew how to cushion the blow of a tragedy. Maybe he'd spent his life doing it.

I put a bone before Setanta but he wasn't interested in it. He was lost like the rest of us, sitting in the silence like a shadow of himself, waiting for time to pass. I watching him gnawing at an old shoe of my father's.

Everyone seemed to forget the reason they were there as the day went on. Tongues became loosened with the drink. I heard one or two people laughing. They told stories about him – his gruffness, the way he took people on, his refusal to bow to authority.

After a while the talk dwindled. Everything had been said. People started to move out, their duty done.

Sean Glynn came over to me. He gave me a hug.

'I know what you're going through,' he said, 'My father died two years ago. It was his heart. He was luckier than yours was. He went suddenly.'

As I looked at him I forgot all the things I'd disliked about him over the years. He was just a person now like the rest of us. Was this what death was about - removing all the trappings of our lives and making us the same as one another? Now that he was free of the need to impress me with where he'd gone in life a burden was removed from him.

'It's the worst thing in the world to lose someone you love,' he said.

'People keep telling me he's gone to a better place. That doesn't sound too good for the rest of us still stuck here.'

'We have to make the best of it. What choice do we have?'

Ger Dempsey was the last to leave. He wanted to help with tidying up but Greta wouldn't let him. Betty bustled in and out of the kitchen. She emptied trays of food, putting uneaten sandwiches into tin foil. Empty bottles were stashed in a binliner beside the Rayburn.

Before we knew it everyone was gone. There were just the three of us left. Greta heaved a sigh of relief.

'No matter how nice people are,' she said, 'it's a relief to be left to yourself.'

It was strange not having my father to worry about. A sense of emptiness replaced the fear. We tried to fill it by talking about the people who'd just left. Betty liked some of the ones I didn't. The same was true of Greta.

Memories from the past came back to us, things they'd said to us in years gone by and things they'd done. Our conversation became frivolous as the night went on. We almost forgot what happened.

'We're making small talk to take our mind off it,' Betty said. Maybe it happened at all funerals.

'We gave him a good send-off,' she said.

I looked at the drinks cabinet. There was only one bottle of Guinness on it.

Greta raised it up in the air.

'To Daddy,' she said, 'I hope you're happy, wherever you are.'

'Amen to that,' Betty said, 'He'd have been delighted to see so many people ringing his praises.'

'He told me never to speak ill of the dead,' I said, 'That's why we have to cut hell out of them while they're alive.'

They laughed.

'That would be Daddy all right,' Greta said, 'He had a wicked tongue on him sometimes.' her hand.

We continued to toast him. Betty stayed until after midnight. I felt a great warmth towards her, a warmth my father never allowed me to express. I was able to do it now.

She talked to me about the sadness of her love life, the way her father forbade her to marry the man she loved. I asked her if she was bitter but she said she wasn't. Certain things were destined not to be. 'Maybe we wouldn't have been happy together,' she said, 'you never know the way things can go.'

I argued with Greta again the following morning. It was as if Betty's presence kept us civil with one another. Now that she wasn't there the old tensions came back.

After she had her breakfast she said she was going down to the church to say some prayers.

'I thought you said he'd have no Purgatory,' I said to her.

'Stop picking on me,' she said, 'They're not for him, they're for the rest of us.'

'I'm not picking on you.'

'Religion is a dirty word to you, isn't it?'

'It's neither clean or dirty. I have a problem with people who grasp it too easily.'

'Like me.'

'Maybe.'

'So what should I do, start agonising about it?'

'There's no need to be sarcastic.'

'I know the way you think of me.'

'I don't think of you any way. All I ask is for you not to try and impose your beliefs on me.'

'When was the last time I did that?'

'You never stop doing it

'That's not true. I didn't even ask you to come into the oratory with me that day when Daddy was dying.'

'I appreciated that.'

She wiped a tear from her eye.

'I wish you knew how much I agonised over my faith when I went into the convent first. Or after Mammy died. I don't bother talking about things like that to you because I know you wouldn't be interested. Did you know I wanted to be a doctor but that there wasn't enough money to send me to university?'

'Are you saying being a nun was your second choice?'

'Don't put it like that.'

'What other way can I put it?'

'You're twisting what I said - like you twist everything.'

'It's you that's twisting it.'

'You know about one per cent of how I think about life. That's probably all you want to know. Anything else would disturb all your preconceptions about what an idiot I am.'

Maybe she was right. Maybe I never took the trouble to get to know her. Because I was younger than her I'd always been threatened by her. My mother used to say that boys with older sisters didn't behave as well as girls with older brothers.

'I feel sorry that you don't have my faith,' she said, 'It would make life so much easier for you. I'm not talking about the mushy beliefs you accuse me of. I'm talking about things that have come to me from my pain. You could have them too if you open your heart to God. It's a lonely life without anything to hope for at the end of it.'

'Maybe it's a more honest one.'

'That's your opinion. I can feel God inside me now as surely as I see you standing in front of me.'

'Do you never think he might be an illusion?'

'Why should I think that?'

'A lot of people do.'

'Not the kind of people I know.'

'That's the point. You live in a restricted environment.'

'Why do you have such a chip on your shoulder? You've always had some sort of a gripe about religion, haven't you?'

'How do you make that out?'

'Oh come on. Everyone knows you have. Right back to your experiences with the priests in the college.'

'I like Fr McGinty.'

'He's the exception that proves the rule.'

'Really? So everyone in a dog collar is Public Enemy Number One to me. Is that what you're saying?'

'Even the way you say "dog collar" has anger in it. Why do you use these kinds of words? Is my veil a dog collar to you too?'

'I couldn't care less if you wore a bowl of gardenias on your head. It's what's under it that matters.'

She shook her head in frustration.

'For someone who has doubts about God's existence,' she said, 'you spend a lot of your time acting like him.' It was like a comment I would have made myself. She was starting to ape my sarcasm, the pupil outdoing the master.

'Your faith is the Big Lie,' I said, 'God is the heavenly father you invented to make up for the fact that your earthly one let you down.'

'What book did you get that ridiculous theory from?' she said.

She started to cry. I hated when she did that. My father called tears a woman's rhetoric. He said there was no answer to it. Tears won every argument even without trying.

'I didn't get it from a book. It's the way I think. Sorry if it offends you.'

'Let's not argue anymore. What good can come of it? We never get anywhere.'

'I won't bring up the subject again.'

'Is that a promise?'

'Cross my heart and hope to die.'

We were quiet with one another for the rest of her visit. I tried to stay away from her in case there were any flash points coming up to her departure.

I spent some time trying to repair a tractor that had fallen into disuse. Maybe I'd be able to sell it, I thought, if I got it going. There was a trailer I tried to fix up as well. One of the wheels was falling off.

I walked through the fields remembering all the times I'd saved the hay with my father, all the other things I'd done with him and my mother before the accident.

A cow calved one day. I drove Betty to town to get food. In the execution of small details I forgot my anger with Greta.

I gave his clothes to charity. She said to empty the pockets first, that there might be money in them. I didn't find any of that, just betting slips.

There were lots of his hand carvings in a wardrobe in his bedroom. Behind one of them I found the statue of the man on the horse. He'd kept it all that time. When I saw it I cried. I didn't show it to Greta. She knew nothing about it.

She was on the phone to Nebraska a lot. There were letters of condolence about my father that she wanted to answer before going off. A girl she was friendly with from school called to see us. She was jolly and she made both of us laugh, telling stories about a boss of hers who was a cross dresser. There were times I felt our life was totally normal, more normal even than when my father was alive.

We gave his wheelchair to the local hospital. They also took his crutches and the orthopaedic bed. Nothing could be done about the lift. It was as irrelevant now as it had always been. He'd hardly used it a dozen times in all the years.

I went up to her room the night before she went back. She was reading a book when I went in. It was *Little Women* by Louisa May Alcott, one of her favourites. She re-read it every few years. It was like comfort food to her.

'It's unusual to see you up here,' she said.

'There were a few things I wanted to say. If you're busy we can talk later.'

249

She put the book down.

'Is something wrong?'

'No. I just wanted to say it would be a pity if your visit ended with a bad atmosphere between us. I've been hard on you for the last few months, maybe harder than ever before. I don't want you to go away feeling I have a grudge against you.'

It was all I could manage but it seemed to touch a chord. The tears that came so easily to her filled her eyes, making her look strangely beautiful. She took my hand in hers.

'I have more respect for you than you realise.'

'We bring out the worst in each other.'

'Maybe that's better than bottling things up.'

'In the long term it probably is but there's a lot of carnage along the way. I'm sorry about all the times I've hurt your feelings.'

'There's no need to be. I've gone beyond being hurt for a long time now. You say you were hard on me. I was hard on you too. Maybe I'd never have faced up to that if you hadn't made me.'

'There was bitterness in the way I did it.'

'I deserved it. For years I was immersed in my own world. I had an exaggerated sense of my importance. That was the thing I accused you of. For what it's worth, I don't anymore. So for all that I say, *mea culpa.*'

Her voice became different when she uttered the Latin words. As I listened to her I imagined her on the altar taking her vows, a nun instead of my sister, acknowledging the mark of Cain with a bent head.

'I've got a fair bit of *culpa* myself,' I said.

250

I drove her to Dublin the following day. She said she'd get the train but I wanted to make the gesture. Both of us were unusually polite to one another on the journey, cordial to the point of a different kind of tension than we usually felt now that all the drama was over.

We stopped to eat on the way. As we sat over tea and chips I asked her about her work in Nebraska. It would have been the first thing my mother would have enquired about. With me it was the last. She spoke about people I'd never heard her mention before, about her daily routines, the strain she went through leaving the hospital for the quiet life of prayer and contemplation.

The table we were sitting at was wobbly. When she put down her teacup the tea spilled onto her lap.

'My new dress!' she gasped, 'I was saving it for today.'

It was good for me to hear her being human. It reminded me of the way she was before she entered. Maybe none of us ever fully changed. I handed her a tissue. She was still brushing it as we got to the airport.

I carried her bags from the car park to the departure area. Her flight wasn't going for a while. After she checked in I suggested going for another snack.

The restaurant was crowded. There were so many conversations going on we had trouble hearing one another. I bought her a cup of coffee in a plastic cup.

We watched the people around us. Many of them had tears in their eyes, tears of happiness if they were

251

arriving and of sadness if they were leaving. As I looked at them I tried to imagine what their lives were like, what kind of people they were, what experiences they'd had. I often did that in public places. It was tempting when so many emotions were laid bare, when people's situations were exaggerated in the nakedness of the terminal.

There wasn't anything out of place in her luggage. It was as neatly packaged as I expected it to be, each bag containing just the amount of contents that would have been advised for it. She was concerned that it wouldn't be overweight even though her Order paid for the excesses. The address labels were filled in in her impeccable handwriting, the letters as straight as pillars.

'It's necessary,' she said when I complimented her on them, 'I don't know how many things I've lost over the years due to labels being indecipherable. The ink gets smudged as well, especially if it's raining. A case of mine ended up in Idaho once. I had to have it Fed Exed to the convent.'

Flights were announced over an intercom. We watched names and numbers on a screen, digits and destinations appearing and disappearing almost before we had a chance to see them. Some flights were delayed, some cancelled due to unforeseen circumstances. The words 'Due' or 'Arrived' put smiles on people's faces.

She powdered her face with the mirror of her compact, dabbing her cheeks to bring up their colour. I wondered if she'd been told to downplay her femininity in the convent. Maybe things had changed that way. For my father they'd changed too much. She wasn't wearing her veil. That always bothered him. He saw it as a betrayal of her vocation, an apology for what she was.

'I hate waiting,' she said,

'It's better than flying.' I was a white knuckler.

'Once you're off the ground it's not too bad. It's the turbulence that gets me.'

'Will you read something on the journey?'

'I usually just sleep.'

'Are you looking forward to going back?'

'Yes and no. Every move is a wrench. Sister Immaculata had a new roof put on the convent. I'm looking forward to seeing it.'

'When do you think you'll get back again?'

'It depends. There are very few of us in the convent now. Two elderly nuns died last year. Sister Immaculata likes to have as many of us as possible around.'

'They were hardly doing the garden work in their nineties.'

'You don't understand. It's a community.'

She gazed at the screen. More numbers appeared. They were gone almost as quickly.

into the distance.

'You mightn't be back for a while then.'

'Probably not.'

'Will that bother you?'

'Not unduly. What's there to come back for in a way. With Daddy gone I mean. I miss him so much. He gave me a hard time sometimes but he had a heart of gold. At the end of the day he was harmless.'

The number of her flight came up on the screen. She'd been watching it closely.

'That's me,' she said.

A voice said, 'Boarding now' over the tannoy.

'I hope I haven't delayed you too long,' she said.

'What else would I be doing?'

She was returning to a world that was orderly, somewhere light years away from my own frenetic one. A world of predictable problems and solutions. Each day would mean the same routine as the day before - Matins, a walk in the grounds, reading of the Scriptures, some work in the garden, preparation of meals, phone calls to other convents to arrange new postulants, the gradual winding down to Vespers and a night alone in her room.

I carried her bag to the departure area. A man with dark skin checked her passport. He waved her on. She put her arms around me.

'Phone me,' she said, 'We only have one another now.'

She was right. Whatever badness there was between us, we had memories nobody else could have, shared moments of good and bad things that can never come again. Even bitter experiences become cherishable to us when we're the only ones who have them, or when they're so long into the past as to be forgiveable. We cling onto them in the absence of anything else being available to us.

'I will,' I said.

Her squat shape waddled down the gangway. She waved once before disappearing into her other world.

11

Everything moved fast in the next few months. There were a lot of practical details to be ironed out. I busied myself with the probate from my father's will. He left the farm to me. Greta got his savings. 'Don't let any of the other nuns get their hands on them,' he wrote in a codicil. It made her smile. He didn't leave anything to Betty. She was neither surprised nor bitter at this. 'If he had I think I'd have got a heart attack,' she said, 'I always expected him to maintain Radio Silence when it came to me.'

Setanta followed me everywhere I went. He clung to me as the last piece of my father, the last link to the land he loved. He'd been gaunt since he got sick, as gaunt as the day we rescued him from the ditch after he'd been thrown from the car. He reminded me of a greyhound as he slunk from room to room.

I watched him pawing my father's chair. He barked at me sometimes if he woke from a bad dream. If I brought him for a walk he lagged behind me. I didn't think he'd last long. He refused everything Betty left in his dish for him. I asked her to mind him for me. He was pulling me too deep into the past every time I looked at him.

She asked me what I was going to do with all my father's things. I hadn't thought about them before she said it. The longer I kept them, I knew, the harder they'd be to dispose of.

'Be ruthless,' she said, 'It's the only way. Everything you keep is going to bring back a memory.'

I knew she was right. He was hardly a fortnight dead before I gathered everything I could find and put it onto a skip.

Anything to do with his book I burned. That was an exorcism of sorts for me.

'It has to die with him,' I said to her. She agreed. We both felt his father had a lot to answer for. If he'd taken the trouble to get to know him when he was growing up there may never have been a need to immortalise him in a book.

The question of what to do with the farm took longer. For a while I thought I'd work it, at least part time, but after a few weeks I realised that was impossible. If my interest in it was minimal while my father was alive it was nil now.

I let it be known around the town that I was interested in selling up. One night a relative of my mother called. He made me an offer for everything, lock stock and barrel. It was an insult in market terms but I wasn't in the mood to argue. When I accepted it without trying to beat him down he could hardly believe his ears.

'You're not like a farmer,' he said. He was referring to the way most of them pretended to be insulted by offers they were secretly delighted with, walking away from people on fair days as if they weren't interested and then turning back again a minute later.

He'd made my father a few offers for it over the years and they were laughed off.

'I'd have laughed them off too before now,' I said.

'Then I'm lucky to have come along now.'

Despite everything, I was sad to see it go. I rang Greta to tell her. She was sad too.

'The convent was always my second home,' she said, 'Now it's my only one.'

I took whatever I wanted from the house over the next few weeks, storing everything in Betty's house. I stayed with her as the sale was going through. On the night before my mother's relative moved in we got drunk together. We sat out on the verandah remembering the good times and the bad ones, the whole crazy carnival our life had been. Now that the past was distant from us it didn't seem threatening anymore. It just made us feel sad. She told me things I never knew about m father and I told her things she didn't know. It amazed me how two people could have such different experiences of the same person.

'Is everyone like that?' I asked her.

'No,' she said, 'Your father was a one-off. He was a prism.'

I thought that was a good way of putting it. Betty had great insights into people. Maybe it came from not being married. I often thought married people were so immersed in their worlds they couldn't see the wood for the trees. Single ones had more of a bird's eye view of things.

I didn't know how I'd be without the farm to go back to. I'd spent more time away from it than on it in recent years but it was still an anchor for me. So was my father. Betty said I shouldn't be thinking like that.

'You can do things now that you never could when he was alive,' she said to me.

I was sad on the morning I left for London. It wasn't as bad as leaving my father but it was still emotional for me. I'd told her a lot about myself since he died. She'd become more of a friend to me than an aunt.

'You taught me more than anyone about how to deal with things,' I said to her at the door. I meant it. Her philosophical attitude about all the things that went wrong for her in her life was an example to all of us.

She thought it would be easy for me to pick up where I left off in London but it didn't work out like that. I learned that you couldn't step off a merry-go-round after the music stopped and expect to get back on when you liked.

As soon as I arrived I felt a hole in the pit of myself. I'd never been there before without the knowledge that I could go home if I wanted. Now there was no home. I was flying blind.

I felt rootless without the farm. The freedom I thought I craved was only valuable to me when it was conditional. Absolute freedom meant absolute nothingness. I had nothing to contrast it with, nothing to make it relevant. How could you escape from a prison when there was none there?

When I got to the apartment my key wouldn't work in the door. A man came out.

'Can I help you?' he said.

I told him I lived there.

'Ah,' he said, 'The Irish boy.'

He was the new tenant. I'd been away too long for the landlord to hold it for me. When I got on to him on the phone he said he'd tried to ring me a number of times but couldn't get through.

He'd put my possessions in storage. I retrieved them and put them into a new place I rented. It was a flat in the east of the city beside an industrial estate. It was cheap but depressing. I did my best to make it cheerier by putting in soft lights and cushions on the chairs but even these failed to lift its aura of darkness. I remembered something my father used to say: 'You can put lipstick on a pig but it's still a pig.' I smiled to myself as I thought of him. He hit the nail on the head with so many of his expressions.

The money I got from the farm meant I had enough to buy a house in London if I wanted. I wasn't sure if I was ready to make that kind of commitment. I looked at a few but they were either ridiculously expensive or unsuitable for some other reason. I didn't want to do anything hasty. Once you signed along the dotted line with an auctioneer you were in effect signing your life away. What if I wanted to go back to Galway or travel farther afield in the years to come? I remembered my father saying about Aisling, 'Once a voyager, always a voyager.' Maybe it applied to me too.

I visited the Corncrake one day. Most of the people I knew were gone. The clientele was younger now. That would have been Justin's doing. The juke box was replaced with a video machine.

The building itself had been solidified. No longer did the floor shake when the Tube passed. I almost missed that. There was no atmosphere in it. As I sat at the counter nursing a glass of bitter I felt I was in a train station.

I asked the barman if he knew anything about Malcolm.

'Know anything about him?' he said, 'Not really except for the fact that he's six foot under.'

I thought he was joking.

'What do you mean?' I said.

'He was stabbed to death in the chokey.' He said it in a matter-of-fact way as if I shouldn't be surprised.

'I don't believe you.'

'It was going to happen sooner or later.'

I realised to my horror that he was serious.

'What happened?'

'He tried to touch up one of the inmates. It was the wrong guy. He found himself on the receiving end of the broken shards of a tin can.' Shortly afterwards he'd died of gangrene poisoning.

I was shocked. And yet in another part of me I saw the barman's point. He was always skating on the edge of danger. It was a sad end to a pathetic life.

I asked him if Justin was still around.

'Not him either,' he said, 'He's gone to greener pastures.'

'What do you mean?'

'He's cash and carried. To a Montessori teacher from Surrey, I believe.'

'Has he left bar work?'

'I think he's in computers now.'

Before I left he gave me his phone number.

'Don't ring him until after tea,' he said, 'He does all his gardening at this time.'

'Gardening?'

'His latest passion.'

I rang him later that evening. It was a while before he picked up the phone. He sounded stressed.

'I was sorry to hear about your father,' he said.

I'd left without telling him. He didn't say how he found out.

'Thank you. He had a good innings. What about yourself? I believe you got married.'

'Guilty as charged.'

'So you couldn't deal with the loneliness of life without me.'

'Now you have it. I suppose you'll be next.'

'That's unlikely.'

'I presume you're in London.'

'I am.'

'We'll have a jar some night.'

'That would be good.'

I heard a woman's voice in the background.

'Is that your wife?' I said.

'If it isn't I'm in trouble.'

She seemed to be soothing a baby. There were squawks.

'Surely you haven't had a child already.'

'It's hers, not mine. I'm one of those Instant Family husbands.'

'Somehow I can't see you as a father.'

'That makes two of us.'

I refrained from asking him if she turned into a pizza after sex.

'Does she have you changing nappies as well?'

'If I don't she locks me in the dungeon downstairs.'

I asked him if he was still on the 'wacky baccy.'

'Keep your voice down,' he said, 'I'm off all that stuff now.'

I told him I'd heard about Malcolm. He was as blasé about him as the barman in the Corncrake.

'Whoever snuffed him out did him a favour,' he said.

'What kind of sentence is the man who killed him going to get?'

'None. They're going to give him a medal of honour.'

I asked him about his job. He was evasive about what it entailed, refusing to divulge any details to me except for the fact that it paid well. He said he intended to be as rich as Croesus within a few years. That was the only way he could justify keeping his head down in a white collar post for employers who didn't have two brain cells to rub together.

'You know me,' he said, 'I don't stand still too long. When I get enough loot I'm going to buy out the people above me.'

He went on talking about money. It was a subject that bored me. Maybe he was using it as an excuse to avoid talking about anything else.

He yawned when I mentioned the past. It was as if it was dead to him, as dead as his old personality. I mentioned the nights we'd spent driving to West End parties.

'Before I go,' he said, 'I must tell you about the new Volvo I just bought.'

He yammered on about power steering and wheel locks. I thought he might firm up a time about meeting but he didn't. He asked me for my phone number but without much conviction. A part of me felt he'd have been happier if I hadn't made contact with him at all.

After I left down the phone I wondered if I should have sounded more enthusiastic about the Volvo. Somehow I doubted he'd be driving it to clubs in the West End at the dead of night. It would more likely be going to market garden centres in the suburbs on Sunday mornings.

He didn't ring me. In a way I was relieved. The man I knew was gone. He once told me he saw domesticity as death. Maybe he was ashamed of himself for giving in to it.

I didn't ring him either. What would have been the point? Over the next few months I worked in different jobs. I started them with the enthusiasm with which I seemed to start everything in life but then it faded. I threw in the towel when I began to get established.

I worked as a delivery man in a pizza parlour for a while. It didn't pay much but it kept me on the move. It was like the courier job except with food. That made it pressurising. Pizzas got cold. Parcels didn't.

A job as a cinema usher on the Holloway Road was more enjoyable. I got to see the films after leading people to their seats. It was like being paid for something I'd be doing anyway. At the weekends I distributed food to people in a homeless shelter for a charitable organisation. Maybe I was trying to salve my conscience about my father.

I never stayed at anything for long. My concentration kept faltering. There was a voice inside me telling me to move. The problem was that it never told me where to move to.

Betty phoned me a few times. She was minding Setanta all the time now. A vet had given him some supplements to help him put on weight.

She told me there was always a bed in her house if the 'wild colonial boy,' as she called me, ever decided to return. Whatever about being colonial, I was hardly wild anymore. If anything I was living a more introverted life in London than I did back home.

I didn't see her offer as an option. She probably threw it at me out of sympathy. We were, after all, blood. She thought I deserved credit for putting up with my father for so long. Now that he was gone she wanted me to cultivate a new identity without him. It sounded good in theory.

I asked her if she passed the farm much. She said she went by it nearly every day.

'It looks better than it used to,' she said, 'but I'd prefer it the old way if you know what I mean.'

'I do. Dirty.'

'I didn't say that.'

'You didn't have to.'

'Is there any sign of you to get married?' she said at the end of one call.

I told her it was lonely coming home to the empty flat every night but I'd always seen myself as a bachelor.

'Better to be miserable on your own than with someone else,' I said, 'Didn't someone famous say that?'

'If he did he was an idiot. Don't end up like me, an old bag of bones with nobody to cuddle up to on a cold night.'

Aisling rang me one night. I couldn't believe it was her when I picked up the phone. Her voice sounded nervous. If she hadn't said her name I wouldn't have known who it was. When she said it I became nervous too. For a second I was going to drop the phone.

'A blast from the past,' I said.

'More like another life,' she said.

'How are you?'

'Not too bad. I thought of ringing you so many times but I couldn't pluck up the courage.'

'How did you get my number?'

'From Betty. I ring her now and again. She's under orders not to tell you.'

'She's obeyed them well.'

She said she was sorry to hear about my father.

'I wanted to go to the funeral but I couldn't bring myself to.'

'You should have.'

'It wouldn't have been fair to you. You had enough to contend with.'

I thought she was ringing from Ireland but she said she was actually just down the road. It was another shock to me.

'I live here now,' she said.

It was as if a parallel life, a dream life, was appearing before me. She might have been a creature from a film or a play. Even in my past she'd been unreal. Now she was unreal in a different kind of way. My second life had come back to me. I didn't know whether to welcome it or not.

'Did you get married?' I asked her. I didn't know why.

'No,' she said. After a pause she added, 'Betty told me you didn't either.'

She said she thought my father's death would have given me the freedom to bring some lady down the aisle.

'You can't just get married for the sake of it,' I said, 'It wouldn't make sense.'

She said she'd love to meet me to catch up on everything. I wasn't sure it was a good idea but I said I would. A part of me wanted to know if I was totally over her. For years I'd been telling myself I was. Was it true or was it just wish fulfilment?

We met at a wine bar near Piccadilly Circus. When I saw her first I didn't recognise her. The hips that once swung so loosely on her were gone. She had more of a womanly shape now. Why did time change us so much? Had I a right to expect her to look the same?

She was wearing a leopardskin skirt. A matching handbag hung over her shoulder. Her hair wasn't parted in the middle anymore. She'd had it styled. It was in a top knot style.

'What have you done to your hair?' I said.

'I had to tie it up to get it out of my eyes.'

'It makes you look different.'

'Better or worse?'

'If I don't say "Better" I suppose I'll be in trouble.'

'You certainly would.'

She gave me a hug.

'I've missed you so much,' she said, 'You look great. I was so horrible to you that time I didn't think you'd turn up.'

'How could I not?'

We went into the bar. A sign said, 'Wait To Be Seated.'

'You're wearing lipstick,' I said to her.

'So?'

'You usen't to.'

'There are a lot of things I do these days that I usen't to. Do you not like it?'

'Don't be silly. I just have to get used to it. You've changed your image.'

'I never knew I had one.'

'You've turned into a woman.'

'As opposed to what – a man?'

The bar was a yuppie place full of businessmen. They were all dressed to the nines. A waiter approached us. He asked us if we wanted a meal. We said no. It meant we had to go to another end of the bar. It was darker down there.

We sat in a corner on red velvet seats.

'It's more cosy here,' she said.

It was like the old days for a moment. But then it wasn't.

She said she was sorry for the way we ended.

'I don't know what went wrong,' she said.

'Neither,' I said, 'do I.'

I ordered a bottle of Beaujolais. Adrenalin made me drink faster than usual. She started talking like a clock. After a few minutes I fell into her flow. Before we knew it we'd gone through the bottle between us.

'Let's get another one,' she said, 'It's a special occasion.'

No sooner had I flicked my finger than a waiter came over.

'Just what the doctor ordered,' she said.

Her manner became more animated with the second bottle. She reminded me of my father when he'd had a few brandies.

I asked her if she was still sailing.

'I gave it up,' she said, 'I'm strictly a land animal now.'

'I'm disappointed to hear that.'

'Have you still got the boat?'

'I've hardly been in it since you left.'

She asked me where I was living.

'In a tip,' I said.

'Come on.'

'I'm serious. I'll get a decent place when I know what I'm going to do in the long term.'

When I asked her if she'd been with many men after me.

'A few,' she said.

She didn't want to go into any details. There were experiences she'd been through that she couldn't talk about. She was still feeling the pain.

'Not everyone is as nice as you, you know,' she said.

Some men she'd met had done her head in. She was only coming back to herself now.

'Was it Tony you went away with that day?' I asked.

'Yes. We went back to Athlone. He's from there too.'

'I'm sure your parents were glad to see you.'

'Over the moon. They hardly let me out the door for the first few weeks.'

'It must have reminded you of life with my father.'

'In a way. They worried about me when I was with you. I was often on the phone to them from Galway.'

'You didn't tell me that.'

'I didn't want to upset you. They thought I was too young to get so involved with someone. My father thinks your father is a maniac.'

'He's not the only one. What about your mother?'

'She thought it was no life for me being copped up in the house all the time.'

269

'Did I not bring you out as much as I could?'

'It wasn't your fault. It was the situation. He knew how much of a free spirit I was.'

'So you moved in with Tony.'

'For a while. It didn't really work out.'

'Why not?'

'He was even more controlling than you were.'

'Thanks.'

'Sorry. You know what I mean. I seem to bring out the father in men.'

'How long did you stay with him?'

'Less than a year. We drifted apart. He got with someone else then. She was another Athlone girl. I was glad for them.'

'What about you?'

'I worked with my mother for a while. She had a creche.'

'But you didn't stay at that either.'

'Kids are great but they drive you mad if you give them an inch. Athlone was never for me in the long term. It's a goldfish bowl. I kept running into Tony with Irene.'

'Is that his new girlfriend?

'His wife actually.'

'It didn't take him long to get over you.'

'I think Irene might have been pregnant. He was shifty when I asked him about it. She was terrified he'd leave her for me.'

'Was she right to be?'

'Maybe. I think he still had a torch for me.'

'Was it mutual?'

'I'm afraid not. I thought I loved him but I mustn't have.'

'Do you think he married Irene on the rebound?'

'I don't know. He rang me one night. It was after they got married. He was crying into the phone.'

'Did he ask you to meet him?'

'He hinted at it but I knew it wouldn't be right.'

She said she never saw him again.

'I left Athlone soon after that.'

'Where did you go?'

'Here, there and everywhere. I worked as an au pair in Bordeaux for a year. Then I did a TEFL course.'

'What's that?'

'Teaching English as a foreign language. I was getting big money for it in Dubai. Mostly from rich Arabs.'

She said she had a relationship with the father of one of her pupils. He used to beat her. She wasn't able to understand why she didn't leave him. He told her he was a widow but it turned out he had a wife.

'She was living in Venezuela. I was some fool. She turned up at the college one day with a baby in her arms. When am I going to get sense?'

'Do any of us ever? Look at me.'

'You're not the worst of them.'

In everything she said I felt she was sending out a signal to me that she'd like to get back with me. The idea made me feel nervous with her. It was if she'd sampled life and found it wanting. I was now her choice as consolation.

I found myself becoming bored with her the more she talked. Whenever I said something, even something banal, she over-reacted.

She told me she was studying geology at a Polytech. I couldn't understand how that would appeal to her. She said she wanted to be a lecturer eventually.

'I've put all that juvenile stuff behind me,' she said.

'What juvenile stuff?'

'All that crazy travelling.'

'Why do you call it crazy? It was one of the things I liked most about you.'

'It's just a phase you go through, isn't it?'

'Maybe for you it was. I don't think I'd ever tire of it.'

'Why don't you do it now?'

'I'm not the type.'

'You're just looking for excuses. You romanticise it because you haven't done it. If you did you'd see the drab side of it soon enough.'

It was like a conversation we'd had after we first met. I saw the old glint in her eye that had once attracted me to her so much.

I ordered a third bottle of wine. My head was spinning. I knew I'd pay for it in the morning but I didn't care.

'There's still time if you want it enough,' she said.

'I don't think I have the motivation.'

We talked about my father, the hold he had over us.

'He changed our lives so much,' she said.

272

I wasn't sure how he'd changed hers. Did she mean if it wasn't for him we'd have ended up together?

She wanted to find out more about London. I didn't open up about it. The wine loosened had my tongue but I put the brakes on about some things. She knew so much about me I needed to keep some things from her. Otherwise, I feared, she'd get in on me like she had before.

'Let's dance,' she said.

There was a corner of the bar set aside for that purpose. It was a kind of apron stage. There were strobe lights above it. A man sat on a stool playing a piano.

She gave him a wink as we passed him.

'Have you been here before?' I said.

'That'd be telling.'

I was unsteady on my feet. She held me close to her. I got the smell she used to have. Was it perfume?

She started kissing me.

'We're like two winos,' she said.

'What do you mean *like*? We're the real deal.'

I felt my desire for her growing. She looked beautiful under the lights of the stage.

'Would you like to come back to the flat?' I said.

'That would be lovely. Why should the night end here?'

We left the bar. I took her hand in mine the way I used to. We walked to a taxi rank. I thought of the boathouse, the swans on the bay, the beguiling light of the moon.

A taxi arrived after a minute. She lay in my arms the whole way to the flat. I wasn't sure if she was sleeping or not. When we got there I lifted her out of the car.

I paid the driver.

'She looks like a good one,' he said, 'Take care of her.'

He drove off.

'Why did I drink so much?' she said.

'For the same reason I did. You wanted to.'

'That makes sense.'

We went inside. I turned on a lamp.

'So this is the tip,' she said, 'I don't know why you were giving out about it. It's lovely.'

She slumped into a chair.

'You need a cup of black coffee,' I said. 'In fact we both need a cup of black coffee.'

'No. More wine.'

'That would be stupid.'

'I'm sick of being sensible.'

I put on some music. She moved her hands to it.

'I love that song,' she said.

It was Tony Bennett. She moved her hands through the air as if she was conducting it.

'Do you think we could ever get back to the way we were?' she said.

'How were we?'

She laughed.

'Now you're being bold.'

I stared at her.

'Why are you looking at me like that?' she said.

'Like what?'

'Like that.'

'I'm not looking at you any way.'

'Yes you are.'

'I'm drunk.'

I wasn't sure if she was pretending to be drunker than she was. Maybe she thought I'd like her more that way.

'So am I.'

'Don't look at me like that.'

'All right.'

The kettle came to the boil. I brought a cup of coffee over to her.

'Is there wine in that?' she said.

'There's coffee in it.'

'I don't want it. Take it away.'

She started laughing. I gripped her by the arm.

'If things were as great as you say they were,' I said, 'Why did you walk out on me?'

'I ask myself that question a hundred times a day.'

'And how do you answer yourself?'

'With a question mark.'

I sat down beside her.

'You ripped my heart out of me,' I said.

'I know. It was wrong and it was inexcusable. Can you forgive me?'

'Why did you do it?'

'I had no choice. You were gone past listening to me about your father. Every time I said things couldn't go on as they were you ignored me.'

'You should have told me to my face that you were going.'

'If I had my life to live over again I would.'

Her eyes were gone back in her head from the drink. She started to open the buttons of my shirt.

'I don't think that's a good idea,' I said.

'Why not?'

'It's not the right time.'

'When is?'

'I don't know.'

'What's the problem?'

'I'm feeling sick from the wine.'

'You want me,' she said, 'I know you do. I can see it in your eyes.'

She opened her blouse. Her bra was so small I could see most of her breasts.

'Well,' she said, 'what do you think?'

'Of what?'

'Me.'

'I think you're very beautiful.'

'And?'

'And I think you should close your blouse.'

'Do you not find me attractive anymore?'

'Of course I do.'

'Make love to me,' she said, 'Make love to me like you used to. Nobody can say anything to us now. There's just us.'

I walked away from the bed.

'What's wrong?' she said.

'I told you. I'm feeling sick from the wine.'

'Do you not find me attractive anymore?'

'It's not that.'

'What is it then?'

'I'm a different person now.'

'What's that supposed to mean?'

'You came back into my life from nowhere. Do you realise how many years we've been away from one another?'

'That's the whole point. I want us to get back what we had. It's too good to lose.'

'You were the one who let it go.'

'I know. That's why it's so important to me to make up for that. Can we not pick up where we left off?'

'Maybe sometime. Not now.'

She put her head in her hands. I thought she was going to cry.

'Okay,' she said.

She stood up. Her hair was tousled. She examined herself in the mirror.

'I'm a mess,' she said.

She buttoned up her blouse.

'It's too late to get a taxi,' she said, 'Can I stay here? I won't bother you.'

'Of course.'

I went into the spare bedroom. She stumbled into it behind me.

'Sorry for putting you to all this trouble.'

'It's no trouble. Sorry for getting annoyed with you.'

'I deserved it.'

She fell onto the bed. I put a duvet over her. Her eyes started to close.

'I'll be asleep in ten seconds,' she said, 'It's the wine.'

I went into the other room. Was I being unfair to her? Maybe not. I tried to get my mind off her, to fend off the eerie sensation of having her in a bed beside me after all the years. It was ages before I fell asleep.

When I woke up the next morning she was sitting in the kitchen. She looked as if she'd just got out of bed. Her make-up was smudged.

'I was really out for the count last night,' she said, 'I could have slept for Ireland.'

Her hair was down on her face. It was like it used to be when I got to know her first. For a moment I felt like we were in the boathouse.

'What about you?'

'It took me a while to get off.'

'Sorry about the way I behaved. I don't usually do things like that.'

'You were fine.'

'I don't know what came over me.'

'Sorry if I was rude to you.'

'You weren't rude. I acted like a slapper.'

I put two slices of bread in the toaster.

'What are you doing?' she said.

'Blotting paper.'

'I'm not hungry.'

'You need it.'

It popped up. I gave her some tea with the toast. We started eating.

'There's so much I want to ask you about yourself,' she said. 'Now that I'm sober maybe you'll tell me.'

'There's not much to tell.'

'How hard was it to break away from your father?'

'Not as hard as you might think. He got easier to deal with after you left.'

'Was that why?'

'No.'

'How long did you stay after I left?'

Long enough. I used to go away for breaks. When he got used to that I thought I might go away for a longer stretches and see how he was.'

'London was your salvation; it was like a new lease of life for you.'

'Why do you think that?'

'I just do.'

She asked me what life was like for me in the Corncrake. I didn't know how she knew I was working there. She mentioned things I couldn't even remember telling people. It was as if she'd been checking up on me. I started to feel ill at ease. She mentioned Justin and Malcolm. How did she know about these people?

'What about girls?' she asked.

'What about them?'

'I want to hear all the dirt.'

'I went out with a few but I was thinking of you when I was with them.'

'I don't know whether to feel flattered or guilty.'

'You should feel guilty.'

She giggled.

'I heard you got involved with two drug dealers,' she said then.

'How did you hear about that?'

'Never mind. What were they up to?'

'If I told you,' I said, 'I'd have to kill you.'

She giggled again.

'Now you're beginning to sound like a character from a bad movie,' she said.

'It's the truth.'

'Do you find yourself attracted to danger?'

'Why do you ask that?'

'Because I am.'

'I'd never have had you down for masochism.'

'Why would I have stayed with the man who beat me otherwise?'

'Are you saying you enjoyed it?'

'No, but I wasn't able to leave him.'

'I've heard of situations like that. It's more about control than anything else.'

'I felt trapped,' she said, 'almost like you were with your father. Then one day I just upped and went. He didn't know what hit him. One minute I was there and the next - bazoom.'

'You're good at that,' I said. I couldn't resist the dig.

'Now you're doing it to me.'

'Don't put it like that.'

'What other way can I put it?'

'When I outgrew the need for my father it was like I didn't need anyone else either.'

'You say that as if it's a boast.'

'It's not a boast or an apology. It's just the way I am.'

'Or maybe the way you think you are.'

'You're getting very analytic. Isn't that my department?'

'Maybe I'm turning into you.'

She started to kiss me. I held her back.

'Remember last night,' I said.

'Sorry. I'm sober this time.'

She asked me what I planned to do for the rest of the day. I said I didn't know, that my head was so scrambled with the wine I'd probably just vegetate.

'I suppose it wouldn't be on for us to spend the day together.'

'I wish I could, Aisling.'

'Ouch. I get worried when people call me by my name.'

'Why?'

'It means they're about to say something serious. Or have just done so.'

'Let's play things by ear for the moment.'

'That famous ear.'

'We don't want to make a mistake a second time.'

'I agree. It would be a disaster.'

She put on her coat.

'See you sometime,' she said.

I wanted to tell her to stay but something stopped me, some cruel voice inside my head Was it revenge? I thought of the way she was with Tony the night he rang her after marrying Irene. It was as if she was tony now and I was her.

I dated other women afterwards but there was no spontaneity in it. That was the only way I could enjoy their company. I went so far and no further. Even if I slept with them there was no emotion in it. I played them like instruments and they responded in kind. I explained my position from the outset and if they didn't like it they were free not to pursue things. Sometimes I ended relationships and sometimes they did. Either way there were no recriminations. I didn't hurt them and I wasn't hurt by them. They were injections of company I needed every so often. It was like the way you felt the craving for a certain kind of food.

I didn't contact Aisling again in case she'd misinterpret the signals. One night when I was feeling lonely I rang her number but when she answered it I hung up. I don't know why. Maybe I was afraid I'd start to need her again.

Betty rang me every so often. One night when I picked up the phone her voice was different. I knew immediately there was something wrong.

'What is it?' I said.

'I don't know how to say it.'

'What do you mean?'

She paused. When she spoke again there was a catch in her voice.

'It's Setanta.'

She didn't need to say anymore.

'Is he dead?' I said. Maybe I was even expecting it.

'He was run over by a car last week.'

I felt a wrench of emotion as great as if it was a human being she was talking about. My chest tightened.

'I wanted to ring you but I couldn't find your number. It's probably cold comfort to you but he didn't suffer. The poor creature died as soon as the car hit him. He went out like a light.'

'How did it happen?'

'It was at that bad bend beside your house. He used to go back there a lot. He never really left the farm in his head.'

'Was he on the road?'

'In the middle of it. He gave the driver no chance.'

I put the phone down on the table. My head was burning. I thought of the last time I'd seen him, his leanness. I should have paid more attention to it.

'Are you there?' Her voice was faint. I picked up the receiver.

'Sorry. I was gone for a second.'

'I feel bad for not telling you before now.'

'It wouldn't have made it any better.'

'He hadn't been himself for a long time. I think he lost the will to live when your father died. Your going away was the last straw.'

'I shouldn't have left him.'

'What could you do? You had your life to live.'

'Thank you for looking after him so well.'

'I'm afraid I didn't do too well that day.'

'He was always wandering away. It wasn't your fault.'

'He gave me great comfort in my life. In some ways we were suffering from the same problem.'

I hadn't been able to cry at either of my parents' funerals. Now I did. The tears came out of me like water. Maybe the emotion had been building up in me. It was waiting for something like this to get itself out.

Setanta was gone. Everyone was gone. Anything I ever cared about had been taken away from me.

'Poor Setanta,' I said, 'He lasted for as long as it mattered.'

'He's in the back garden now,' she said, 'He'll be in my thoughts forever.'

She didn't say anything else. The click as she put the phone down was like the end of another phase of my life. I felt I was running out of things I could cope with.

12

The next few years are a blur to me. I know I spent some time in London and that I travelled home to Galway now and then but everything else is mixed up. I've forgotten conversations I had with people even in the recent past. Sometimes I think things happened to me that didn't. Other things I think didn't happen did.

It must be three years ago now since I first went to a doctor. He told me I was under severe stress as a result of all the things that happened to me in my life. The pills he put me on relaxed me but I needed more and more of them as time went on. It was like when Justin used to supply me. They made me not want to do anything

I drank after taking them sometimes. The mixture made me mellow for a few days but then it wore off.

I started to increase the dosage. That's where things get confusing for me. I lost some jobs as a result of being groggy. After a while I got to a stage where the pills weren't working at all. I felt my heart palpitating. My sleep was disrupted. I woke in the middle of the night.

'I'm taking you off everything,' the doctor told me one day, 'You've developed an immunity.'

'If I have,' I said, 'you're responsible.'

He didn't want to hear that. Maybe he felt guilty about putting me on them. Maybe he was afraid I'd report him to someone.

Without the pills I felt strange. I started to imagine people were talking to me who didn't even know me. Sometimes I wondered if I knew myself.

I walked across roads when the traffic was at its peak, weaving in and out between the cars like someone who wanted to get knocked down. Whiskey stopped me shivering from the withdrawal symptoms but it was a vicious circle. A different kind of shivering followed.

I was walking through Galway one day when I felt dizzy. My mind started to race away from me. I sat on a wall to catch my breath. Everything was swimming in front of me. The tar on the road made the air look fluttery.

I went into a hotel for a drink. The barman said, 'You've had enough already.'

'That's ridiculous,' I said, 'I haven't had any at all today.'

I'm not sure what happened next. I saw him falling down in front of me but I wasn't aware of having hit him. Someone struck me from behind then. I was knocked out.

When I woke up I was in a police station. A man in a uniform was questioning me.

'Do you normally go around hitting people?' he said. 'You nearly broke his skull. Are you on drugs?'

I couldn't believe what I was hearing. If I hit him I'd have known it.

'It must have been someone else,' I said.

'He's lucky to be alive.'

'I can't remember doing it.'

'Then maybe we'll jog your memory.'

He threw me against the wall. I fell to the ground. Another man came in. He kicked me until I lost consciousness.

It was a different day when I came to. I was in a bed surrounded by men in suits. They were all staring at me.

'You've been in a coma,' one of them said, 'What happened to you?'

I told him I remembered nothing. He said I'd been found dumped on a road three days before.

'You were raving,' he said, 'We thought you were a goner.'

I was moved to another building. The days passed in a fog. I have vague memories of a doctor appearing now and again. Nurses jabbed me with needles.

Some time later I was moved to another place. I had a room of my own there. One day a man I'd never seen before came in. He took out a file that contained information about me. When I asked him where he got it he just smiled. After a few minutes he started asking me about my father. What kind of man was he, how many years had I spent with him, that kind of thing. I thought that was none of his business. I didn't see what it had to do with anything.

Every time I said something he jotted it down in his notebook. He paused before each question in case I had anything to add. That annoyed me. I always know what I'm going to say before I open my mouth. Another thing that annoyed me was the way he spoke. He enunciated his syllables very slowly as if I was of limited intelligence.

'Do you know who you are?' he said at one stage. I thought that was hilarious.

The next time I was interviewed he rigged me up to a machine. Wires were put on my wrists. A needles fluttered up and down on a graph. I asked him if it was a lie detector test but he didn't answer me.

There was one question he kept coming back to. Did I feel bitter about my past? I said, 'Of course not. Life doesn't work out like you plan it. Some things work out for you and some things don't. It's as simple as that.'

He wasn't happy with that. Maybe he wanted me to say I blamed my father for everything. That would probably have given him more fodder for his research. I didn't humour him. All I told him was that I was basically content with my life, that the only time I ever felt really lonely was when I was among groups of people.

He looked out the window.

'That'll be all for today,' he said.

Afterwards I was moved to the place I now inhabit. I've been here for eleven years.

I have all the comforts of home here. My room is like an apartment. Downstairs there's a conference room. It's all very elaborate. I don't know how much it costs. Greta takes care of that. She's back in Ireland now. I put her in charge of everything after I fell into bad health.

My world has shrunk to the dimensions of this room. All it has in it is a bed and a wardrobe. I can walk the length of it in fourteen steps and the breadth of it in twelve.It only locks from the outside.

The people in the rooms on either side of me behave strangely. The man next door makes noises in the middle of the night. I bang on the wall to make him stop but he doesn't. My pleas don't have any influence on him. If anything they only make him noisier.

The man on the other side is quieter. That makes me more wary of him. He spends a lot of time talking to himself. When he opens up to the rest of us he makes no sense. He had a stroke last year. It made his face go funny down one side. But even without the stroke he always looked odd. I don't know what his problem is. Greta puts it down to drink.

I wish she wouldn't fixate on that subject so much. She believes all the evil in the world is a result of it. That's probably because of my father. She thinks my own problems began with Justin. 'He caused everything,' she says. That isn't really true. I was well able to raise a glass to my lips without his help.

I'm treated with respect here. The staff accept me for who I am. Sometimes I see the orderlies giggling when I pass them in the corridor. I can live with that.

I tell my problems to Dr Gupta. He's the man I go to for therapy. There are sessions once a week. He was assigned to me shortly after I was admitted. Over the years we've built up quite a camaraderie. I tell him all the things that come into my mind. He either tapes me or jots down notes on what I've said. Sometimes I think he knows more about me than I do myself.

There are women in another wing. I'm attracted to some of them. Dr Gupta thinks I won't be ready for a relationship for a long time yet. That's nonsense but I have to agree with him. Otherwise privileges will be taken away from me.

One night he put a clamp over my head. He ran something through me. I felt as if I was being electrocuted.

'This will make you feel better,' he said, 'It will take away all your pain.' Afterwards I didn't remember much.

He often makes me delve deeper into the past than I want to. That annoys me. It's reassuring to know he's interested but I hate it when he takes notes. He looks at me so earnestly sometimes I find myself saying things I didn't intend to just to keep him happy.

When I'm agitated I scream out loud. If I do that he gives me an injection.

Sometimes I plead with him not to give me one. If he's in a good mood he gives me pills instead. That's as far as he's willing to compromise. He writes out a prescription and it's given into the pharmacy. The next thing I know a bottle is left beside my bed.

They have me on so many pills in here I feel like an astronaut. There are pills for when you're down, pills for when you're up and pills for when you're not sure how you are. I think they cancel each other out. Occasionally I get a good reaction from one of them but the next day there tends to be a hangover effect. The more dependent you get on them the higher a dosage you need. That's why I only pretend to take them sometimes. I put them in my mouth and raise a glass of water to my lips. I've become quite skilful at slipping them under my tongue and then spitting them out afterwards.

They give me bad dreams. There are times when I think dreams are my reality and everything else is an illusion. When I feel like it I can watch myself having them, making them up as I go along.

There are moments between sleep and wakefulness when I'm aware of what's happening in the dream. It's up to me whether I prolong it or not. If the thing that's happening is upsetting I stop it. One time my curiosity got the better of me and I let it run. I shouldn't have done that because when I did it went out of control. I woke up screaming. They had to give me another injection that day.

Afterwards I became nervous of going to sleep. I imagined another person inside me that I wasn't aware of, living inside me all the time. He came out at night when my defences were down. It's a scary thought, having a lodger inside your head like that, waiting for his chance to pounce.

The worst dream I have is set in London. It's back in the eighties. I'm walking down a one-way street in this deprived neighbourhood. All of a sudden I come to a dead end. I try to turn back but there are two men standing blocking my path. One of them is rattling a chain. The other has a switchblade. They're dressed in leather. After a while they start talking about my father. They say things about him that are lies, that they know to be lies. They're laughing like maniacs. I know they're trying to goad me. One of them rattles his chain beside my ear. Then he grabs me around the neck. At this stage the dream is hazy because he seems to turn into my father. Then he becomes me. It doesn't make sense.

I only have this dream when I've had a stressful day. Most of the things in it stay the same. The only thing that changes is the amount of time it goes on for. Now and again it continues until the man starts rattling his chain. If it goes on for longer we all change our identities. I prefer it when it comes to a halt at the dead end. It's like when you have that dream when you're falling off a cliff. It always stops before you reach the bottom. What would happen if we could programme our minds to go on just that little bit further and you actually hit the bottom? When I think about it I don't really want to know.

I have another dream where I'm at a railway station. It's winter. There's snow all over the ground. Trains keep coming and going but none of them stop. When one does I'm not allowed on. Three people come out, two women and a child. One of the women puts her arms around me. The other one sneers. We walk down a ramp. The woman tries to hold my hand but I'm not interested. I push her away from me. When I start to cry the child runs to comfort me.

In a third dream I'm being brought somewhere in a car by Aldo and Denis, the two people Justin introduced me to in London. I'm in the boot with a bag over my head. Bumps on the road make it lurch back and forth.

We drive through the city in the rain. The radio is blaring. Aldo and Denis are screaming at one another about some deal that went wrong. When we get to our destination it isn't London anymore. It's Galway. My father is standing over me. Greta is in the background. 'We haven't seen you for so long,' she says, 'How is Aisling?' I try to answer her but I can't. Aldo is trying to strangle me. 'Don't worry,' she says, patting me on the head. She leaves the room. Then Aldo comes over to me. He offers me a cigarette. 'For old time's sake,' he says.

The dream always stops at this point. In other versions of it Denis is replaced with Malcolm and Greta with Betty. The locations shift too. Sometimes I'm in a train instead of a car. But it always ends with Aldo saying 'For old time's sake.' That's the part I like best. It's as if nothing really changes in life. The places we're familiar with may close down and the people we know move but at the end of the day you're left with the substance of your old life. That's what keeps us going through all the rough times.

Greta calls to see me when she gets a break from the convent. We just sit and talk in my room. If Dr Gupta is in a good mood he lets her bring me down the town. It always looks strange to me because I see it so seldom. It's all modern buildings now. It's lost most of its character.

We sit looking out over the bay. Boats pass by. I wonder where they're going. I think of the days when I used to wish I was on them. That's not the case anymore. I just want my days to be the same. That way there are no surprises. Life can't hurt you.

When people see us they stop what they're doing. Some of them stare. Greta fends off the ones I don't want to talk to. We enjoy going to a restaurant for a cup of tea. When we're waiting for it to arrive she always asks me the same question: 'How are you?' I say, 'Fine'.' Then she says, 'No I mean how are you *really*?' That really gets me going.

Sometimes I ask her if I'm being kept here by force. She says not to be so silly.

'Why don't you take me out for good then?' I say.

She says that will happen in its own good time.

One day I asked an orderly, 'Could I walk out now if I wanted?' He said, 'Of course.' But I notice that if I go too far beyond my room there are people in uniforms looking at me disapprovingly. They go out of their way to avoid being seen. If I approach them they sneak away.

Aisling visited me once. It was many years ago. She kept saying, 'My God, what happened to you?' I don't know why she said that. She had no reason to.

She didn't say much else. A lot of the time she just kept looking into space. At one stage I caught her crying. I worry about her. Life didn't go the way she planned.

'I'm going to get you out of here,' she said to me at one stage.

I started laughing.

'Is that all that's wrong with you?' I said.

I explained to her that there was nowhere I'd prefer to be. She nodded her head. I knew by her expression that she didn't believe me. When she was leaving she put her arms around me. She hugged me the way she used to. I kept asking her what was wrong with her but she wouldn't say. As she walked away I found myself wondering if I'd ever see her again, if there was any way we could work out our problems. Maybe we were destined to fail. Some things work for you in life and some things don't. It's as simple as that. You can't do anything about it.

I sit in my room tonight thinking about all the things that went right and all the things that went wrong. I look out at the farm and remember how I was when I was growing up, walking through the fields and wondering what the future held. In some ways it all seems like yesterday. It's as if I went straight from school to here without any interruption. All the other events - the accident, Aisling leaving me, London, my father's death - are hazy. I try to make them clearer to myself but something blocks me. It's like having a trapdoor inside my head.

On clear days I can see the farmhouse. It makes me sad to think that there are new people in it now. Anytime I pass it with Greta I say, 'Let's ask the new owners if we can have a look inside.' She always says no.

The night is quiet. Leaves tremble in the trees. The traffic lights on the road go green, yellow, red; green, yellow, red. People pass by on the road in the distance. They're quiet too, like ghosts in a play.

The sun is going down now and with it the memory of another negligible day. In a few minutes it will sink under the horizon, the last breath of warmth on a stunted landscape. The shadows that remain will play tricks with the leaves on the trees. Then the dark will settle in, bathing all of us in its uniformity. I'll soak myself in the comfort it brings. After that the rain will begin, casual at first and then intense, a brittle dance that will last for an hour or so and then stop. Droplets will crawl down the wall like spiders.

In the silence of the night I'll replay my life as I replay it every night like a film inside my head, occasionally changing the spools depending on the mood I'm in, inserting a subplot here and there that may or may not be relevant.

I look out the window. The moon is shining down benignly. I feel myself becoming one with the water in the bay, the cold grey light of the town. It's the same view every night, the same undulations of the shadows, the same unmoving water. There's a comfort in it. I like to know that these shadows and shapes, the co-ordinates of my existence if you like, will always be there when I look out at them no matter how I might feel inside.

Sleep will come soon. Or maybe not. Some nights I nod off without trying to. On others I lie awake almost till dawn, watching the landscape re-define itself as the sun hints. If that's the case I'll reflect once again on all the incidents I've recounted here, the incidents that might one day approximate to a pattern for me.

I'll think of my mother and father and Greta and Aisling and all the other people who passed through my life for however short a time. Memories are all I have now in the same way they were all my father had at a certain point and maybe his father too. I'll create scenes out of them to make sense of them, dangling the characters in them like marionettes on a string, putting them into situations that may either reform or destroy them or both.

The wind swirls around me. I look out at it rustling the leaves of the trees, swishing them into the air like girls' skirts. As I watch its movement I'm aware suddenly that nothing can make me lose control of myself now, neither passion nor malice. Not even, as I once thought feasible, the cushioning of love.

Sometimes I blame my father for the way things turned out. Sometimes I think it's all in the fates. Then there are the times I feel a kind of excitement in the fact that I myself was responsible for it all, all the wastefulness and all the rot. It gives me a sense of pride to realise that I've made some kind of protest at the way things have been for me, that I've risen above myself to cry out. I feel as if I've purified myself by reneging on the opportunities life threw at me, that I've decided nothing was preferable to little, that impotence was my reaction to the fact that what was given to me was less than the All.

At times like this, my heart beating with a kind of perverse thrill, I experience the pleasure a man might get when he flagellates himself, when he destroys in one fell swoop what it's taken him a lifetime to build.

Remorse has sweetened my drinks.